THE BLACK MASK LIBRARY

THE EARLY YEARS (1920–26)

The Man in the Shadows: The Complete Black Mask
Cases of Terry Mack *by Carroll John Daly*

Zigzags of Treachery: The Complete Black Mask Cases of the
Continental Op, Volume 1 *by Dashiell Hammett*

THE SHAW YEARS (1926–36)

Blood on the Curb *by Joseph T. Shaw*

Black Harvest: The Complete Black Mask Cases of Jules Tremaine *by Norvell W. Page*

Boomerang Dice: The Complete Black Mask Cases of Johnny Hi Gear *by Stewart Sterling*

The Case-Hardened Samaritan: The Complete Black Mask
Cases of Dal Prentice, Volume 1 *by Roger Torrey*

Dead Evidence: The Complete Black Mask Cases of Harrigan *by Ed Lybeck*

Laughing Death *by Raoul Whitfield*

Luck: The Complete Black Mask Cases of Oscar Sail *by Lester Dent*

Murder Maze: The Complete Black Mask Cases of Jerry
Tracy, Volume 2 *by Theodore A. Tinsley*

The Price of a Dime: The Complete Black Mask Cases of Ben Shaley *by Norbert Davis*

Somewhere in Mexico: The Complete Black Mask Cases
of Jerry Frost, Volume 1 *by Horace McCoy*

South Wind: The Complete Black Mask Cases of
Jerry Tracy, Volume 1 *by Theodore A. Tinsley*

That's Hollywood: The Complete Black Mask Cases of
Bill Lennox, Volume 1 *by W.T. Ballard*

White Talons: The Complete Black Mask Cases of Tex of
the Border Service *by Katherine Brocklebank*

THE LATER YEARS (1936–51)

Dead and Done For: The Complete Black Mask Cases of
Cellini Smith, Volume 1 *by Robert Reeves*

Dog Eat Dog: The Complete Black Mask Cases of Cellini Smith, Volume 2 *by Robert Reeves*

The Hound with the Golden Eye: The Complete Black Mask
Cases of Luther McGavock, Volume 2 *by Merle Constiner*

It Happened at the Lake *by Joseph T. Shaw*

Let the Dead Alone: The Complete Black Mask Cases of
Luther McGavock, Volume 1 *by Merle Constiner*

Murder Costs Money: The Complete Black Mask Cases
of Rex Sackler, Volume 1 *by D.L. Champion*

Murder on the Midway: The Complete Black Mask Cases of
the Human Encyclopedia, Volume 1 *by Frank Gruber*

Murder Pays 7 to 1: The Complete Black Mask Cases of
Rex Sackler, Volume 2 *by D.L. Champion*

MURDER PAYS 7 TO 1

The Complete

Cases of Rex Sackler

1942–43

D.L. CHAMPION

---

introduction by Karl Schadow

illustrations by Peter Kuhlhoff

cover by Rafael de Soto

BLACK MASK

2023

Table of Contents

Rex Sackler's Sole Appearance Outside of the Pulps: Via the Airwaves On *The Mollé Mystery Theatre* / *i*

1   What's Money? / *1*

2   Murder Pays 7 to 1 / *49*

3   Blood from a Turnip / *93*

4   Killer, Can You Spare a Dime? / *139*

5   Murder by the Ears / *183*

6   Come Out of the Grave / *225*

Rex Sackler's Sole Appearance Outside of the Pulps: Via the Airwaves On *The Mollé Mystery Theatre*

DURING THE INTRODUCTION to the July 3, 1945 episode of *The Mollé Mystery Theatre*, host of the radio series Geoffrey Barnes stated: "Tonight I have selected a story by D.L. Champion entitled REX SACKLER, DETECTIVE. It's a fast-moving riot of suspense and thrills, and in it, you will meet two of the rarest characters of detective fiction, Rex Sackler and his assistant, Joey Graham." Rare would indeed be an understatement as this duo's only appearance on radio, and in any other media occurred, on this program. Readers of this duo's exploits were first introduced to their antics in pulp magazine stories written by Australian-native D'Arcy Lyndon Champion who was attributed under the moniker—D.L. Champion.

In the pulp stories, Joey Graham narrated the cases in which he and his boss known as the "Parsimonious Prince of Penny-Pinchers" were engaged. However, for the radio episode, this point of view was rewritten with third person narration being incorporated into the script. In this episode featured on the *Mollé* series, Joey was the first one to speak even before the drama began. He presented a thirty-second public service announcement (under the auspices of the Office of War Information) warning listeners that idle talk would jeopardize our military secrets and aid our enemies. In assessing the Sackler adventure, both the script and also the audio were consulted.

It should be noted that the version of the latter is courtesy of the Armed Forces Radio Service (AFRS) in which an edited version was broadcast via the AFRS *Mystery Playhouse*.

Having commenced September 7, 1943, *The Mollé Mystery Theatre* (often referenced by its abbreviated title, *Mystery Theatre*) had been thrilling NBC Tuesday night audiences for some ninety weeks prior to the appearance of the Sackler exploit. The program was developed by the Young & Rubicam advertising agency and bankrolled by the agency's client, Cummer Division of Sterling Drug Company. Mollé Brushless Shave Cream was the primary product promoted during the show. Each Tuesday evening the program featured: "…one of the great mystery stories; selected from either the famous classics or from the best of the moderns." Sackler and Graham certainly belong to the latter category as they first entertained readers in the July 1, 1939 issue of *Detective Fiction Weekly*. After three stories were published in that magazine, Champion submitted his next yarn in the series to *Black Mask*. Between 1940 and 1950, a total of twenty-six cases of Rex Sackler appeared in the pulpdom's most prestigious detective title.

The host of *Mystery Theatre*, crime connoisseur Geoffrey Barnes, stated that he personally selected the stories for each of the weekly radio thrillers. Though promoted by the NBC Press Department as a real person, Barnes was actually a fictional creation portrayed by Roc Rogers, a character actor known as the medium's "master of menace and mystery" for his work in several series including *Gang Busters*, *Ellery Queen* and *Famous Jury Trials*. Additionally, the stories for the radio program were culled from a vast range of sources including slick magazine short stories (*Collier's* [January 19, 1924], *The Most Dangerous*

Game, Richard Connell), stage plays (*The Cat and the Canary,* John Willard), novels (*The Leavenworth Case,* Anna Katherine Green), and the tattered pages of pulp magazines. Within this arena, scripts were transformed from *Baffling Detective Mysteries* (March 1943, *The Death Rose,* Cornell Woolrich), *Real Detective Tales and Mystery Stories* (August 1927, *The Eleventh Juror,* Vincent Starrett), *Weird Tales* (July 1943, *Yours Truly—Jack The Ripper,* Robert Bloch) and *Black Mask.* Stories of the latter heard on the program were from the works of Raymond Chandler (*Spanish Blood,* November 1935 and *Goldfish,* June 1936) and Cornell Woolrich (*After Dinner Story,* January 1938).

The *Mollé* chillers were adapted by free-lance radio scribes including Everett George Opie, Constance Smith and Jacques Anson Finke, among others. Noteworthy is that the duo of Walter B. Gibson and Ed Gruskin transfigured the 1937 Rufus King Doubleday Crime Club novel *Crime of Violence.* For the *Mollé* series, writer Palmer Thompson chose the story *What's Money?* from the January 1942 issue of *Black Mask.* It commences this current volume of Rex Sackler pulp adventures. Thompson had extensive experience crafting radio scripts both on a local basis for the 1939 *Radio Play Guild* series (WNEW, New York) and later for such network programs as *The Kate Smith Hour, First Nighter* and *The March of Time.* The Sackler piece was submitted while he was a member of the Army Air Force Medical Administrative Corps.

Thompson's rendition of *What's Money?* was approved by *Mystery Theatre* producer/director Frank Telford who had assumed the program's reigns in July of 1944 from its former leader Day Tuttle. Under Telford's helm, the series had steadily moved up in various ratings to a very respectable level within the top twenty. In his 1946 assessment of detective genre on radio, author and critic Ken Crossen coupled the *Mystery Theatre* along with *Suspense* as: "… two programs that occasionally afford a glimpse of the quality that is possible in the air mystery drama." In promoting the upcoming Sackler adventure of July 3, 1945, the NBC press release reprinted verbatim in newspapers across the country included the following from the *Richmond Times Dispatch* which stated: "A smart but tight-fisted detective gets the runaround from his underpaid assistant in 'Rex Sadler, Detective' the NBC-WMBG Mystery Theater presentation at 9 P.M. Palmer Thompson adapted his script from the D.C. Champion's story of a group of hard-boiled people, all equally unscrupulous and greedy." Though perhaps unnoticed except by the staunch followers of the pulp stories, is that both Sackler and his creator's name were misspelled in this announcement. The reasons for these errors are still unknown but it was not uncommon for press releases, whatever the original source, to contain such mistakes. In the script and the subsequent on-air performance, both names were stated correctly. In introducing the episode for the AFRS version, Elliott Lewis (as host T4Y) thought the program had: "… good pace, good chills and some good fun."

In that NBC Press Release, Palmer Thompson's name was spelled correctly. It is interesting to note that while many of previous pulp stories utilized in the *Mollé* series had their originating story titles identified in the script, a generic title was incorporated for the Sackler session. Originating from WEAF, the NBC flagship station in New York, the cast which varied from week-to-week was culled from The Big Apple's finest etherwaves thespians. In his role as director, Telford consulted NBC Casting Director Eleanor Kilgallen (younger sister of showbiz columnist Dorothy Kilgallen) in selecting these individuals. Though no cast members were mentioned in the press release and none are acknowledged in the script nor during the on-air broadcast, most have been identified by this author.

Two of radio's most-accomplished actors were chosen to portray the detective duo: Frank Readick for the boss and Kenneth Lynch as his assistant. Readick had been in radio since the late 1920s performing in numerous CBS dramatic anthologies. He was also the second actor, following James La Curto, to play The Shadow when that ominous voice was the narrator of the *Detective Story Magazine Hour*. In the 1932 *Joe Palooka* series, Readick played the champ's manager Knobby Walsh. Later he held the leading roles in the 1939 juvenile adventure series *Smilin' Jack* (based on Jack Mosely's newspaper strip) and the comedy, *Meet Mr. Meek*. Readick may be best remebered as reporter Carl Phillips in the Orson Welles Mercury Theatre production, *War of the Worlds*. He was also a regular supporting cast member of both *The Cavalcade of America* and *Gang Busters*. Readick's strident, tenor voice was the perfect impersonation of what readers may have thought of Sackler.

As Joey Graham, Ken Lynch voiced the perfect foil for his boss. Previously, Lynch played a reformed convict—co-starring with Richard Gordon (as a retired clergymen) in *The Bishop and the Gargoyle*. He also had a regular supporting role as the mechanic Tank Tinker in the *Hop Harrigan* series. Lynch also appeared in numerous episodes of both *Gang Busters* and *Words at War*. Prior to their roles in the Sackler story, both Readick and Lynch had been in several *Mystery Theatre* episodes. As transformed by Palmer Thompson, the radio script followed the basic plot of the pulp story, though some of the meeting places for certain scenes were changed. These alterations were made to assist the listening audience in following the plot during the thirty-minute session. Not all of the characters from the pulp story were carried over to the radio version. Additionally, some character names were changed. Supporting cast included Barry Hopkins as attorney Edwin Mayer (Elmer Justis from the pulps), Larry Haines was Mike with Ralph Bell his fellow thug, Hymie. James Van Dyk was killer Spider McGraw (Big Joe Angers from the original story). Jerry Macy may have played the role of Inspector Wooley. The actress who voiced Alice Grattan is still unknown. Most importantly, much of the banter between Rex and Joey was retained in radio play, at times verbatim. A prime example is the armed robbery of both Rex and Joey by Mike. Even though Joey is the often the brawn of the duo, he balks when Rex tells him to chase after the gun-toting Mike as his boss simply does not pay him enough dough to get shot.

After amassing some ninety-one mysteries, the Sackler escapade was a fitting finale of that first elongated *Mollé* series. The program then took a summer break and returned for three additional successful seasons on NBC. Unfortunately for fans of Rex and Joey, the duo did not make a second appearance during this time. However, the Champion story "Who Took the Corpse?" (*Black Mask*, January 1944) was performed on November 2, 1945. It was adapted by Frederic Methot. Prior to both *Black Mask* stories, Champion's yarn *The Sergeant's Reprimand* (*Esquire*, September 1943) had been read on air by story-teller Nelson Olmsted in 1944, twice during the NBC program, *Your America* and once on the same network's War Bond Drive program. It was also interpreted by Sgt. Larry Powell on a local USO show in October of 1945 from station KLPT in Paris, Texas. As of this writing, no stories from Champion's other major characters, Inspector Allhoff or Mariano Mercado have been adapted for radio. Interestingly, according to Australian radio historian, Ian Grieve, there was a series of *The Phantom Detective* broadcast in that country during the mid-1930s. The episodes for this program may have been adapted from the pulp adventures of Richard Curtis Van Loan which Champion wrote under various pseudonyms. Of note is that *The Phantom Detective* radio series was a major focus of Champion's March 1968 obituary. To their dismay, Rex and Joey were not mentioned in this brief tribute to their creator.

— Karl Schadow

What's Money?

About to be blasted by Hymie the Gunsel, Joey was deeply touched by Sackler's passionate plea that his assistant be spared. Then he remembered he was worth ten grand on the hoof to his nickel-nursing boss—

1

Check and Double Check

SACKLER CAME INTO the office, his face as long as a hundred years and his shoulders bowed beneath several tons of invisible sorrow. He ignored my greeting. He hung up a hat which still bore the marks of rain that had fallen at Hoover's inauguration and sat down with a sigh dragged from the very roots of his being. He was the spirit of gloom.

I watched him with a critical eye and diagnosed the melancholy with facile accuracy.

"Well," I said pleasantly, "who took you?"

He lifted his dark thin face. He regarded me with suffering black eyes. He ran his long white fingers through his ebony hair. He said inquiringly: "Who *took* me, Joey?"

I nodded. "A natural question," I told him. "Of the several million troubles in this world only one ever bothers you. That's money. When I see you come into the office looking rather like a sentimental collie dog might be expected to look on the day Albert Payson Terhune feels blue, it occurs to me that someone has dealt you a savage blow in the pocketbook."

He looked at me distastefully as if I were a bad egg he had been served for breakfast. He sighed again and said: "Money? What's money?"

Considering the fact that money was his life's blood, his God, his mistress and something for which he would eagerly barter his right eye, I dismissed this question as rhetoric. Sackler withdrew a small sack of tobacco from his pocket, then spying the deck of cigarettes on my desk thought better of it and put the sack away again. He snatched one of my cigarettes before I could move the package out of the danger zone.

"Joey," he said, "you're so ethically deficient it's impossible for you to understand what principle means."

"Usually," I said, "it means that someone's squawking about a buck and pretending they have a much more noble motive."

"That is cheap and cynical, Joey. I am disturbed this morning over a matter of principle purely. The amount of money involved is negligible. As a matter of fact, two cents. Can you conceive of my worrying over two cents?"

"With no effort whatever," I told him. "If someone has chiseled you out of two cents it was doubtless done at the point of a howitzer."

"Very funny," said Sackler in a tone which indicated it wasn't. "As I stood on the subway station platform this morning, I dropped a penny into a chewing gum machine. No gum came out. I tried another machine with the same result. The point is that I have been swindled by a large corporation. As a matter of sheer principle, I am annoyed."

I grinned at him. Sackler prating of principle where money was involved sounded like a press release from the Wilhelmstrasse concerning the nobility of Hitler's battle to save civilization. Sackler sat on every nickel he made like a hen sitting on its eggs.

His money was not trusted to banks. That, for Sackler, was a trifle too risky. He scattered his earnings about in Postal Savings accounts all over the country. Revolution alone was going to rob him. He rolled his own cigarettes

"You're Sackler, ain't you?"
said the burly stranger.

when he wasn't grubbing mine in order to evade the state tax and he wore a suit of clothes until the threads literally parted.

But now, I thought, he'd reached the apogee of it all. He was actually beating his breast because he was out two cents. His misery brought cheer into my heart.

"Write them a letter," I suggested. "A stiff letter. They'll undoubtedly give you a refund."

He smiled the sad bitter smile of a man resigned philosophically to his fate.

"I thought of that," he said. "But do you realize it costs two cents for the stamp alone, not to mention the stationery?

Moreover it would cost a nickel to telephone them. No matter how I handle it, I don't break even."

My laughter rocked the room. "I thought it was a matter of principle," I said. "Purely principle. I notice, however, that you've figured out the cost of your protest very neatly."

"You have a moron's mind," said Sackler. "I'm damned if I know why I put up with it."

He took the makings from his pocket once more. He glanced over at my desk but this time I was too fast for him. I had the deck of cigarettes in the drawer before he could get out of the chair.

WE SAT IN silence for a half-hour. Sackler, apparently, was so upset about his losing struggle with the slot machine that he failed to suggest some form of gambling. It was his custom to leave no effort unexpended in order to win back from me during the week the meager salary he paid me each Wednesday. Usually, he was quite successful, too.

We looked up simultaneously as the outer office door slammed shut. There was a gleam in Sackler's eye. A polite professional smile spread itself over his face. His nostrils distended as if he were trying to smell the amount of the fee his potential client could afford.

The door of the inner office opened and Sackler's smile fell from his face. His eyes lost their glitter. A uniformed police officer stood on the threshold, a gold badge gleaming bravely on his broad chest.

Sackler said glumly: "Hello, Wooley. What do *you* want?"

Inspector Wooley sat down. He greeted Sackler cordially, which was odd. He disliked Sackler only a trifle less than

Sackler disliked him. Wooley envied Sackler's income and his success in a score of cases where Wooley and his men had failed. There was something suspicious about his attitude this morning.

"Well," he said with all the sincerity of an Axis diplomat signing a nonaggression pact, "and how's the boy, Rex? How's business? How's everything?"

"Terrible," I said. "He's ruined. He dropped a fortune this morning in slot machine speculation."

Sackler shot me a glance more deadly than malignant virus. Wooley, not realizing it was a gag, shook his head and clucked commiseratingly.

"Too bad, old man," he said. "Too bad."

He was laying it on so thick by now that Sackler became suspicious.

"Look, Wooley," he said. "What do you want? Now that you've smeared me up nicely for the past few minutes you may come to the point. Though I'll tell you in advance if it's a favor I can't do it. If it's money I haven't got it."

"Rex," said Wooley gravely, "you're a private detective. I'm a public servant. Yet we both work toward the same ends, don't we?"

"You sound like an editorial in the *Sun*," said Sackler, "and it worries me. I don't like it. What the devil do you want?"

"Look," said Wooley, "you seen the papers about the Grattan killing, haven't you?"

"Yes. But you picked up a guy on that. Bellows, wasn't it?"

"We let him go this morning. Insufficient evidence."

"Well," said Sackler, "what do you want from me? You're talking like a guy who wants something."

"Even," I put in, "like a guy who wants it for nothing."

"Here's the setup," said Wooley. "This guy Bellows was engaged to Grattan's daughter. The old guy didn't like the idea. He and Bellows had quarreled. Long and often. Moreover, the old guy's dough goes to the girl after his death. She's nuts about Bellows. With one bullet he can get rid of the old man's objections to the marriage, and also fix it so that his wife has a pretty dowry. See?"

"What do you mean, insufficient evidence?"

Wooley scratched a head which held very little hair. "Alibi," he said, "and it's a screwy one. Bellows has this alibi: It seems someone called him from a downtown poolroom just before the killing. Four guys saw him in that poolroom. Every one of those guys is a bum. The lousiest assistant D.A. we've got could discredit their testimony in twelve seconds flat."

"So," said Sackler, "what are you worrying about? Pick Bellows up again. Discredit the testimony of his witnesses and stop bothering me."

"Wait," said Wooley. "Through sheer accident Bellows has one good witness. As he was entering the poolroom General Barker passed him in the street. Now do you get it?"

WELL, NOW IT was rather obvious. The alibi testimony of some poolroom punk was one thing. The evidence of General Barker was another. Barker was not only an army officer with a national reputation, he was an upright guy with a tremendous reputation for integrity, probity and all the other virtues emblazoned in the copy-books. An alibi from Barker was as good as a reprieve from the Governor.

Sackler said as much. He added: "What makes you think

Bellows is guilty, then? You don't think Barker's lying?"

"He may be mistaken. He came forward after seeing Bellows' picture in the paper. He'd never seen him before. He just recalled bumping into him accidentally the night of the killing. If Barker's right the time element would have precluded Bellows' having anything to do with it."

Sackler shrugged. "All right," he said, "why not assume Barker is right? Drop the case."

"The D.A. wants a conviction. The case is spectacular. The papers are playing it big. An election rolls around this fall. The D.A. and the commissioner would like a conviction. And it's quite possible Barker is mistaken." Wooley scratched his pate again, and added a note of wistfulness in his tone: "If Barker *hadn't* run into Bellows, we'd have a cold case."

"Look," said Sackler suddenly. "By any chance is the police department retaining me?"

"Retaining you? The department can't retain a private detective, Rex. It'd look awful."

"All right," said Sackler, "then go away. I've listened to you for twenty minutes free. I have no interest in the case. No one is paying me and if you're merely unburdening your soul take it to a priest, your wife, or a sympathetic bartender. But go away from here."

Wooley looked wounded. "Rex," he said and his voice quivered with hypocrisy, "after all we're both fighting crime. We must work together."

"That," said Sackler, "is a beautiful gossamer thought. What is it you want from me?"

"Well, Rex, this Bellows is going to retain you."

Sackler's eyes lit up. He was performing some heart-warming

mental arithmetic. One client equals one fee. One fee equals more dough in the bank. More dough in the bank equals three gallons of dreamy gloating happiness. He leaned over his desk and addressed Wooley with more affability than he had yet shown.

"What's it worth, do you figure? Has the guy any dough? What ought I ask him? What—"

"Wait a minute," said Wooley. "Let me tell you my angle. We still believe Bellows is guilty. The case is open and shut, save for Barker's testimony. We figure that if Bellows retains you, you'll be in a good spot to keep an eye on him. We want you to work with us, to keep in touch with us. You should be able to dig up something on the case. He'll be freer with you than with us. If you can do it, pin that murder on him. We'll be grateful, Rex. The D.A.'ll be grateful. It won't do you any harm."

Sackler took a deep breath. He looked very much like a man enjoying a moment for which he has waited many years. As a matter of fact, he was.

"For years," he said, "I have been harassed by an incompetent police department. For years their envy of my ability and my financial success has caused them to frustrate me at every opportunity. Now, in the person of Inspector Wooley, that department comes crawling to me on its stomach to help them solve a case they can't handle themselves. I laugh, uproariously."

He got out of his chair, took two paces toward me and snatched one of my tailor-made cigarettes before I could stop him. He lit it, smiling. Then turned again to Wooley.

"Moreover," he said, "you're damned insulting. I am a professional man of integrity. My client's interest is my own. Your implication that I would betray my client merely because the

D.A. is worried about an election is outrageous. After such a suggestion I cannot countenance your presence in my office."

He drew himself up like a Victorian parent ordering the poverty-stricken lover from his daughter's drawing-room. Wooley, all his phoney beneficence gone, glared at him and stood up.

"All right," he said. "Ride me. But you'll regret it, Rex. You're only figuring how much dough you can take Bellows for. If I offered you more you'd sell him down the river like Uncle Tom."

"That," said Sackler, "is a foul lie. I serve my clients all the way whether they pay or not. Don't I, Joey?"

I searched my conscience very carefully before I answered. Then I looked him squarely in the eye and said, "No."

Wooley, still glaring at Sackler, marched from the room. Sackler didn't even bother to become annoyed at me. He sat down at his desk, leaned back, grinned happily and waited for the advent of William Bellows with his fee.

HE DIDN'T HAVE long to wait.

Wooley had been gone less than half an hour when the outer office door opened. I sprang up, went to the anteroom and admitted two men. Bellows, I recognized, from the picture which had appeared in all the tabloids at the time of the murder. He was rather tall and in his early thirties. He was good-looking in an ordinary sort of way. His face was thin and closely shaven. His eyes were alert and, at the moment, shadowed with worry.

His companion was short, middle-aged and well-dressed. He wore a pair of tortoise shell glasses through which two shrewd blue eyes peered and questioned. I led the pair of them into Sackler's presence. He bowed suavely like an undertaker silently estimating what price to put upon the funeral.

Bellows introduced himself. He indicated the short man and said: "This is Elmer Justis. He was Mr. Grattan's lawyer. He is now advising me."

Sackler unleashed his oiliest smile and I dragged up a couple of chairs for the company. Bellows drummed his fingers on the arm of his chair. He spoke jerkily.

"You of course know, Mr. Sackler, that I've been questioned in the Grattan murder. Luckily for me General Barker came forward and told the D.A. he'd seen me on the night of the killing. However, the thing still hangs over my head. I want to feel that I'm completely in the clear. I want you to find Grattan's murderer. Alice Grattan, my fiancée, agrees with me on this move."

"Of course," said Sackler. "I appreciate your feeling. I offer you all the facilities of our office."

The lawyer lit a cigar. "The procedure seems ridiculous to me," he said. "The police have released Bellows. As long as they know the defense will call Barker, they won't dare prosecute even though they're satisfied they have a cold motive. To retain a private operative under the circumstances seems unnecessary and a waste of money."

Sackler paled. This was heretical talk, indeed. He took swift, drastic measures to prevent the fee from slipping away before he had even held it in his grasping hand.

"A man's reputation," he said sententiously, "is his greatest asset. I think it essential Bellows' name be cleared before the bar of public opinion."

Bellows nodded. "That's what we think. I mean Alice and myself. Besides, we should expend all effort to discover the actual murderer. Justis and I disagree on this. We've already argued about it. But my mind is definitely made up."

He reached inside his breast pocket and withdrew his wallet. The ethereal expression on Sackler's face shone with a holy light. He handed Sackler a blue oblong piece of paper. He said, a shade of anxiety in his tone: "Will fifteen hundred be all right?"

Sackler looked at the check with the eye of Romeo regarding Juliet.

"Payable to me," he murmured. "But the signature?"

"Miss Grattan's," said Bellows. "She's helping me finance the investigation into her father's death. She wrote out the check."

"Quite satisfactory," said Sackler. "I shall undertake the investigation. I shall probably want to interview Miss Grattan and both of you gentlemen at my leisure. I shall get in touch with you if you'll leave your addresses with my assistant."

I took their addresses and they left. I brooded at my desk. It seemed to me that money fell into Sackler's lap like manna from heaven. And in this specific case there had been no stipulation made that he must solve the case. The fee was his no matter what. And since the police had been able to unearth no suspect beyond Bellows, it apparently wasn't going to be easy.

AFTER ABOUT TEN minutes Sackler got up and reached for his hat. I didn't bother to ask him where he was going. I knew. Rex Sackler kept no checking account. Moreover, he wasted no time in turning a check into immediate cash ready for deposit in one of his several Postal Savings accounts. Now,

I knew, he was heading posthaste to Alice Grattan's bank to exchange the blue paper in his pocket for green bills. It would be utterly impossible for him to put his mind on the case until that detail had been taken care of.

He walked to the door, said over his shoulder, "Back in a few minutes, Joey," then stopped dead on the threshold.

A burly figure moved in from the anteroom. The door closed behind it. The burly figure fixed Sackler with a pair of cold black eyes. Two thick lips moved and a strong Brooklyn accent said: "You're Sackler, ain't you?" Sackler nodded. The stranger came farther into the room forcing Sackler back with him. He was flashily dressed in a light brown suit with pockets looking as if they'd been slashed in the fabric with a sword. His tie was bright yellow and the red scar that rippled down his cheek from temple to chin added no beauty to his appearance.

He thrust, suddenly, a heavy hand into the right pocket of his coat. He withdrew it again, gripping an automatic. Its muzzle aimed at a spot of space directly between Sackler and myself.

"All right, you guys," he said. "Give me your dough."

Sackler stared at him as if fate had slammed him over the head with an invisible baseball bat. Stunned amazement was in his eyes. It was bad enough for him to face the threat of having money removed from his person. But a stickup in the office of a private detective was only slightly better than a heist in the Second Precinct House.

Our holdup man's eyes flickered with impatience. "Youse guys will empty your wallets on the top of the desk," he announced. "If there's enough dough there, I won't bother with the rest of the joint. Now get started."

Sackler glanced at the automatic. Then he turned his gaze on me. "O.K., Joey," he said as if he were a German general telling the boys to knock off Switzerland, "take him."

I lifted my eyebrows. "Take him?"

"It's your department," said Sackler. "I furnish the brains and the financial backing. You're the strong man."

I removed my gaze from Sackler and studied the muzzle of our visitor's automatic. I estimated roughly it would take him all of four-fifths of a second to pump me full of lead. Conservatively, it would take me three seconds longer to open my desk drawer, grab my own gun and start shooting.

I moved my left hand slowly toward the inside breast pocket of my coat. To remove any possible misunderstanding, I announced clearly: "I am reaching for my wallet."

I emptied the wallet on the desk. I tendered the sum of nine dollars to the stickup guy. I said, "That's the roll," folded my arms and let Sackler play out the rest of the hand.

Sackler looked at me like a child who has discovered that his mother's morals are not what he supposed. He opened his mouth preparatory to casting bitter reflection on my physical courage, but before he could articulate the words, the thug spoke impatiently.

"All right, you. Hand over the dough. We ain't got all day."

SACKLER TOOK HIS wallet from his pocket with all the enthusiasm of a debutante picking up a rattlesnake. He put its contents on his desk. Rather to my disappointment the cash totaled only six dollars besides, of course, the Bellows check.

Our holdup man, maneuvering his gun, moved carefully across the room and picked it up. Sackler, a catch in his voice, said: "You don't need that check. It's made out to me. You can't cash it."

The scar-faced man sighed wearily as he picked up the check and the money.

"Why don't you mind your own business," he asked petulantly, "and leave me mind mine. Now, I'm going. You better stay here for at least five minutes because you don't know how long I might wait in the hall ready to plug youse guys if you come out."

He backed to the door and through it, slammed it and disappeared. Sackler fixed me with a halibut's stare. "After him," he said. "Go get him."

"I shall not. He is a professional thug. It is more than possible he will stand outside for a few minutes ready to shoot if I come out."

He looked at me as if he had nailed me red-handed with a jimmy at the poorbox. He brought up a sigh of resignation from his heels.

"Joey," he said heavily, as if more hurt than angry, "my opinion of your mentality has never been high. My estimate of your morals has been none too optimistic. However, I never believed that, with all your faults, you were yellow."

"That," I said, "we won't argue. But you might revise your opinion of my mentality. Since that mug could have plugged us both while I was still going for my gun, you might grant that I'm not a complete moron."

"You sat there," he said accusingly, "while he rolled me for fifteen hundred and six dollars."

"He rolled me for nine. He rolled you for six. You can have payment stopped on the check and get yourself another."

"The money, Joey, is nothing. It is a matter—" He paused. Then as if reaching the conclusion he was wasting valuable time, he snapped: "Get that Grattan woman on the phone. Tell her we were robbed. Have her stop payment at once and mail us another check. Hurry, Joey."

"Why not," I suggested, "phone the bank first, and tell *them* that you want payment stopped on the Grattan check at once?"

Sackler looked pained. "Joey, your ignorance of financial matters, at times, appalls me. A bank will not stop payment on a check except by order of the person who issued it."

I shrugged and picked up the phone. I reported a moment later that Alice Grattan wasn't in.

"All right," said Sackler, "keep ringing her every twenty minutes until you get her. Don't leave that phone for a minute."

I called Alice Grattan without success the rest of the day. I resumed calling, on Sackler's frantic instructions, early Saturday morning. Shortly after noon, I got her and reported to Sackler that another check would be put in the mail immediately. It was only then that Sackler relaxed, sighed, and put his mind to the solution of Grattan case for the first time.

2

Ten Grand on the Hoof

IT WASN'T UNTIL Monday, however, that he went into action. Alice Grattan's second check had arrived in the mail, had been duly cashed and cached. Sackler sat at his desk buried in thought. He sighed, looked up, and glanced at the package of cigarettes on my desk. I snatched them up quickly. Sackler sighed again and took the makings from his pocket. Slowly he rolled a cigarette. He came out with something that looked like a fat wet worm.

"Joey," he said, "on Sunday night there was a robbery at Grattan's. A wall safe behind an oil painting in the library was forced and emptied. Miss Grattan did not even know of the safe's existence until it was broken."

"So," I said, "are you arguing that someone knocked off the old man so that they could roll his safe several days later?"

"Joey," he said, "you are a fool. Grattan, I have ascertained, was a big independent dealer in diamonds. He kept large sums of money on hand and one hell of a lot of valuable ice."

"I thought you were retained to find out who killed him."

"That," said Sackler, "is precisely what I am finding out. And now after weeks of idleness—weeks during which I have still paid your salary—I have a task for you."

"Which is?"

"See Barker. For some reason Wooley thinks he may have been mistaken in his identification of Bellows. The D.A. would undoubtedly like a conviction and Bellows is a cinch save for Barker's testimony. See the old guy. Find out whatever you can. And hurry. After that I've got a couple more angles for you to work on. In the meantime, I'll find out what I can from the Grattan girl, from Bellows and that lawyer."

Nothing loath, I hurried. I had been cooped up for two weeks in the office with Sackler. Adding what he had won from me at rummy, at dice and the cigarettes he had grubbed it hadn't been a cheap two weeks.

I went downstairs, climbed into the coupé and headed for General Barker's apartment house.

On the fourteenth story of an upper Park Avenue apartment house, I stood before Barker's door and stretched my finger forth to push the bell. From within the apartment a voice sounded through the door. It was a cultured voice, a gentle voice, withal there was a note of fear in it.

"Your motive," it said, "I do not understand. Your punishment I understand quite well. You will be executed for this. You will surely lose your life if I lose mine."

My finger froze a tenth of an inch from the bell. My right hand reached inside my coat to my shoulder holster. My ear pressed against the panel of the door. I heard a second voice—hard, tough and vaguely familiar. "Buddy, there's only two people ever going to know who knocked you off. And, from here on in, you don't count. You don't count at all."

Three shots sounded almost simultaneously. The first two came from within the apartment. The third was fired from my own automatic and its bullet blew the lock off Barker's door. Gun in hand I charged headlong into the apartment.

General Barker lay upon the floor. His head was cushioned

on an expensive Axminster, the color of which was changing slowly from a deep blue to a dark red. Standing over him, a thirty-eight in his hand, was Big Joe Angers.

BIG JOE TURNED his head as I raced into the room. He made a movement as if to swing his gun in my direction. He recognized me and didn't. My automatic already covered him and Big Joe knew me well enough to know I could shoot fast and accurately.

"Drop it," I said. "I thought I recognized your voice."

Big Joe dropped the thirty-eight. It fell with a padded thud upon the body of the man he had just killed. I regarded him over the muzzle of my own weapon and wondered just what I'd walked into.

Big Joe watched me with hard and calculating eyes. There was a taut expression on his face. The body at his feet did not disturb him. Big Joe had killed too many men for that. He was the town's ace killer. And he had at least one thing in common with Rex Sackler. Within the limits of his profession, which was murder, there was nothing he would not do if the price was right.

Now, he cleared his throat. He looked significantly down at the corpse of General Barker. He said hoarsely: "How much, Joey?"

God! How our reputation traveled!

"In a case like this," I said, "there isn't any price. I'd be an accessory and liable for the chair myself. I'm taking you in, baby."

Big Joe's eyes narrowed. "The cops ain't ever going to burn me, Joey," he said. "That's something I promised myself a long time ago. Let's make a deal. I got a lot of dough, Joey."

I sighed. The reputation of Rex Sackler and Company had certainly spread. Big Joe seemed quite convinced that I would risk putting my own body in the death cell if he handed me a certified check.

"No," I said, "you're coming in, Joe. You—" Then I committed the gravest error in all my career as an assistant private detective.

I took a pace across the floor toward Big Joe. The Axminster slid along the highly polished floor. I slid with it and lost my balance. As I strove to recover, Big Joe lashed out with his foot and caught me on the end of the spinal column. I fell, without dignity and dangerously, upon my face.

Big Joe sprang at the thirty-eight on the floor. He picked it up as I rolled over on my back and fired twice. I missed exactly the same number of times. Big Joe retreated to the doorway. He blasted at me as I ducked behind a huge armchair. I heard a bullet plow into the overstuffing. Big Joe shot once again, then I heard the door slam. Big Joe was beating a hasty retreat before anyone came to investigate the shots. For that I was profoundly grateful.

I stood up and used a handkerchief to wipe the cold sweat from my brow. There were footsteps at the door and an elevator boy and a copper burst into the room. The policeman looked at the body. He looked at me and of course recognized me.

"Ah, Joey," he said, not without satisfaction. "A corpse, and you with a gun in your hand. Wooley will be delighted. I'll be a sergeant in no time."

"Take it easy," I said. "I've got a tale to tell."

I told him about Big Joe. He seemed rather unconvinced until I showed him a hole in the wall where a bullet from the thirty-eight had landed. I pointed out that there was another slug somewhere in or about the chair. I drew attention to the fact that my gun was an automatic. Then I asked permission to call Rex Sackler.

Sackler listened to my recital, sighed heavily and said: "Well—it's too bad, Joey."

"What's too bad?"

"My God, you were right on the scene when a murder was committed and we haven't got any client who wants to know the answer. There's not a fee in it anywhere."

"It breaks my heart," I told him. "What am I supposed to do now?"

"Go in with the copper and tell your story to Wooley. If we can't get a fee we may as well ingratiate ourselves with the department. I don't think they like us, Joey."

Which was the understatement of the week.

AFTER I HAD spent an hour or so at headquarters, it dawned on me that we were being pushed around. Sackler had met me at Wooley's office, where I had told my story. Later, we waited outside in the anteroom, with a uniformed copper standing over us, while Wooley made a number of private telephone calls.

Finally, he joined us again. He smiled and there was malice in that smile. There was an odd twinkle in his eyes.

"Come on," he said. "We're going over to the courthouse."

"For what?" asked Sackler. "I'm busy on a case, Wooley. You've heard Joey's story. There's nothing to add to it. What do you want us for?"

"Perkins, the assistant D.A. wants a word with you," said

Wooley. "Come on."

Puzzled, we went along with him. A few moments later we sat in the chambers of Judge Morrow. The judge, gray and exuding a beneficence which had enabled the machine to elect him several dozen times, sat behind his desk, toying with his watch chain.

Perkins and Wooley held a whispered conference in a corner of the room. Once Perkins looked at Sackler and me over his shoulder. The smirk on his face duplicated the expression on Wooley's.

My feeling that something screwy was going on strengthened. Sackler looked annoyed.

"Look here," he said suddenly. "Why are we being held here? It's sheer malice, Wooley. You don't like me because I make more money than you. You're wasting my time merely to annoy me." Wooley didn't answer. Instead he winked at Perkins. Perkins moved over to the judge's desk, cleared his throat, and spoke like a congressman addressing the electorate.

"Your Honor, a prominent citizen has been murdered. It is an important police case. This man, Joey Graham, was a witness to that murder. The prosecutor's office needs his testimony to convict. I ask that you hold him in ten thousand dollar bail as a material witness."

Sackler's jaw fell open. His eyes gaped open. There was stark horror written on his face.

"Ten thousand dollars!" he exclaimed. "That's utterly ridiculous. It's—"

The judge hammered severely on the desk with a pencil. "I shall be the judge of that, Mr. Sackler," he said. "In cases of this sort I am guided by the advice of the district attorney's office.

I'll hold this man Graham in ten thousand dollar bail. Where are the papers?"

Perkins, Wooley and the judge grinned widely. Of course, it was a put-up job. It was a cinch I wasn't going to disappear. But I saw their point quite clearly. Asking Sackler to put up ten thousand dollars was a really beautiful thing. I grinned myself. Then suddenly I asked myself what the hell *I* was laughing for.

If it were a matter of my languishing in a cell for a few weeks or of Sackler withdrawing ten grand from his various Postal Savings accounts, I was as good as a prisoner right now.

"This," said Sackler, "is persecution. I'm working on a case now. I'm working on the side of law and order. I need my assistant badly. I should think the police department would want to aid the cause of justice, not hinder it."

"It shouldn't work any hardship," said Wooley. "You've got the ten thousand. You get it back later. It doesn't cost you a nickel."

That was true enough. But even the idea of withdrawing money from his accounts sent a tremor of horror down Sackler's spine. The judge wrote something rapidly on a form which Perkins had handed him.

"All right," he said. "Commit this man."

Perkins waved the paper. "Well," he asked, "are you bailing him or not?"

Sackler looked like a man who is offered the choice of hitting either his mother or his wife. He shook his head slowly.

"If only I wasn't working on a case," he said. "But I might need you, Joey. I guess I'll have to spring you. But for God's sake don't leave my side. If you get lost or anything I'm out ten thousand dollars."

"My pal," I murmured, "my great golden-hearted pal."

They held me in the detention pen while Sackler scurried around town and returned with the money. As we left the building, he linked his arm through mine. It was a most unusual gesture for him. But I understood it.

A few hours ago I was just Joey Graham, his underpaid, long-suffering assistant. Now I was a valuable property. I was worth ten grand on the hoof. And for once Rex Sackler was going to take very good care of me.

WE WENT UPTOWN again. We walked into the office to find two men sitting there. They were sitting quite calmly with their legs crossed. Each of them held his right hand balanced delicately on his left knee. In each of those hands were guns.

Sackler stood upon the threshold and blinked.

"My God," he said, "are we going to be held up again? This, Joey, is too much. I can bear no more."

I looked over his shoulder. One of the thugs I recognized. It was the scar-faced individual who had stuck us up a few days before. He stood up now, held his gun in my direction and spoke to the tall dark man with the Celtic face who was with him.

"Mike," he said, "there's two of them. What are we supposed to do?"

Mike got out of his chair. He looked at Sackler for a thoughtful moment. "Hymie," he said, "we better take them both. Otherwise, this money here"—he indicated Sackler with his gun muzzle—"will start howling copper right away and they might pick up our taxi on the way out."

Hymie nodded gravely. "O.K. Come along, both of you."

"Look," said Sackler, "I'm getting damned tired of having

guns stuck in my stomach. Now what the devil's it all about this time?"

"There's a pal of mine in this town," said Hymie, "who ain't got any intention of burning in the chair. The coppers are looking for him. They'll probably find him. But if this here guy Joey is put where he can't talk, it don't matter whether the cops find my pal or not."

I felt a sudden emptiness at the pit of my stomach. It didn't take a genius to figure out what was going on. Sackler opened his mouth to speak again but Mike prodded him gently in the stomach with a thirty-eight. Sackler shut up.

"All right," said Hymie, "come along, you two. Going downstairs we'll have our rods in our pockets. But we'll stand so close to you we couldn't miss anyway. I don't expect any funny stuff."

We went along. In the elevator I could feel Mike's gun pressing into my back. I was, at the moment, one scared assistant shamus. I looked at Sackler. He didn't resemble any conquering hero himself.

3

Anything for a Pal

IT WAS A long silent drive across the Manhattan Bridge deep into the heart of Brooklyn. Sackler and I sat in the back seat with Hymie between us. Facing us from the collapsible seat was Mike, his hand in his pocket, through the fabric of which I could see the outline of his gun.

Sackler stared at the back of the hack driver's neck in brooding silence. He registered deep thought and I hoped to God he was accomplishing it. No one would need to pass a civil service exam for detective-sergeant to figure out the object of this snatch. I was the only living guy whose testimony could send Big Joe Angers to the chair. Without me he was clean.

There was a queasy emptiness at the pit of my stomach, and my pulse beat at least ten strokes above normal. For once I was praying that Sackler would master-mind a way out of the jam we were in. For once I wasn't hoping that he'd make a humiliating mistake.

The cab drew up at a ramshackle house somewhere in Bay Ridge. Hymie and Mike escorted us up to the porch as the cab drove away. As we entered the house I shot a swift glance at Sackler, asking with my eyes if he'd figured anything. He gave no response. I entered the house with the reluctant step of a man walking the plank.

We sat in a living-room furnished in the early Garfield manner. A flight of stairs ran down into the room from the other story. A small hall led to the rear into, I supposed, a kitchen. Mike held his gun on us while Hymie went through our pockets. He appropriated my automatic and tossed it clatteringly onto the imitation marble mantelpiece. Sackler still stared into space as if he were about to conjure up a legion of angels to rescue us. I licked my dry lips and wondered somewhat hysterically why it was that fear freezes the salivary glands.

I said in a voice that I fought to keep steady: "How about a glass of water?"

Mike nodded at Hymie. "Take him in the kitchen and give him one. If there's any of that rye left bring me out a slug."

Hymie tapped me on the shoulder with a thirty-eight. I rose and preceded him into the kitchen. I helped myself to a glass of water at the sink. Hymie picked up a bottle of cheap rye which held about four ounces of whiskey and drained it. Then he drank a glass of water. We marched back into the living-room.

Hymie met Mike's eye. "Not a drop," he said. "The bottle was empty."

Mike frowned. "That's damned funny. I—" Then Sackler came to vocal life for the first time since we had left the office, and interrupted him.

"Look," he said abruptly. "What are you guys going to do with us?"

"Well," said Mike, "I ain't got the final orders yet. But I can give you a pretty good idea."

For that matter, I thought hopelessly, so can I.

"With you," went on Mike, "I guess we ain't going to do nothing. We got no orders about you. I just brought you along so you wouldn't have the coppers on our tail right away. I guess after we've done what we're going to do we'll just let you go."

Sackler nodded. His air of preoccupied worry remained with him despite Mike's information. He said: "What about Joey, here?"

"Well," said Hymie slowly, "he knows too much. You know how it is in cases like that."

"I know," said Sackler, "but just what are your plans?"

"We'll take him for a little ride," said Mike. "But he don't have to worry. Bang, bang. He'll never know what happened to him, see?"

WELL, THAT WAS just lovely. Bang, bang, and I'd never know what happened to me, see? I felt a strong urge to charge in with both fists flying and at least go out on my feet. I restrained myself. On several occasions I'd seen Sackler pull a miracle out of a hat. I was praying he hadn't lost his touch.

Sackler bit his lip, knitted his brow. There was an expression on his face approaching anguish.

"Look," he said, "listen to reason. You can't knock off Joey. Joey's a sweet character. He never did anything to you guys. Let's cook up some sort of a deal on this. I'd do anything rather than have anything happen to Joey."

Despite the fear which still dripped along my spinal column I looked at him curiously and not without affection. For years we had bickered, fought and haggled vehemently about money. But beneath it all, I realized now, there had always existed a strong bond of friendship.

Hymie made a gesture of futility. "You know better than that, Sackler. You can't cook up a deal in a case like this. You can't trust a guy who's seen a murder committed. How can you guarantee to keep his mouth shut?"

Sackler sighed and ran his fingers through his hair. "I'll be responsible for him," he said and the sincerity in his voice moved me. "You *can't* kill him. You *can't*."

He spoke with a terrible zealousness. There was the slightest hint of moisture in my eyes. Sackler the tough guy, Sackler the selfish mug who never thought of anything but himself and his fees, pleading with every nerve for my life. It touched me oddly.

"Take it easy," said Mike. "It's a job that's just got to be done. You been around long enough to know that, Sackler."

Sackler sighed again. He looked utterly miserable. I felt as if I were in the middle of a big dramatic scene. I tried to play up to it.

"Rex," I said, "it's O.K. Forget it. I'm just stuck with it, that's all. I can take it, all right."

He did not meet my eyes. He turned to Hymie and said: "All right, if you do kill him what are you going to do with the body?"

Hymie shrugged. "Plant it somewhere. Hide it out in Long Island or drop it in the bay. All the better for us if there's no corpus delicti."

"No," said Sackler, a hint of desperation in his voice, "you don't have to do that. Leave the corpse here. Or anyway tell me where you're going to leave it."

"Look," said Mike, "if the coppers find the body, they'll tie it up with Big Joe and Barker's murder right away. There'll be a stink raised. Why should we stick our necks out?"

"What if I talk?" asked Sackler. "What if I tell the coppers the truth?"

"Your word'll mean nothing. There's no legal evidence to tie us up with Big Joe. Besides, without a body nothing you say'll make any sense. There ain't no proof of a murder. Anyway, if you're worried about a decent burial, Hymie and I'll bury him neatly ourselves."

"Thanks, anyway, Rex," I said. "I—" He didn't let me finish. He was out of his chair, smashing his left fist into his right palm and roaring at the top of his voice.

"Burial! Who the hell cares about a burial? Do you realize I'm in for ten grand on Joey's bail? Do you realize I have to produce a live man, a death certificate, or a corpse? Do you realize if I don't I lose that dough? *Ten grand?*"

He sank back into his chair, clapping his hand to his brow as if the thought were too much for him. I glared at him with hell's own fires of hatred in my heart. I felt at that moment as if I were all the Gestapo and he was Jan Valtin. In one hundred years I shall never be as angry again.

"You louse!" I yelled. "All the time I thought you were worrying about me! A hell of a lot you care how many bullets they blast me with. When I'm lying at the bottom of the East River you'll be beating your yellow breast about your filthy money. Hymie, for God's sake, grant me a dying wish. Let me take one smack at him before I go."

SACKLER POSSESSED THE unmitigated gall to look at me reproachfully. "Now, Joey," he said, "they're going to kill you anyway. I can't do anything about it. Since you're going to get it, you may as well save me my money. There's no sense in both of us suffering. Ten grand's a lot of dough."

"On Judgment Day," I said bitterly, "you'll crawl from your grave and offer the guy who's keeping the books two and a half bucks to square yourself. You'll be astounded when he belts you with his halo."

"Take it easy, fellows," said Hymie. "We don't want no trouble." He glanced down at his watch. "It's time, Mike. Go upstairs and call. Tell him it's O.K. We're ready."

Mike nodded. He tucked his gun away, rose and climbed the stairs. Hymie, his thirty-eight in his hand, took over the guard duty. Sackler's face was gray. There was pain in his eyes. I came to the astounding conclusion that he was sicker about losing his ten grand than I was about losing my life. I found a single consolation. When Mike's first bullet exploded into my brain it was going to cost Rex Sackler the sum of ten thousand dollars. The grave would be warmer for that thought.

Hymie leaned back in his chair smiling. Our argument, apparently, had amused him. His right hand rested on his knee and his gun dangled carelessly from it. I glared over at Sackler again. He winked with his left eye and jerked his head in my direction. Then I looked around and realized what he was driving at.

My automatic still lay on the mantelpiece where Hymie had tossed it. From where I sat it was a reach of about eight feet. Hymie, still smiling, was not, at the moment, paying a great deal of attention to either of us. I knew, however, that any sudden move on my part would bring the thug immediately back to the alert.

But here was a case where I had absolutely nothing to lose. If I grabbed the gun and shot it out the chances were, say, two to one against me. If I didn't, they were infinity to nothing. I took a deep breath and moved like a pursuit plane.

I grabbed the automatic at precisely the same moment that Sackler threw his ancient hat full in Hymie's face. Hymie sprang from his chair and his thirty-eight fired a single shot into the floor. By that time I was pressing the automatic into his side.

"All right," I said, "you're licked, Hymie. Pipe down."

Sackler took the thirty-eight from his hand.

From the upper story came Mike's voice. "What the hell's wrong down there? What the—"

Footsteps sounded on the stairs. "Take him, Joey," said Sackler. "But here, use this."

He pressed Hymie's thirty-eight into my hand and relieved me of the automatic. He slugged Hymie, quite unnecessarily, over the head with the butt of my weapon, but I had no time to protest then. I raced to the edge of the stairs and ducked down behind the bottom newel. Mike was a cinch to handle.

I had the gun in his back before he had even reached the last step. I relieved him of his gun and the pair of them stood there disconsolately while I covered them. Sackler was beaming from ear to ear.

"Hold them there, Joey. I'm going upstairs to make a phone call," he said cheerfully.

I nodded. I said: "Why did you switch guns on me? I'm used to that automatic."

"Oh," said Sackler, as calmly as if he were telling me what he'd had for lunch, "that automatic wasn't loaded. Mike knew it."

"It wasn't loaded! Do you mean to tell me you had me jump Hymie with an unloaded gun?"

"Mike unloaded it when Hymie took you to the kitchen for that water. Hymie didn't know about it. You were in no danger."

"I am speechless," I told him. "Is there any way in which you wouldn't gamble for my life?"

"Joey," he said, "you hurt me. After all it was the only chance of saving your life. I took it."

"Saving *what?*"

"Your life, Joey."

"Saving your bail, you mean. For God's sake, go upstairs before I slug you."

He went upstairs registering the misunderstood beautiful soul, far too good for this mundane world.

THE SITUATION WAS reversed in the hack going back to town. I enjoyed it infinitely more than the ride out. Hymie and Mike sat huddled together, glumly facing the gun I held in my hand. Sackler hummed a lilting tune far off-key.

I said: "I don't know why we're bringing these monkeys into headquarters. Why didn't you have them send out a wagon?"

"We're not going to headquarters, Joey."

"Where *are* we going then? Roseland?"

Sackler shook his head. "We're going to Alice Grattan's apartment. I just phoned Wooley. He's meeting us there along with Bellows and that lawyer guy, Justis."

"Why? If it's a cocktail party I'd sooner go to O'Shaughnessy's Bar and Grill."

"It isn't social, Joey. It's professional. You may have forgotten that I've been paid a fee to find out who killed old man Grattan. Well, now I'm going to tell them."

I raised my eyebrows. "You're going to *tell* them? You haven't worked a minute on the case. We've been held up. We've been kidnapped. We've been held in ten thousand dollar bail. When did you find time to discover who knocked off old man Grattan?"

"I've been thinking," said Sackler. "A process you wouldn't understand, anyway, Joey. Besides, I made a couple of phone calls earlier today. I spoke to Alice Grattan and the Second Federated Bank. Also to a number of wholesale diamond dealers."

"And I suppose they told you who murdered old man Grattan," I jeered at him.

Sackler sighed happily. "In a manner of speaking, Joey, they did," he said smoothly.

4

Sackler Shares the Wealth

EIGHT OF US congregated in the huge book-lined study at the Grattan apartment. Hymie and Mike, subdued and apprehensive, sat together on a sofa looking very much like the Katzenjammer kids awaiting a sound spanking. Alice Grattan, an ash blonde with wide blue eyes, relaxed in an armchair and turned an adoring gaze on young William Bellows who stood over her chair. Elmer Justis, well-dressed and pompous as when I had first seen him, smoked a cigar and looked thoughtful.

Wooley leaned upon the mantelpiece and regarded Sackler with disfavor. Sackler himself strutted up and down the floor exceedingly pleased with himself. I still wasn't sure why. If he had found the time to turn up the answer to Grattan's murder between our adventures of the past few days, I was prepared to admit that he had half the brain he claimed he had.

Sackler cast a swift glance around the room. His eye lighted on a japanned box of cigarettes. He took one and lit it.

He bowed in Wooley's direction and said: "First, I want to know about Big Joe Angers. Have you broken-down Monte Carlo coppers got a line on him?"

"They're on the way to pick him up now," said Wooley. "We got a tipoff to his whereabouts right after you called me. He'll be in the can within the hour. But what's that got to do with the Grattan killing?"

"That," said Sackler, "is something I wouldn't expect a police inspector to understand."

"Do you really know who killed father?" said Alice Grattan. "You know the Association of Diamond Dealers has offered a twenty-five hundred dollar reward for the arrest and conviction of the killer?"

Sackler's eyes glittered like green neon lights. He sighed contently. He sat down and inhaled on the cigarette, savoring its flavor, primarily, I supposed, because it was free.

"Look here," said Elmer Justis petulantly. "I'm a busy man. The inspector asked me to come here as a favor and I've come. Will someone come to the point?"

"Frankly," said Wooley, "I doubt if there's a point to come to. As I see it we can hold Bellows for murder. With Barker dead the defense can't produce a reputable witness to support his alibi. The motive's perfect."

Alice Grattan's eyes flashed. Bellows opened his mouth to say something. But, as usual, Sackler was in there first with the dialogue.

"Bellows didn't kill Grattan," he said. "Not that it matters a great deal to the D.A. However, I know who did and I can prove it. Moreover, I can get a conviction."

"For twenty-five hundred dollars reward," said Wooley bitterly, "you can do anything. Have you brought those two thugs, Hymie and Mike, here to confess the killing?"

Hymie and Mike looked very uncomfortable. Sackler stood up and faced his audience.

"All right," he said, "let's get started. Let's begin with the day I met my client, Mr. Bellows. He gave me a check for fifteen hundred dollars, signed by Alice Grattan. He gave it to me on a Friday morning. At eleven o'clock."

"Daylight saving time," sneered Wooley.

"Daylight saving time," said Sackler blandly. "A few moments later, Hymie over there walked into my office with a gun and stuck me up. He took six dollars in cash and that check. Now, what would a legitimate stickup man want a check made out to me for? He couldn't cash it. If he tried he'd be walking right into the arms of the law."

"Is this a puzzle?" said Justis. "I tell you I'm a busy man."

"It's a puzzle to everyone in this room but me," said Sackler. "After the holdup, I called Miss Grattan to have payment stopped, to have a new check issued. I couldn't get her on Friday. I couldn't get her on Saturday until the afternoon. Where were you then, Miss Grattan?"

Alice Grattan stared at him in complete bewilderment. For that matter, so did I.

"Why, I told you that on the phone, Mr. Sackler. On Friday, Mr. Justis sent word for me to come to his office. He was detained for some time. I waited a long while for him to return. I remained with him all day. Had dinner with him and his wife and stayed overnight at their place. Saturday morning, I also spent in his office going over some of my father's papers."

Sackler waved his hand like a magician who has just pulled a dragon out of a child's hat.

"There," he said. "See?"

WE LOOKED AT each other. It was evident that we all saw with the clarity of a blind man in London at midnight during a blackout. I realized that at least a third of my salary was paid for playing straight man for Sackler, so I came in.

"Could you make it a trifle clearer?" I asked him.

"Ah," said Sackler grandly, "excuse me. There are times when I forget the mentality of my auditors. Justis makes an appointment with Miss Grattan for Friday, during a period when he knows he will be out of the office. He keeps her waiting. He keeps her out of her own house until Saturday afternoon after the banks have closed. Now do you get it?"

"No," I said.

Sackler's sigh held compassion for all the deficient mentalities of the world.

"When I was first given that check there wasn't sufficient money in the bank to clear it."

Alice Grattan frowned. "That's a little-used account, Mr. Sackler," she said. "There's usually a considerable balance in it."

"So you thought," said Sackler. "So Justis intended you to think. He tried his best to talk Bellows out of retaining me. Failing that, he sent a thug—Hymie over there—to get the check back by force. He kept Miss Grattan out of the way so I wouldn't receive another check from her until Monday when the account would once more have money in it."

Justis slammed his fist down on the table. "That's absolutely ridiculous," he thundered. "What have I to do with it? And if there's no money in the account on Saturday, how would there be any Monday?"

"You put it in Monday morning," said Sackler sweetly. "As soon as the bank opened."

"My God," said Wooley. "Assuming he did it, why couldn't he deposit the cash Friday? Why Monday?"

"He didn't have it Friday," said Sackler. "He didn't get it until Sunday night."

A little light filtered into my brain. "Where did he get it on Sunday?"

"From the wall safe in this room. You recall it was broken into on Sunday night. He cashed in a fortune in diamonds and replenished the account he had been looting."

"You accuse me of embezzlement," said Justis. "You accuse me of robbery. Are you going to accuse me of murder next?"

"Precisely." Sackler beamed. "Thank God someone gets it at last."

Wooley wiped his forehead with his hand. Sackler's circuitous method of expatriation invariably exasperated him.

"Keep talking," he said. "If you're accusing Justis of killing Grattan, the police department would like to know about it. The motive and the method particularly."

"Sure," said Sackler. "I shall use the simpler fragments of my vocabulary, so you will understand it. Justis was Grattan's lawyer and confidant. He also held his power of attorney, looked after his bank accounts and business. Moreover, he was named executor of Grattan's estate. These things I was told by the Second Federated Bank on which that check was drawn. They also told me that a check for fifteen hundred bucks on Miss Grattan's account could not have cleared on Friday."

"All right," said Wooley. "You've already told us most of this."

"Justis," continued Sackler, "had been rooking Grattan for years. Then came a crisis. I don't know whether Grattan got on to it, or whether Justis' stock market losses were so big he had to do something about it. Anyway, he hired Big Joe Angers to kill Grattan.

"He knew just when Grattan would have a fortune in

diamonds in that wall safe. So did one of the wholesale dealers from whom I got my information. Moreover, he had a made-to-order suspect in Bellows. He framed that phone call to Bellows, to lure him to a poolroom frequented by thugs. That sort of an alibi would be no good whatever. During that time he had Angers kill Grattan."

"Then," I said, "why didn't Big Joe force the safe that night? Why wait so many days after the murder?"

"Justis isn't fool enough to tell Big Joe about that safe. Joe could've kept all the swag that way. No, with Grattan out of the way, Justis could take his time about the safe. He had the freedom of the house, was a constant visitor. His hand, however, was forced by two things."

"You mean the check?" I asked. "He couldn't permit it to bounce because it would arouse Miss Grattan's suspicion?"

"Right. Undoubtedly he had visited the house often since the murder, awaiting his chance to open the safe which Miss Grattan didn't even know existed. He never had the chance. Possibly she was in the room with him all the time. However, he had plenty of time. So he thought. He knew he didn't have plenty of time after she wrote that check for me."

ELMER JUSTIS LAUGHED. Not too heartily, I thought. "And I suppose I had this Angers kill Barker also?"

"Is this a confession?" asked Sackler. "You and I know just how right you are."

"Motive?" snapped Wooley.

"Obvious," said Sackler. "He knew how anxious you mugs were to convict Bellows. He knew you'd do it without Barker's testimony. He was already in for one murder, why not two?

With Bellows already burnt, it'd take an awful lot of evidence before the D.A. would open the case again, admit he burned an innocent man, even if Justis' peculations ever came out."

Wooley scratched his head. "It sounds logical to me," he admitted reluctantly. "And examination of Grattan's accounts, of Justis' books, ought to prove it pretty well."

"Wait a minute," said Justis. "You forget that I'm a lawyer."

"You seem to have forgotten it once or twice yourself," said the Grattan girl bitterly.

"I'm a lawyer," said Justis again, "and I don't see that you have any case. Bellows' motive is as strong as mine. The case against him is as good. The whole theory is pretty conjectural from a legal point of view."

Wooley looked inquiringly at Sackler. There was an unpleasant degree of truth in what Justis had said. Sackler, I observed, appeared very calm. He looked as if he had at least one more rabbit in the hat.

"Big Joe Angers is cold on Barker's murder," he said. "Joey's testimony will burn him. He has a better chance if he comes clean in a courtroom. I have no doubt he'll drag Justis down with him."

Justis' face was pale. Wooley nodded slowly. He strode across the room to the telephone. "I'll see if they've picked up Big Joe yet."

He put the call through, spoke for a moment, then hung up slowly. "Rex," he said, "there goes our case."

"My God," exploded Sackler, "I solve a case for you. Do you mean to tell me your coppers are so dumb they can't get a known crook like Big Joe Angers?"

"They got him all right," said Wooley. "But with bullets. He's dead."

Sackler clapped a hand to his head. The blood came back into Elmer Justis' cheeks.

"He came quietly enough at first," said Wooley. "But on the way to the station-house the boys told him what you'd already told me. That Joey's snatch hadn't worked. Big Joe said he was damned if he was going to burn. He snatched a copper's gun and started shooting. They shot back. Big Joe's in the morgue at this moment."

Sackler's shoulders sagged. His face was suddenly haggard and there was pain in his eyes. He uttered a groan that would not have been out of place at the Wailing Wall.

"Well, Mr. Sackler," said Bellows, "it certainly isn't your fault, even if we can't get a conviction. At least I'm cleared. That, after all, is what we were paying you for."

"*You're* cleared?" said Sackler as if that were the last thing he had been thinking of. "Who gives a damn about clearing you? The Diamond Dealers' Association says specifically: arrest *and* conviction. Those dumb coppers are plucking twenty-five hundred slugs out of my pocket."

"Well, gentlemen," said Justis rising, "if there isn't anything else at the moment, I'll be running along."

"Wait," said Sackler. "Wooley, don't let him go. I'll think of something. I *must* think of something."

I smiled happily. I examined the innermost core of my heart. I discovered that my interest in the triumph of justice was not so intense as my desire to see Sackler lose twenty-five hundred dollars.

All of us, even Justis, watched him with interest. There was anguish in his eyes and the tortured frown on his brow was shaped like a grieving pretzel. Every brain cell had been drafted in a titanic battle for twenty-five hundred dollars.

HE LOOKED UP suddenly. There was a familiar glint in his eye and his brow was clear again. He glanced across the room to Hymie and Mike. Then he looked at me. His eyes clouded again for a moment. He reached in his pocket, withdrew a worn leather purse and extracted fifty cents.

"Joey," he said, "will you run down to the corner and get two decks of cigarettes? I'm all out and you can get one for yourself."

"There are plenty of cigarettes here," said Bellows. "In that box there."

Sackler shook his head. "I've been smoking yours all afternoon," he said apologetically. "Go ahead, Joey."

I blinked at him. Sackler's worrying about smoking someone else's butts astonished me. Moreover, he'd never bought me a package of cigarettes since I'd known him. I took the fifty cents from his hand, suspicion welling up within me like erupting lava.

I donned my hat, walked from the apartment and closed the door behind me. I stood in one place and moved my feet up and down achieving the sound effect of diminuendo footsteps. There was something very screwy going on in Sackler's mind. I wanted to know what it was. I jammed my ear against the panel of the door and listened.

"I should have seen it before," Sackler was saying. "Hymie and Mike are the answer, Wooley. It's easy."

"Explain it," said Wooley.

"They're Angers' thugs. They were in on the deal all the way. They probably did none of the killing. Big Joe always does that himself. But they stuck me up for the check. They snatched Joey and myself. They know the whole story as well as Big Joe himself. They'll talk."

"I ain't saying nothing at all." This was Hymie's voice.

"Oh, yes, you are," said Sackler. "Look at it this way. Talk and you'll be open for an accessory rap. Since you've turned state's evidence, you'll beat it with a few years."

"Rot," said Justis. "If they don't talk you can't put a finger on them. Why should they turn state's evidence?"

"If they don't talk," said Sackler, "God help them. They'll be held on a kidnapping rap. They'll get life."

There was a long silence. Then Mike said: "You mean if we play it your way you'll keep your mouth shut about the kidnapping?"

"Exactly," said Sackler. "Now will you sign a confession implicating Justis, here and now?"

There was a second silence. Then, "Yeah," said Mike. "Yeah," said Hymie.

"O.K.," said Sackler. "Wooley, get a stenographer."

I grinned happily to myself. I tossed the half dollar Sackler had given me and caught it gaily. I went out of the house and bought two decks of butts. I took my time about coming back.

I TIMED MY entrance nicely. The police stenographer had just pulled the typewritten sheets out of his portable type-writer. Wooley took them and handed them to Mike and Hymie. Justis, across the room, stared at Sackler as if he were a snake.

Sackler saw me, nodded hastily, and forced his fountain pen into Hymie's hand. I drew a deep breath and made my play.

"By the way, Inspector," I said, "I want those two men there held for kidnapping. They snatched me forcibly this afternoon."

Hymie dropped the pen as if it were a scorpion. Wooley

uttered an oath, Sackler glared at me and there was sudden hope in Justis' eyes.

"Well," said Mike with finality, "that sort of changes things."

"Listen, Joey," said Sackler, "I don't think you ought to press that kidnapping charge."

"No? I thought we stood for law and order. I thought we stood for virtue. I thought—"

"Shut up," said Sackler, "I know what you're driving at."

"Good," I said. "How much?"

Sackler licked his lips and swallowed something in his throat. Wooley said testily: "What the devil are you guys talking about?

Sackler said, not without a terrible effort, "Ten per cent?"

I said, with no effort whatever, "Twenty?"

It may have been a trick of the sunlight but I thought I saw a tear in his eye as he nodded.

"Very well," I said. "I was not kidnapped. I went with those two mugs of my own free will. I say this before witnesses. I shall make no attempt to press my trumped-up charge."

Wooley picked up the pen. "All right," he said. "Now will you sign?"

I beamed happily around the room as they signed. It was difficult to tell at the moment whether Justis or Sackler was more disturbed.

ON THE WAY back to the office, Sackler said, low fury in his tone: "Joey, you are a low, black-hearted eavesdropper. You listened at the door."

I smiled sweetly. "That I did."

"You are a blackmailing hound. You have no loyalty to your employer."

"Loyalty?" I said. "What about you? I was the guy they wanted to snatch. I was the guy to make the complaint, if any. Not you. You deliberately got me out of the room, hoping everything would be in the bag by the time I got back, so I wouldn't know what you were doing. You didn't even care if I did make the complaint after you had the confession signed and sealed. You were afraid I'd do what I did do. Threaten to screw up the signing until I got my rightful cut of the reward."

He shook his head and sighed. "What about the cigarettes? And my change."

I gave him a deck of cigarettes. I gave him eighteen cents change. He weighed it in the palm of his hand for a long time.

"Joey," he said slowly, "under the circumstances I think you should pay for your own cigarettes. Give me another sixteen cents."

Personally, I believe that all Scotsmen are a horde of profligate spendthrifts.

Murder Pays 7 to 1

When the pudgy little man retained Joey's tightwad boss to solve a murder that hadn't yet been committed—and the only possible suspect had two perfect alibis—Joey saw a chance to gloat over Sackler's lost fee. But love will find a way—and Sackler's feeling for do-re-mi amounted to a Grande Passion.

1

Sackler Takes a Chance

REX SACKLER CAME into the office, said "Good morning," as if the two words were costing him full cable rates and sat down at his desk. I ignored him. I stuck to my task of picking the winners of those ten football games for which feat the *News* offered a C-note.

I completed my calculations, put them in an envelope and turned around to argue Sackler out of a two-cent stamp. He sat, bent over his desk, running his thin fingers through his ebony hair. There was a frown on his brow and his piercing black eyes stared at the paper before him, engrossed as a monk at a burlesque show.

I stood up, crossed the room and said: "Let me have a stamp, will you? I—"

I broke off abruptly and blinked as I noted the title of the paper. I said, in the tone of a man watching the sun rise in the west: "What in the name of God are you reading?"

He lifted his sharp-featured face. "This is a *Racing Form*, Joey. It tells all about horses."

"Since when are you interested in horses?"

"Well," said Sackler, "horses are primarily gambling instruments. Gambling amuses me. Of course, the bookmakers have a cold ten per cent against you. But after all, what's that matter? It isn't important whether you win or lose. It's the fun of the game that counts, isn't it?"

I clapped a hand to my head and took a dazed step backward. Sackler's regard for money was a little less than his regard for his right arm. Torquemada's rack could not have forced him to disgorge a Confederate dollar from his Postal Savings accounts. I found my voice and said as much.

"Nonsense," said Sackler. "You speak, Joey, from ignorant prejudice. You envy my freehandedness. To prove you thoroughly, completely wrong, I am about to take a flyer this afternoon."

I stared at him incredulously. "You mean you're going to place a bet on a horse?"

"I am," said Sackler firmly. "And to win. None of these piker place or show bets for me."

I LOOKED AT him for a long time. I shook my head. I said: "There are two possible angles. One, quite remote, that you've had a horrible dream. Like Scrooge in *A Christmas Carol*. The other, far more likely, that you know something. That every horse in the race, except yours, will be wearing a sponge in its nostrils—that the one you bet on will have a half gallon of caffeine coursing through its veins. If you're betting on a horse the race is as fixed as the law of gravity. I'm inclined to risk a dollar myself."

Sackler smiled. "Ah," he said, "I was about to speak to you about that, Joey."

Suspicion welled up in me like a tear in a True Story reader's eye. Whenever I became involved in financial transaction with Sackler, I invariably came out on the short end. Sackler paid me a totally inadequate salary every Friday afternoon, then devoted the rest of the week trying to win it back. With no little success, either.

A scream rent the air. "Good God," I said, "what's that?"

Sackler stood up abruptly, moved in the general direction of my desk and snapped up one of my cigarettes before I could grab the package. He said: "Jocy, I know the winner of the fourth race. I should get eight to one."

I was still wary. Avarice, however, overcame my better judgment.

"What's the horse?"

Sackler narrowed his eyes and looked like a Balkan conspirator. "Well, Joey," he said, "you don't expect me to *give* away valuable information like that, do you?"

"Good God," I said indignantly. "Are you in the touting racket now? Are you actually selling tips on horses?"

"Well," he said, "not exactly. Not for cash anyway. In exchange for my information I simply require you to lay a twenty dollar bet for me."

"Oh," I said. "It doesn't matter whether you win or lose. It's the fun of the game that counts. I take it, you're letting me have all the fun."

Sackler shrugged his shoulders. "All right," he said. "I'm merely trying to let you in on something. I got this direct from Charlie Harrison, the bookmaker. However, if you don't want it—"

I went back to my desk and sat down. I fought to keep my mouth shut, to take no part of this deal. Something warned me that, as usual, it was going to cost me dough. However, there's a lot of sucker blood in me. I turned around and met Sackler's mocking expectant eye.

"I am putty," I said. "I'll bet twenty for you. What's the horse?"

"Mayfair II," said Sackler. "Get the bet down before three o'clock, though."

"All right. I'll bet twenty for you, Shylock, and twenty for myself. Are you certain the horse will win?"

"Certain," said Sackler. "My God, I'm betting twenty dollars of my own money!"

That was enough for me. If Sackler was siphoning twenty bucks from one of his Postal Savings accounts to bet on a horse, that horse was going to win by seven lengths. Rex Sackler was the sort of guy who would wager, without hesitation, that Christmas came but once a year or that the ocean contained a certain percentage of salt—always provided the odds were right.

Rex Sackler's regard for money made the affection of Abelard for Heloise pale into a casual relationship. Mindful of the dire happenings of 1929, he eschewed banks. His money was safely salted away in a score of post offices. Nothing short of revolution was going to snatch Sackler's cash away from him.

His pain at disgorging a nickel was only equaled by his ecstasy in hoarding it. He spent a dollar with the agony of a man having a cancer removed sans anesthetic. His suits— both of them—were snappy little numbers, tailored when La Guardia was still a congressman. His hat was a misshapen mass that he had picked up off a Bleecker Street barrow while Cal Coolidge sat silent and smug in the White House. His shoes, which he repaired himself with some patented rubbery substance, had been wrought on a last which had been discarded eight year's ago.

Considering all these things, I came to the inevitable conclusion that if Sackler was prepared to wager twenty slugs of his own money on Mayfair II the race was as safe as an election in Jersey City. I decided to throw in twenty of my own money. Mentally I multiplied that twenty by eight and came out with a figure that seemed eminently satisfactory, considering the depleted condition of my own bank account.

I donned my hat and coat, collected the twenty from Sackler, added forty of my own funds to it and went down the block to lay the bet.

I GOT BACK to the office just as the client came in. He was a little pudgy man with a round face and a suit that had cost at least twice as much money as Sackler's entire wardrobe. I bowed to him politely and escorted him to the inner office from the outer. Sackler lifted his eyes and stared.

He was engaged, I knew, in a task at which he was peculiarly proficient. He was looking with his X-ray eyes through the exterior of the client right to the heart of his credit rating. He smelled money at a hundred yards. He showed all his teeth in an obsequious smile. He indicated a chair with a wave of his hand. He said: "Sit down, Mr.—"

"Mellish," said the pudgy man. "George Pinkerton Mellish."

"Ah, Mr. Mellish," said Sackler, "the talents and facilities of this office are at your disposal. Aren't they, Joey?"

I said, "Yes," with no enthusiasm whatever. Inwardly, I hoped that what Mellish had to offer us was a modicum of work and a meager fee. There were times when Sackler's making money annoyed me almost as much as it pleased him.

Mr. Mellish sat down. He looked around the office with a pair of bright blue eyes, which, I thought, held an odd expression. He sighed deeply and lit a cigarette with fingers that twitched slightly.

"This is an unusual matter," he said heavily. "Secrecy is of the very essence."

"Our discretion," said Sackler with the oiliness of a congressman in October of the even numbered years, "is equaled only by our ability."

I refrained from observing that the policy of our office in regard to discretion and everything else was controlled solely by the fact of who was paying whom how much and how fast.

"I'm glad to hear that," said Mellish. "The case I offer you is, I'm afraid, murder."

Sackler's eyes lit up and his spirits rose in direct ratio as mine fell. And for the same reason, too. Murder, the gravest crime on the books, commanded the biggest fee. The idea of Sackler sinking another juicy check into his already bloated accounts made me slightly nauseated.

He shot a swift glance at me and there was gloating in his eyes. He turned deferentially to Mellish. Mellish once again cast his sharp blue eyes around the room. He stroked his chin thoughtfully.

"I have every reason to believe that a man was murdered this morning in a house on Charlton Street."

Sackler licked his lips. "You want us to find the killer?"

"In the event that my theory is correct, I do."

"Details," said Sackler, trusting they were complicated enough to warrant the asking of a fat fee in advance.

"There is a man named Lomax," said Mellish. "Arthur Lomax who owns the Charlton Street house. I am of the opinion that he was stabbed to death this morning in his bedroom. I want you to find out if this is true. If so, I want the killer uncovered."

The smug expression on Sackler's face nettled me. I risked his wrath by saying: "If a murder was committed, if you know about it, Mr. Mellish, why don't you tell the police?"

Sackler glared at me like a headlight. Mellish could command the services of the police department free. There was always the possibility that Mellish hadn't thought of that. From Sackler's viewpoint I was engaged, at the moment, in snatching a well-buttered piece of bread out of his mouth. Mellish's next words flooded him with relief.

"There are reasons why I prefer this handled privately," he said. "I haven't much faith in the abilities of the police. Second, it's barely possible they've already been called in."

"Barely possible?" said Sackler. "You mean the people in the house know murder's been done, yet they haven't notified the police?"

"That," said Mellish, "is a distinct possibility."

"Why?"

"If the killer is the man I think he is, he is a close friend of the family. They will be inclined to hush it up if possible."

Sackler's face lit up. He was going to have the name of a suspect delivered to him before he began. That made the task much easier. But Mellish's answer to his question, doubtless, disappointed him.

"I'll mention no names," said Mellish. "Mine is only a suspicion. I'm interested in this matter because Lomax' wife is a niece of mine. I want this murder investigated. I have told you all that I shall tell you. If you want the sort of fee I'm prepared to pay, you'll have to earn it."

SACKLER CALCULATED QUICKLY. "The fee," he said, "will be two thousand dollars."

Mellish nodded. "Send the killer to the chair," he said, "and the money's yours."

Sackler blinked. It was an old habit of his to collect the fee in advance. Mellish, apparently, wanted results first. Sackler explained suavely that advance fees were a rule of the office. Mellish to my delight was as adamant as the Rocky Mountains.

"I am a businessman," he said. "I do not pay for failure. I offer you two thousand dollars to find out who killed Arthur Lomax. Further, I make the provision that my name does not appear in the investigation at all. That you don't even get in touch with me at my home or office. I don't want it even suspected that I'm behind the investigation. I'll phone you every day to see what you have. Two thousand dollars. Do you take it?"

Sackler nodded glumly. "But," he said. "How do I know you'll pay me? I must have references as to your financial standing."

Mellish stood up. "Fair enough. Have all you want. Here is my card. My bank is the Third National. I'm rated in Dun's and mentioned in *Who's Who*. Check me up to your heart's content."

He tossed a card on Sackler's desk. He walked to the door. He said over his shoulder: "Remember, if you violate any of the conditions I've laid down the contract is void. You get no fee."

His blue eyes stared frigidly at Sackler. Then the door slammed and he was gone. Sackler sighed heavily and shook his head.

"Joey," he said, "I don't like it."

"You don't like what? The fact that you have to work before you get paid?"

"Partly. I don't like the whole setup. This guy Mellish knows of a murder, apparently, almost as soon as it is committed. Moreover, he seems very anxious that no one knows he's putting a shamus on the killer's trail."

I shrugged my own shoulders. Sackler's worries were not mine. Win, lose or draw, I drew precisely the same salary each week. Obviously Mellish knew more than he had told us. But I knew quite well why Sackler hadn't plied him with questions. There were a hundred other private detectives in town. All of them more reasonable than Sackler. The idea of driving a client away to the opposition was, to him, as repulsive as making love to a rattlesnake.

Sackler's eye fell on the package of cigarettes on my desk. Hastily I put them in my pocket. He sighed and took a sack of Bull Durham from his desk drawer and proceeded to roll one of his own with clumsy fingers.

"All right, Joey," he said as he lit it. "We've got a case. Make the first move."

"Which is…? Going over to that house on Charlton Street?"

"That question," said Sackler, "is the answer to why you'll never be in business for yourself. The first move is to check Mellish. How the hell do I know he's *got* two thousand bucks?"

I picked up the receiver and went to work. I issued an eminently satisfactory report a few minutes later. Mellish was president of an iron works in Jersey City. His financial rating was AA1. His bank spoke of him in awe. Sackler wore a complacent smile as he listened to me.

He stood up and put on his ancient hat. "Come on, Joey," he said. "We have a duty to perform. We are working in the interests of justice, law and order."

"Not to mention two grand," I said disgustedly as I followed him from the room.

But he didn't answer me. He was filled with a vision of greenbacks. The rustle of folding money was sounding in his ears.

2

Too Early for Murder

A MAID ADMITTED us to the Lomax house on Charlton Street a little before eleven o'clock. Sackler asked for Mrs. Lomax and we were escorted through a magnificently furnished hallway to the breakfast nook. Two people sat at the table. Lomax' wife was small, blond and arrayed in negligée which more than hinted she was possessed of an excellent figure. Across the table from her sat a man of middle age, well-dressed and with streaks of gray in his hair. Mrs. Lomax looked up at us. She said with no cordiality whatever: "I am not accustomed to interviewing strangers at this hour in the morning."

Sackler glanced about the room. He caught my eye for a moment. It was obvious what he was thinking. It was quite apparent that if murder had been done here an hour or so ago, the coppers were certainly unaware of it. Homicide's routine would take at least two hours.

He bowed to the blonde. "This is not a social call," he said. "I would like to see your husband."

"He's in bed. He never rises before noon. Why don't you see him at his office?"

Sackler ignored the question. "May I ask if you've seen him this morning?"

The blonde glared at him. "I suppose," she said angrily, "you'd also like to know if I slept with him last night. Is it any of your damned business?"

Sackler tugged thoughtfully at his ear lobe. "It might possibly be the business of the police department," he said, and watched with hawk eyes for the reaction. There wasn't any.

The middle-aged man coughed and stood up. "I am Doctor Deeling," he announced. "Alienist of some repute. The Lomax family physician for several years. I called on Mr. Lomax this morning. I'm staying here for breakfast. If this is a legal matter perhaps I can be of some help."

Sackler fixed the doctor with his gaze. "Then you've seen Mr. Lomax this morning?"

Deeling nodded. "I left him less than fifteen minutes ago."

"How was his health?"

"Excellent."

Sackler blinked. With a two thousand dollar fee in the offing he was going to be most disappointed if he had been gypped out of his corpse. After all, he couldn't solve a murder case if it developed that no one had been murdered.

The blonde's teeth crunched hard on a piece of toast. "Look," she said, "is this my house or isn't it? Copper or no copper, I demand to know what you're doing here. You'll either tell me or get out."

Sackler turned on all his oily charm. "Madam," he said, "we but do our duty. We were notified that Mr. Lomax had met with a serious accident. Foul play was hinted. We are here to aid you. To investigate."

Alice Lomax looked at the doctor. "Arthur was all right when you saw him, wasn't he?"

"Perfectly."

Sackler ran worried white fingers through his black hair. No one ever wished Hitler dead more heartily than Rex Sackler wished there was a corpse in Lomax' bedroom at that moment.

He said, in the tone of a man hoping against hope: "May we see him?"

Deeling shrugged. "Why not? He'll probably be sore at being awakened twice in one morning. But I suppose the police are entitled to certain privileges."

The blonde got up. She and Deeling led the way up the stairs. I said to Sackler, *sotto:* "After all, what's a lousy fee if a human life has been saved?"

He looked at me like a hotel credit manager when One-eyed Connolly passes through the lobby. We gained the upper story. Deeling knocked hard upon a closed door, then opened it. The four of us filed into a bedroom.

A BODY MOVED beneath a rumpled sheet. A head, tousled, lifted itself from a twisted pillow. A pair of angry, sleepy eyes blinked at us. Lomax, looking very much like a man with a crashing hangover, opened a pair of dry lips and said: "My God, I'll have a traffic light put in this bedroom. What the devil is it now?"

The fact that Sackler had no corpse lifted my spirits. With a deliberate desire to needle him a little, I said: "We came up here to see if you were dead, Mr. Lomax."

Lomax propped himself up on his elbow and glared at us like Mr. Hyde. "My God," he said. "First Deeling wakes me up to see if I'm ill. Now you come along to see if I'm dead. Well, it's all damned solicitous of you, but it's ruining my sleep." He drew a deep breath and endowed his tone with a few thousand more decibels. "Get out, damn you. Get out and leave me alone!"

His wife backed out of the room. If she was afraid of his

wrath, I figured that Sackler and myself, here under very dubious pretenses, should be even more so. We followed with alacrity.

"You see," said Deeling as we stood in the lower hallway again, "there is nothing the matter with him. I can't understand where you got your tip."

"I cannot understand why my breakfast was interrupted," snapped Alice Lomax. "Can it be possible the police department is as stupid as it's reputed to be?"

Sackler was too crushed to answer. I followed him grinning from the house. We stood out on the pavement. I whistled a blithe tune, enjoying Sackler's misery. He turned on me savagely.

"What the devil are you so happy about?"

"I am happy," I told him gravely, "because I came to this house expecting to find it an abode of sorrow, expecting to find a broken-hearted wife whose husband had been foully murdered. I discover, however, that the husband is well. That crime has failed to rear its ugly head. That happiness crowns the little love nest. Any decent citizen would be happy."

His rage was beautiful. I watched his twisted face with the satisfaction of an art critic standing before a Rembrandt.

"You are a selfish, miserable creature," he said bitterly. "You revel in the fact that I lose a fee. You know nothing of loyalty, of decency, of the finer things of life. You are—"

He was interrupted by an odd sound from the house. It was half groan, half cry. It seemed to emanate from the second story. Sackler looked at me and there was a peculiar expression on his face. We stood in utter silence for a moment. Then a scream rent the air, a high-pitched feminine scream that had emerged, doubtless, from the rouged lips of Alice Lomax.

"Good God," I said, "What's that?"

Sackler drew a deep breath. "I think," he said and his voice vibrated with excitement, "I think it is my reward for a good and honest life. I think, Joey, it might be my corpse."

He turned, led the way back into the Lomax house. Bewildered, and filled with strange apprehension, I followed him.

Sackler regarded the thing on the bed with almost obscene satisfaction. Alice Lomax stood, her back to the bedroom wall, stark horror in her eyes and her hand held against her mouth. Deeling, frowning, bent over the bed, staring at the dead body of Arthur Lomax.

Blood stained the sheet. His pajama coat had been ripped roughly open. Something shining protruded from his chest and he lay very still. It was obvious that he was not going to have his sleep interrupted any more this morning.

Sackler moved toward the bed. He looked at the body carefully. He said slowly: "That's a scalpel sticking in his heart, isn't it, Doctor?"

The blonde took her hand away from her mouth. She said shrilly: "What do you mean? Do you dare insinuate that—"

Deeling said: "Shut up, Alice." He turned to Sackler. "Yes," he went on, "that's a scalpel. It apparently pierced his heart immediately. We heard him cry out downstairs. We rushed up here to find him dead."

I LIT A cigarette and sighed. I felt like a football player whose team has lost the game in the last forty seconds of play. A moment ago I was sure no crime had been committed and that Sackler wasn't going to make a dime. Now I stared at a corpse with a scalpel stuck in its heart with knowledge that a doctor had been in the house. Not only did Sackler have his corpse but he had a made-to-order suspect along with it.

It struck me suddenly that Alice Lomax' mind was moving in the same channels as my own. She looked at Sackler fearfully. "Doctor Deeling had nothing to do with this," she said. "I was with him all the time. Just because the murder was done with a scalpel doesn't mean that—"

Deeling said again: "Shut up, Alice."

Sackler's eyes gleamed suddenly. "I'm sure," he said softly, "we couldn't pin a murder charge on the doctor without a motive. What possible motive could he have for killing your husband, Mrs. Lomax?"

My gaze followed his own to the shapely body in the negligee. It occurred to me suddenly what the doctor's motive might be. Sackler opened his mouth as if to speak, when Deeling crashed his right fist into the palm of his left hand.

"My God!" he exclaimed. "Campbell. He's been out a week now!"

Alice Lomax' sigh was hissing relief. "Of course," she said. "Campbell."

Sackler scratched the palm of his left hand with his right index finger. "You mean you know who killed him?"

"Undoubtedly," said Deeling. "It was Campbell. Motive and everything. It's simple now. I should have thought of it before. Campbell, of course."

"And who," asked Sackler, "is Campbell?"

The color had come back into Alice Lomax' face now. She no longer seemed upset at the sight of the corpse.

"Oh," she said, "that was Minna Campbell's husband."

"Wait a moment," said Deeling. "Campbell used to be a business partner of Lomax. He suffered a nervous breakdown which eventually led to insanity. He always believed that Lomax had cheated him in business, had driven him to madness. A week ago he escaped from an asylum in South Bend."

"And your theory is," asked Sackler, "that he planned revenge, that he came here and stabbed Lomax to death?"

"Of course," said Alice Lomax. "It's obvious, isn't it?"

Sackler took a cigarette from the package on the taboret on the bed. He lit one, inhaled slowly. He made a gesture as if to replace the cigarettes on the table. Then he looked at the corpse and put the package in his pocket. He blew smoke from his mouth and said, "No," very quietly.

Deeling and the blonde exchanged a swift glance. I intercepted it. The warm intimacy I saw there confirmed my suspicion of a moment ago. Deeling faced Sackler.

"Well," he said, "what are you going to do about it?"

Sackler sighed like a tired wind crawling through autumn leaves. "I'm going back to the office to think," he said. "In the meantime I suggest you notify the police."

Deeling blinked at him. "Aren't you the police?"

"In a sense. I'm a private investigator. I devote my life to the cause of law and order."

"At three and a third per cent," I murmured.

Alice Lomax glared at us like an angry searchlight. "You're not coppers?" she said. "You've one hell of a nerve coming around here. Get out. Get out, I say!"

Sackler turned and made his way down the stairs. I followed him. The blonde's invective beat against the backs of our necks as we let ourselves out into the street again.

"Well," I said, "what now?"

"Mellish," said Sackler. "Check him again."

"For what? You don't think he killed Lomax, do you?"

"He knew he was going to be killed. I want you to find out where he was since he left our office."

"I still think you're crazy. Certainly he wasn't going to offer you money to solve a crime he hadn't committed yet. He wouldn't—"

"Shut up," said Sackler. "I have a headache now without listening to you imitate Conan Doyle. Find out where Mellish has been all morning."

I shrugged. "All right. Shall I see him personally?"

Sackler shuddered. "Good heavens, no! Snoop around his office. You can find out without asking him. He specifically forbade us to get in touch with him."

"There's a murder involved," I told him. "I never saw you so fussy about a client's injunctions before."

"My God," said Sackler. "He hasn't paid us yet, has he? Don't antagonize him. Moreover, if you can find out anything else about him—his personal life for instance—do so."

3

Double Alibi

IT TOOK ME two good diplomatic hours to find out what Sackler required about Mellish. I got back to the office a little after three in the afternoon. I found Sackler with his ears bent against the speaker of a portable radio. Clem McCarthy's voice beat through the room.

Sackler looked up. "They'll go to the post in about three minutes," he said. "The price now is seven to one on Mayfair II. What've you got on Mellish?"

"He's clean. He's been in his office since ten this morning."

"Anything else?"

"Nothing save a few facts I picked up about his private life from here and there."

"Namely?"

"He's a bachelor. Doesn't bother with women. Hunter, whiskey-drinking, poker-player type. Hangs out with the boys. That's about all I know. However, a guy with your genius ought to be able to figure out who killed Lomax from that."

"You are a very witty fellow," said Sackler in a tone which indicated I wasn't.

Clem McCarthy's *"They're Off!"* interrupted us. Both of us stared tensely at the radio. All in all we had sixty bucks riding at seven to one. True, Sackler was only risking half as much as I was and he stood to win twice as much. Nevertheless, a hundred and forty bucks would come in very handy.

At the quarter Mayfair II led by two lengths. I sat down and breathed a trifle more easily. Sackler sat tensely on the edge of his chair.

At the half Mayfair II still led by a length. In the stretch Mayfair II led by two lengths. In the final eighth Mayfair II led by four lengths and according to McCarthy's excited voice, was going away. Mayfair II crossed the wire, eased up, and Sackler looked like Rita Hayworth's husband on his wedding day.

"Never forget this day, Joey," he said. "Never again accuse me of taking your money. I put you on to this. I shared my knowledge with you. I have made you one hundred and forty dollars. I shall ask for no commission."

"Old golden heart," I murmured. "Especially since I bet twenty bucks for you. It's the first time in my life that I never begrudged you winning something."

Sackler shook his head and clucked like an old hen. "You place too much reliance in money. You have no concept of the sheer fun of gambling. Had I lost I should have enjoyed the thrill just as much."

I was about to call him a black-hearted liar to his face when Clem McCarthy did it for me.

"They're changing the numbers," said the radio. "A foul has been claimed and allowed. Mayfair II is disqualified. The winner is—"

Sackler shut off the radio with a frenzied hand. He beat his chest with his clenched fists. He raised his eyes to the ceiling and called on heaven groaningly to witness that he was the most unfortunate of men.

I regarded him with inextricably mixed emotions. The fact that he had lost twenty dollars was balm to my soul. The fact that I had lost forty caused a sharp pain in my duodenum. Then I realized, as I recalled the hundred and forty bucks I wasn't going to get, that the agony outweighed whatever glee I may have felt. I dropped my head in my hands and wondered why everything happened to me.

A voice said suddenly: "What lamentation am I interrupting?"

Sackler and I both looked up to see our client. Mellish was staring at us oddly with his sharp blue eyes. He stood close to me and I noted a familiar odor on his breath which I didn't place right away. Sackler said quickly: "You were right about that murder, Mr. Mellish. Lomax was stabbed in his bedroom this morning."

Mellish nodded and it seemed to me, with satisfaction. "Ah," he said, "and the culprit?"

"We're working on it," said Sackler. "I have several angles thus far. You can expect results very shortly."

A shadow of disappointment glazed the bright pigment of Mellish's eyes for a moment. "You have nothing?" he said. "Nothing at all?"

Sackler was watching him alertly. "I think," he said slowly, "I have an excellent suspect. Do you know a doctor named Deeling?"

Mellish's face lit up suddenly, then went deadpan again. "No. Never heard of him."

"Well," said Sackler, "that's all I can give you at the moment. If you get in touch with me tomorrow, I may have something else."

Mellish nodded. "All right. I'm going to drop into that saloon downstairs for a drink, if you and your assistant would care to come along."

ASKING SACKLER TO have a free drink was somewhat like requesting a hungry cannibal to join you in a slice of missionary. In practically no time at all we were leaning against O'Connor's bar across the street. Mellish bought three drinks like a little gentleman. Sackler who always ignored barroom etiquette made no move to reach in his pocket.

"I've got to run along now," said Mellish. "Business."

He reached out his fingers and dipped into a bowl of cloves that were on the bar. As he put them in his mouth I recognized the odor I had noted in the office. He munched the cloves slowly and shook hands with Sackler.

Sackler regarded him oddly. "You're a bachelor, aren't you, Mr. Mellish?"

"Why, yes," said Mellish, as startled as I at the *non sequitur,* "I've always kept away from women."

Sackler stared, absorbed, at the nude behind the bar as Mellish left the saloon. The bartender looked after the pudgy retreating figure and observed: "That guy can sure put it away."

Sackler turned his head quickly. "He's been in here before?"

"Sure—all morning. Came in about ten. He's been drinking steadily ever since."

Sackler blinked and sat down at the bar stool. "Joey," he said softly, "I'm beginning to suspect Mr. Mellish. He's the first man I ever heard of who had two perfect alibis for the same murder."

A tall wide torso suddenly loomed up beside me. A familiar rough voice boomed in my ear.

"Listen, my fine spendthrift friend," said Inspector Wooley of Homicide, "there will come a day when you lose your shamus license and get hit on the head with a rubber hose in a precinct basement. It will quite probably be the same day. It may well be today."

Sackler lifted his head two inches and his eyebrows four. "You had better be extremely courteous to me," he said. "For you, Inspector, are on the brink of disaster."

Wooley regarded him with the suspicious gaze he reserved solely for Rex Sackler.

"What are you talking about, my little prodigal pal?"

"He didn't do it," said Sackler.

"Who didn't do what?"

"Deeling didn't murder Lomax."

"How do you know I've got Deeling in the can?"

Sackler regarded Wooley quizzically. "Haven't you?"

"Yes. But how do you know?"

"It's just the sort of obvious thing you would do. But you've got the wrong guy—"

Wooley hesitated for a moment. When Sackler was right, he was very, very right. That fact had been demonstrated to the inspector on more than a single occasion.

"You're crazy," said Wooley but there wasn't much conviction in his tone. "It was open and shut. From the maid and Deeling's chauffeur we found out that they've been conducting an affair for some time. There's your motive. The scalpel belonged to Deeling. Hell, you can't get around that."

"Give me a day or two and I will," said Sackler.

Wooley eyed him without enthusiasm. Then he remembered what he had started to say.

"I came here to bawl you out, shamus. Not to listen to no lectures. I understand you knew that murder was going to happen before it actually did. You was there looking for the corpse before there even was a corpse. Besides, you was impersonating an officer. Now what've you got to say?"

"This," said Sackler softly. "When I'm ready to prove that you've made a mistake, I'll let you know first. On condition that you shut up."

Wooley's face reddened. He restrained what was on his tongue. He recalled that Sackler's abilities had saved him more than once. "All right," he said. "But if you can't prove I'm wrong, I'm going to have you see the D.A. about whatever you know."

"Leave me alone with my sorrow," said Sackler. "I'm worried enough about this damned case without having your seventh grade syntax pounded into my ear. Go away. I'll keep my part of the bargain if you keep yours."

Wooley retreated into the street, mumbling to himself. Tired of waiting for Sackler's hospitality, I ordered a beer and paid for it myself.

"Well," I said, "where are we? You say Deeling didn't kill Lomax. It's a cinch Mellish didn't. He has, as you observed, *two* alibis."

"I do not discuss cases with mental inferiors," said Sackler. "You will shut up, don your hat and drawers and seek out this Minna Campbell. Find out whatever you can about her husband. When he escaped from that asylum out west and whatever you can about his relationship with Lomax."

I drank my beer. If Sackler was in his superior mood, there was no point in continuing the conversation. As I prepared to go I heard him mutter savagely: "If there were only some way I could frame that hound. I'd collect the fee and he'd burn. And I'd watch him burn myself. The dirty double-crossing dog."

I blinked at him. "Who? Wooley?"

"No," he snarled, "that damned steward."

"What steward?"

"That idiot who disqualified Mayfair II. You don't realize what it is to have hard-earned money snatched out of your hand, Joey."

Which remark, considering I had dropped precisely twice as much as he had, was something of a minor classic in the annals of Sackler's frugality.

MINNA CAMPBELL WAS worried. She was a fat shapeless woman who sat in an over-cushioned living-room with a sex magazine on her ample lap and a five pound box of candy within easy reach. The amount of rouge on her expansive cheeks was only equaled by the amounts of dripping mascara on her eyelashes.

I implied, without actually saying so, that I was from headquarters. She was cordial enough with the simpering cordiality of a woman who hasn't many men callers any more.

"I'm worried," she told me, delicately licking some chocolate from her pudgy fingers. "I've been worried ever since they escaped last week."

"They?"

She nodded. "Yes. Another man escaped with Eric. His name I believe was Dunton. He was what they call a paranoiac, I think. I'm afraid Eric might come here, try to see me. Frankly, I'm terrified of him. I haven't seen him since they put him away years ago."

I lit a cigarette. "Was there anything to this tale of Lomax ruining him? Do you think he killed Lomax?"

She said, "No," emphatically. "I'm sure he didn't kill Lomax.

The killer of Lomax is in jail right now. Everyone knows what's been going on between Alice and Deeling for years. Everyone believed that Lomax just didn't care. But evidently he did. Evidently he told Deeling so and Deeling killed him."

She jammed her big mouth with chocolate creams and subsided. I scratched my head and wondered what the hell Sackler expected me to find out. Then, in utter boredom, I permitted my gaze to wander about the room. It came to a sudden and startled rest upon a huge oil painting hanging on the wall to my left. I blinked and stared at it.

Minna Campbell's eyes followed mine. She sighed like a passionate exhaust pipe. "He was very handsome in his day, don't you think?"

I gripped the edge of the chair hard. I said in a voice that fought for control of my risibilities: "Who? Eric Campbell? Is *that* your husband?"

"Yes. Isn't he virile in that picture? I always said about Eric that—"

I didn't hear her feminine garrulity. I was busily engaged in keeping a straight face. Within me a volcano of laughter fought for release. The muscles in my cheeks ached. When she paused for breath, I stood up and took my leave hurriedly. I left the sickly perfume of the room and went out into the cool air of the street. I leaned up against a tree guard, threw back my head and laughed more heartily than I had since Clayton, Jackson and Durante were a team.

I returned to the office feeling like a kid with a snowball watching the deacon approach with a silk hat. Fighting to keep an expressionless face, I sat down and told Sackler all the details save one. One I was keeping to myself, treasuring to my bosom, to hit him on the head with when the time was most propitious.

Sackler wore a deep frown as he digested my information. He made some meaningless pencil marks upon the pad in front of him.

"Joey," he said, "I think it's in the bag. I know you will be delighted to know that I am on the verge of collecting another fee."

He knew quite well that such statements usually nettled me. But this time I met his gaze squarely.

"Good," I said. "I'm very glad to hear it. You deserve everything you get out of this case."

Suspicion clouded his gaze. He stared at me through narrowed lids and grunted.

"All right," he said. "You can go home now, Joey. I have a little thinking to do. I'll see you in the morning."

I put on my hat. I bade him a fulsome goodnight. I left the office whistling blithely and completely forgetting the horrible tragedy of Mayfair II and the honest steward.

The following morning I arrived at the office a little after ten to find Sackler already behind his desk. He regarded me with an odd smile. I, still clutching my secret to my heart, like a new blond mistress, beamed at him. He beamed back. For the first time in history, it seemed, all the personnel of Rex Sackler's office was happy at the same time.

I sat down at my desk and broke all precedent by offering him a cigarette. Sackler broke no precedent at all by taking it.

ABOUT TEN FIFTEEN we heard the outer office door open and close. A moment later, the pudgy figure of Mellish entered the room. He fixed his little bright eyes on Sackler and said: "I see by the papers that Deeling is in jail for the murder of Lomax. May I ask if that was your doing?"

"Indeed it was," said Sackler. "It is my evidence and mine alone that will convict him."

I put down my cigarette and caught Sackler's eye. He remained imperturbable. I frowned, wondering what he had up his frayed sleeve. Obviously he was uttering a blatant lie. Only yesterday he had told Wooley that Deeling was not guilty. Now he blandly informed Mellish that he was. For a moment I was worried. Then I recalled my own esoteric knowledge in the case and grinned again. No matter what Sackler did he was going to lose this time.

"The fee," said Mellish, "depends upon the conviction."

"Of course," said Sackler with a strange sweetness, "I'd never dream of asking you for the money until then."

That, for him, was a remarkable speech. It should have warned me. Sackler leaned back in his swivel chair. He said: "Oh, by the way, Joey, I have a little job for you. Will you run over to the Renault Building, suite 919. They have a check for me. Pick it up. And take your time. It's going to be a slow day. Nothing at all to do until Deeling goes before the Grand Jury."

I got up and went out, more puzzled than ever. Never had Sackler had a check due in his life without my knowing of it. His anticipatory gloating always took care of that. However, I thoroughly obeyed his injunction to take my time.

I had a spot of breakfast and a drink before I went uptown. I walked slowly up to the Renault Building. I went into suite 919. I came out frowning and thinking hard. I reached absolutely no conclusion.

I got back to the office to find Sackler sitting in the outer room. The door between the pair of offices was shut. Sackler looked tired and vaguely triumphant. I fixed him with an accusing eye.

I said: "Is it my company you object to?"

He looked at me ingenuously. "Why, Joey, what could you possibly mean by that?"

"There's no check for you in suite 919 of the Renault Building. Moreover, there's no one in that office who ever heard of you."

Sackler clucked, phonily sympathetic. "Well, well," he said, "I must have made a mistake. No matter, we're getting right to work. I was just waiting for you."

"Where are we going?"

"Charlton Street, Joey. To the Lomaxes'. You remember the Lomaxes, don't you, Joey?"

There was something in his tone I didn't like. Once again I reviewed the situation as I saw it from my angle. Once again I decided that as far as I was concerned the position was completely tenable. I kept my mouth shut and followed him to the elevator.

4

You Can't Win

I ENTERED THE Lomax living-room with a strong feeling of surprise. Leaning against the mantelpiece was Inspector Wooley. Seated close to him, anxiety written indelibly on his high brow was Doctor Deeling. Alice Lomax sat with magnificent legs crossed in the center of a divan. She wore a blue suit that was molded to her curving body. I looked her over twice.

The other occupant of the room was Minna Campbell. In her lap was a box of chocolates. She munched placidly like an uncomplaining cow at her cud.

Wooley chewed his cigar and looked at Sackler with all the faith and trust of a diplomat signing a treaty with the Third Reich. Alice Lomax and the doctor registered worry and a degree of helplessness. Minna Campbell chewed another chocolate.

"All right," said Wooley, "I've done everything you've asked me. I've got Deeling here, temporarily out of jail. I've gone to one hell of a lot of trouble. You better have something good, Sackler."

Sackler took a free cigarette from a German silver box. He lighted it and said: "I always have something good."

"Sure," snapped Wooley, aware he was in the presence of superior wealth, "especially the fee."

I swung my head around and winked at myself in the pier glass behind me. True, the procedure had baffled me somewhat, but I rather felt like a guy with a royal flush when the table is betting its head off. I didn't know what the hell was going on, but I *did* know I couldn't lose.

Alice Lomax glared at Wooley. "Doctor Deeling is innocent," she said bitterly. "Even a dumb copper should know that."

"I may be dumb," said Wooley heavily. "But I can add. He was your lover, wasn't he? Your husband is found dead, stabbed with a scalpel belonging to your lover. Your lover was in the house at the time of the killing. By God, I doubt if even Rex Sackler can go behind those facts."

"I can go a long way behind them, Inspector," said Sackler. "I shall do so purely in the interests of justice, even overlooking your discourtesy of yesterday. Purely in the interests of law and order."

Wooley sneered audibly. I said: "Inspector, neither you nor Sackler know how true that is."

Sackler looked at me with his keen eyes. "Joey," he said, "I have a feeling you are holding out on me. Moreover, I have a feeling that it's going to cost you money."

"Look," said Wooley. "Will you tell me why this meeting was called? I rather exceeded my authority in letting Deeling out of the can. I won't feel comfortable until he's back."

"Very well," said Sackler walking up and down like a ham actor strutting the stage. "Lend me your adequate ears, Inspector."

Wooley, whose ears were the ears of Clark Gable, flushed. His face swelled up. With an effort he held his tongue. Sackler turned to Alice Lomax.

"Mrs. Lomax, you have an uncle whose name is George Pinkerton Mellish?"

The blonde nodded. "That's true. But I haven't seen him for years. He doesn't think much of me. As a matter of fact he doesn't think much of women in general."

"In any event," said Sackler, "he came into my office at nine o'clock yesterday morning and told me that your husband had been stabbed to death in his bedroom."

The blonde blinked. Wooley said: "That's impossible."

"Of course it is," said Deeling. "The murder wasn't committed until ten."

"All these things are true," said Sackler. "Interesting case, eh?"

"Suppose they are true," said Wooley. "Why is Mellish in your office talking to you about Lomax' murder?"

"He retained me. He offered me a fee to solve the murder—to solve, mark you, a murder that hadn't yet been committed."

"All right," said Wooley, "go on."

"Naturally," continued Sackler, "such an odd circumstance required investigation. I checked Mellish thoroughly to see if he had anything to do with the killings."

"So," said Wooley, "did he have an alibi?"

"He had two."

"Two?" said Wooley. "One of them at least was phoney."

"On the contrary, Inspector. Both of them were solid. Mellish's office claimed he was there from ten o'clock on. A bartender in a saloon across the street from my office is equally willing to swear he was there."

"Damn it," snapped Wooley. "And which place was he?"

"Both," said Sackler evenly. "He was in both of them."

THE BLONDE AND Deeling sat on the edge of their seats, regarding Sackler as a child regards a magician who is just about to produce a miraculous rabbit out of a hat. Mrs. Campbell ate another chocolate with intensity. Wooley ran an exasperated hand through his thick hair.

"Damn you," he said heartily, "will you come to the point?"

"Sure," said Sackler amiably. "Now a week or so ago two lunatics escaped from an asylum in South Bend, Indiana."

"My God," said Wooley. "What's that got to do with it?"

Sackler ignored the interruption. I watched him with rapt attention now. "Two lunatics escaped," he said again. "One of them had been ruined by Lomax. He didn't like Lomax and he wanted to kill him. The second lunatic was a paranoiac."

"I don't care if he was a Methodist," said Wooley. "Will you say something that has some bearing on this Lomax murder?"

"This guy, Campbell," went on Sackler, "Mrs. Minna Campbell's husband, had thought a long time about this. He knew, probably from some friend who had written him, that an affair was progressing between Lomax' wife and Doctor Deeling. That was made to order for him. If he could kill Lomax and plant the killing on Deeling, he was literally killing two guys with one stone. For he didn't care much for Deeling, either."

"Why not?" asked Wooley.

"Because Deeling is the alienist whose testimony sent Campbell away. That's a simple matter of court record. I just looked it up."

Wooley scratched his head. Ideas to him were like half pints of whiskey. He could take them only one at a time.

"All right," he said, "so you've got a theory. Maybe it's sound. But why should I give up an open and shut case like the one I've got on Deeling to take a flyer on what you've figured out?"

He paused for a moment and scratched his head again. "And

what's all this got to do with this Mellish guy? And how did he know the killing was going to be done before it actually was? And how did he have two alibis? And how—"

His mental processes broke down at this point. He stared at Sackler with an expression a congressman might wear trying to read Kant's *Critique of Pure Reason*.

"Easy," said Sackler, "you'll have a breakdown."

I bit my lip and winked at myself in the mirror. So, I thought, would you, my profligate friend, if you realized what I realize. I didn't say anything however. I was biding my time like the guy in Gershwin's song.

"Those two alibis," said Sackler, "made me think. They were both perfect. But two perfect alibis require two guys. One for each. I pondered that for some time. Then, my recollection of Mellish's eating cloves in the bar carried me along to the correct conclusion."

Now he had me reeling along with Wooley.

"Cloves?" I said. "How do cloves fit in?"

"Now look," said Sackler with gentle patience, "why do guys eat cloves in bars?"

I shrugged. "To cover up the fact that they've been drinking, to hide their whiskey breath."

"Good," said Sackler like a radio announcer awarding some moron a dollar for knowing there is water in the Pacific Ocean. "Now from whom would they be concealing the fact that they've been drinking?"

"From their bosses, maybe. Their wives, I suppose."

Sackler turned his palms upward and made an easy gesture. "There," he said, "you see?"

With the exception of Minna Campbell whose jaws were

stuck together with a caramel, we all looked at each other. From the completely blank expressions on each face it was apparent that no one saw anything. Wooley said as much, profanely.

"All right," said Sackler, "Mellish wasn't trying to hide his breath from the boss because he is the boss. He wasn't trying to hide it from his wife because he's never been married. He doesn't go out with women. He's a poker playing, poolroom type. So why in the name of God would Mellish eat cloves in a bar?"

"A straight-man is called for," I said, "and practically instantaneously produced. Why would Mellish eat cloves in a bar?"

"He wouldn't," said Sackler and sat down.

BY THIS TIME Wooley looked as though a mild attack of apoplexy would be a happy relief from his present condition. "How much do you charge to explain?" he said hoarsely. "Maybe I can raise the money."

"It's easy," said Sackler. "Mellish wasn't Mellish."

Wooley looked like a man pursued by a werewolf.

"Mellish—wasn't—Mellish," he repeated in the tone of awed horror affected by George Burns when Gracie Allen delivers one of her more inane aphorisms.

"Look," said Sackler, "Campbell gets out of the nuthouse. He's bent on Lomax' murder. He plans it and comes to me. He hands me a card, gives me a bank reference and tells me he's Mellish. He picked on Mellish because he knew Mellish was Alice Lomax' uncle. That would give him some apparent reason for interesting himself in the affair. Naturally, I believe him. No one checks up on the identity of everyone that comes into his office. Campbell, who was a long-married man, automatically popped cloves in his mouth whenever leaving a bar."

Wooley shook his head like a wet dog.

"But why does he come into your office in the first place?"

"To get the murder investigated. He doesn't dare go to the coppers. They might have dodgers on him and return him to South Bend. He believes that Alice and Deeling might possibly try to hide the death of the husband. They'll know they'll be suspect and they might try to cover it up. He's got to get a dick down there quick. He comes to me."

"It's wonderful," I said. "But you've forgotten something. That office alibi applied, of course, to the real Mellish. It doesn't touch Campbell. But that saloon alibi is all his own. How are you going to break that? If he was in O'Connor's saloon how the devil could he have killed Lomax?"

"Oh," said Sackler taking another free cigarette, "I didn't say he killed Lomax."

Wooley clapped a hand to his head. "I was a happy man when I thought Deeling was going to the chair. Now my head reels. You say Deeling isn't guilty. You build up a lovely case against this guy, Campbell. Now you say he didn't do it."

"Not with his own hand," said Sackler. "You see the time element gave it away."

"I see nothing," said Wooley. "My nose is hazy in front of my face."

"Campbell planned the murder. He somehow swiped Deeling's scalpel. He'd already been working on this other nut, whose name was Dunton. Dunton, as I've already told you, was a paranoiac. That means he was under delusions of persecution. It's easy to build up in a paranoiac mind, by repetition, a grudge against someone, to convince him that that person is responsible for all his ills. Campbell had been pouring poison in Dunton's ear about Lomax for months."

"So Dunton killed him?" I said. "But that doesn't explain why Campbell came into the office *prior* to the murder."

"It's not too hard," said Sackler. "Campbell plotted it well enough. Motive was there. He furnished the weapon. He knew the house and how Dunton could effect an easy entrance through the rear upper story window via the fire escape. But he forgot one thing."

"Namely?"

"Dunton's watch."

The haunted look came back into Wooley's eyes.

"There's an hour's time difference between New York and South Bend," said Sackler. "Campbell put his own watch ahead. He neglected to tell Dunton to do the same. The murder was scheduled for nine o'clock New York time. That was when Campbell came into my office assuming Lomax was already dead. Dunton killed Lomax at nine o'clock Central Standard. In short, an hour later."

Deeling leaned forward in his chair and looked at Sackler intently.

"Can you prove this?" he asked in a husky voice. "My God, have you any evidence to go along with your theory?"

"Of course, I can prove it," said Sackler. "I always prove my cases."

I met Sackler's eye and a great emotion welled up in me. I felt all the power of the superintendent of a concentration camp. I was about to hit Sackler over the head harder than he had ever been hit before in his life. I drew a deep breath.

"Sucker!" I yelled. "You've earned what fee? You overlook the fact that you were retained by a maniac. You can't possibly collect. I knew it all the time. I saw Campbell's picture at Mrs. Campbell's that night. I knew it was the guy who was posing as Mellish."

SACKLER REGARDED ME with a fishy eye. "Judas," he said. I should have been warned by his succinctness.

"I kept my mouth shut," I rushed on. "I didn't tell you because I knew you'd drop the case cold. I sat back and let you work. Let you work for nothing. I feel like a guy full of champagne and absinthe. And how do you feel, spendthrift?"

He looked at me with gleaming eyes. "Why, Joey," he said very calmly, "I feel like a man who is about to collect a two thousand dollar fee. Moreover, I feel like a man who has also won a small bet on a horse named Mayfair II."

I was suddenly very much afraid. I had a swift premonition that something had gone wrong. Rex Sackler was not the man to sit quietly by, when he found out he had lost a fee.

He turned from me quickly and faced Minna Campbell. She met his gaze, munching another piece of candy.

"Mrs. Campbell," he said, "I visited you last night, did I not?"

Mrs. Campbell made an unintelligible sound which doubtless was meant as an affirmative.

"I spoke to you about the danger of your husband being at large? I convinced you that it was best for you to see that he was confined again?"

Again Minna Campbell nodded. I watched her face closely. An empty sensation was creeping up from my lower intestines to the pit of my stomach.

"Very well," said Sackler. "Now will you tell everyone here just what measures you took to insure your husband's capture."

Mrs. Campbell swallowed the chocolate in her mouth. "I offered a reward," she said. "A reward to whoever might capture my husband."

"Ah," said Sackler, "and the amount of that reward, Mrs. Campbell?"

Minna Campbell reached for a nougat. She said: "Two thousand, three hundred dollars."

Wooley started. He was almost as afraid of Sackler in financial transaction as I was. I said desperately: "So what? You haven't got Campbell. Where is he?"

Sackler blew a smoke ring toward the ceiling. "Campbell is in our office, Joey. He is, as a matter of fact, handcuffed to your desk. He is bound and gagged. So is his partner, Dunton, who has already confessed to the murder of Lomax."

I sat down with a thud. I said, incoherently: "How—what—"

"Elementary," said Sackler. "I followed him when he left the office this afternoon. After I sent you on that fool's errand to the Renault Building. It was inevitable that sooner or later he would get in touch with Dunton. Luckily he went immediately to a West Side rooming house where Dunton was hiding. I went along, too. I brought them back with the aid of a gun. Dunton broke down at once when I confronted him with all the evidence I've just offered you. You can pick them both up, Inspector. You, Mrs. Campbell, may mail a check to my office in the morning."

Minna Campbell opened her mouth disclosing brown, stained teeth.

"I certainly shall," she said. "I haven't slept a wink since Eric got out. You're wonderful, Mr. Sackler."

Sackler smiled happily. "I don't do so badly, do I, Joey?"

Personally, I was beyond speech.

WE WERE HALFWAY uptown again before I found my voice. I said, bitterly: "Why the extra three hundred dollars? Campbell offered you a two-thousand dollar fee. You got that hag to lift it to twenty-three hundred. Why?"

Sackler smiled dreamily.

"Mayfair II," he said.

"Mayfair II?"

"Of course. I should have won that bet, Joey. I had twenty dollars of my own bet at seven to one. That, including my original stake, is one hundred and sixty dollars. Then I was entitled to the winnings of the twenty you staked for me. That's a hundred and forty more. A total of three hundred dollars. I simply had Mrs. Campbell, who incidentally is quite amenable to masculine charm, offer a reward that would cover everything."

"You are a miserable creature," I said. "You could just as well have added a few more bucks and got me my horse money back."

"I punish you for your own good," said Sackler. "When I saw that painting in Minna Campbell's living-room, I knew that you must have seen it also. I knew you were keeping your mouth shut, praying I'd get gypped out of my fee. Deliberately I refrained from including your losses in the reward. There are no bonuses in our office for disloyal employees."

I pulled my hat down over my eyes and sat hunched up in the taxi seat. I brooded. I sat sadly with my sorrow as the cab pulled up to the curb. I sat on the street side of the seat and for a long moment I was so immersed in my own woes, I did not move.

The driver said suddenly: "Hey, buddy, ain't you getting out too?"

I looked up. The seat next to me was empty. I looked through the window to see Sackler scurrying into O'Connor's saloon across the street. He had silently let himself out the traffic side of the cab.

The driver said, "Eighty-five cents, buddy," and the horrible truth hit me like a mace.

He had just netted twenty-three hundred dollars and he had left me to pay for the cab!

Blood From a Turnip

Sackler faced the threat of a 15-bucks-a-month rent raise like a man—by docking it off Joey's wages. That's why Joey held out in the kill-solution, trying to chisel a fee for himself—only to reap the bitter rewards of treachery from the champion penny-pincher of all time.

1

Rent Raise

REX SACKLER CAME into the office wearing a beatific expression and a grin wide as the state of Texas. He bade me an expansive good-morning. He sat down at his desk, reached for the mail with one hand, withdrew a cigar from his vest pocket with the other. I stared at him like a Bavarian yokel at the Eiffel Tower.

His geniality puzzled me; the fact of the cigar was stunning.

"I assume someone gave you that panetela," I remarked.

Rex Sackler shook his head. "Why, no, Joey," he said. "I bought it. Ten cents. I feel quite benign this morning."

I believed that. When Sackler who rolled his own cigarettes in order to swindle the state of New York out of a two cent tax actually paid a dime for cigars, he was feeling benign indeed.

I regarded him suspiciously. "Has someone left you a fortune?" I inquired. "Did you find a thousand dollar bill in the gutter, or did a blind newsdealer give you the wrong change?"

He tore open an envelope, puffed clouds of cigar smoke in my direction and preserved his grin intact.

"I glow with righteousness, Joey," he said. "I am aware of a noble, patriotic deed. I bought this cigar as a sort of reward for my sacrifice."

"Sacrifice?" I said. That word falling from his lips was analogous to the Mikado delivering a short homily on the honor and probity of nations.

I saw a hand and a gun show suddenly above the transom.

"Sacrifice," said Sackler firmly. "I have this morning withdrawn every penny in my Postal Savings accounts. I have given every nickel to the government." He puffed on his cigar as I stared at him, incredulous. He added, "The amount was not inconsiderable, Joey."

I blinked and ran my hand through my hair as Sackler busied himself with the mail. Sackler's entire life had been devoted to fighting for money as a bull buffalo fights for his mate. He loved cash as heaven is reputed to love the poor in spirit. He had lived through one depression, and if 1929 had taught the nation nothing, it had taught Sackler not to trust his money to banks. His wealth, all of it in cash, was scattered around the country in Postal Savings accounts. An armed uprising coupled with the collapse of the capitalistic system were the circumstances needed to snatch his dough away from him.

His clothes looked as old as a redwood tree and his shoes had been repaired more often than the tracks of the Toonerville trolley. He spent money with all the wholehearted enthusiasm of a one armed paper-hanger submitting to the amputation of his other arm. He paid me a meager salary each week and devoted the remaining five working days to winning it back at various forms of gambling. At this he was amazingly successful. And now, he calmly announced that he had given every nickel to the government. I sighed and shook my head. Reason tottered.

"You mean," I asked, my voice thick with unbelief, "that you've given every cent to Uncle Sam? That you're broke? That in this time of stress your patriotism proved a greater emotion than your niggardliness?"

He frowned at the last word. However, his expression of smug complacency did not desert him.

"Every cent," he said. "All out of the bank and despatched to Mr. Morgenthau. Every nickel. Even the two per cent interest which had accumulated."

I still couldn't believe it. I wracked my brains and smoked two cigarettes during the process. Then, suddenly, a light flickered across my mind. I took the cigarette from my mouth and fixed him with an accusing eye.

"Wait a minute," I said. "Do you mean that you've bought Defense Bonds? Is that it?"

He became suddenly interested in the circular he was reading. He avoided my eye. "Why, yes," he said. "Invested every penny in them, Joey. In times like these I think it the duty of every citizen to—"

"Wait another minute," I said. "Isn't it true that Postal Savings pay only two per cent interest while those bonds pay three and a third?"

SACKLER THREW THE circular in the waste paper basket. He opened another letter.

"Why, yes, Joey, I suppose that's true. Though I didn't bother to investigate. The country needs cash and that was the only motive which actuated me. I hope you don't think I considered the matter of interest. I—"

My laughter rocked the room. "No," I said, "not at all! You didn't consider the matter of interest. You considered it as little as you'd consider the loss of your right eye. So now the Sackler fortune picks up an extra one and a half per cent each year. No wonder you felt you could afford a ten cent cigar. You're a noble patriot, Rex. Statues have been erected to guys for less."

Sackler's smile had vanished. A frown was on his dark brow. He ran slim fingers through hair black as the raven's wing. He said, "Joey, I don't know why I put up with you. You show neither respect nor loyalty to your employer. Because your own soul is gross you constantly impugn my motives. It is outrageous. It is lousy. It is— Oh, my God!"

The last expletive, I gathered, was not directed at me. Rather, it was aimed at the letter he was reading. By now all his previous geniality had left him and was at least eight blocks away. His smile had given way to sullenly set lips. The sparkle his eyes had worn was masked by a dejected film.

He read the letter through as if it were a government

communication informing him of a capital tax. He slammed the letter down upon the desk. He said, bitterly: "This is a damned holdup."

I looked at him inquiringly.

"Christie," he said. "That damned old penny-pinching curmudgeon. He wants more rent."

I brightened up somewhat at that. I experienced almost as much pleasure seeing Sackler spend money as he did in hoarding it.

"Good," I said. "How much?"

"Fifteen dollars a month. For this slum. The man is out of his head. However, his letter seems firm enough."

"Well," I said, "are you going to pay it?"

"Pay it?" he shouted and looked at me as if I had asked if he planned a small job of matricide. "Of course, I'm not going to pay it. I stand on my rights."

I eyed him speculatively. Watching him stand on his rights in an argument with Doctor Christie, our landlord, was going to be something of a spectacle. Christie was no man to toss fifty cent pieces in the Hudson River, either.

"You say Christie is firm in his letter," I said. "How do you plan on making him change his mind?"

Sackler ran a hand over his lean jaw. "I am thinking," he announced. He frowned and rested his chin in his palm. He registered superior intelligence.

"In a pinch," I suggested, "we can always move."

"Are you mad, Joey? Moving all our junk would probably cost us twenty-five bucks. No. I've got to figure out some way that's absolutely free."

"I've got a lot of faith in your ability," I murmured, then went back to the morning paper leaving him alone with his anguish.

After five minutes had elapsed, Sackler took a last reluctant drag at the thousandth of an inch remaining of his cigar, put it out and announced, "Joey, I have an idea."

"Which is?"

"Naturally, what with war and present conditions the operating expenses of this office will be higher."

"What operating expenses? You say you'll pay no more rent. The only other expenses you have is my salary and stamps. Stamps won't go up."

HE IGNORED THAT. He rolled himself a cigarette with all the deft aptitude of a palsied man dealing a bridge hand while wearing a set of boxing gloves. He lit it, inhaled, and said: "Joey, you're young. You have your whole life before you. For a lad, you live too luxuriously. You—"

"Oh, no," I said. "I see it all too clearly. If you think you're talking me into a cut, you're crazy. I live like a low caste Indian on the salary you give me. You're not economizing at my expense."

"Hear me out," said Sackler. "I don't say that we'll have to cut you. Only if the rent is raised. Naturally, if the rent remains the same, so will your salary."

I eyed him with distaste. "What am I supposed to do?"

"You see Christie. He likes you. He doesn't like me. You have far more chance of talking him out of that rent raise than I have."

"And if I won't do it?"

Sackler shrugged his shoulders. He said, a note of phoney regret in his tone: "Then I shall be forced to cut your salary fifteen dollars a month to make up the difference in the rent. Nothing personal, of course, Joey. Purely a matter of business."

I lit a cigarette and considered this. Not for a moment did I doubt that he would do it. Every time he was confronted with an unexpected item of expense, he masterminded some method of getting someone else to pay it. Now, I was the victim. Getting another job at the salary I drew here was going to be difficult. I'd never been trained for anything special and because of my association with Sackler, whom even Dale Carnegie wouldn't like, the other shamuses in town would want no part of me.

I stood up. I gave him a look that would have made an adulterous worm hang its head in shame. Sackler merely grinned back at me. "All right," I said, "I'll go and see him. I warn you I'll tell him why I'm seeing him instead of you. I'll let him know exactly what kind of a cheap thus and thus you are."

Sackler's smile persisted. "Tell him I thrash my mother regularly. Tell him I'm in direct communication with the Japanese high command. Tell him I'm ravished by wriggling bacilli but for heaven's sake—and yours, Joey—tell him to forget about that fifteen dollars."

I left the room, a slow wrath crawling over me and a firm resolve to evolve some scheme which would make Rex Sackler pay dearly for this humiliation. Downstairs, I took a bus to Doctor Christie's office.

I came back a half-hour later in a condition of uncertain emotion. I didn't know whether I was worried or not. I waited for Sackler's reaction to let me decide. He lifted his head eagerly as I entered the office. He said, "Well?"

"I didn't see Christie."

"Why not?"

"He wasn't in."

"Why didn't you wait?"

"I didn't want to wait that long. I was afraid you'd dock me."

"Don't be an idiot. Why should I dock you? He'll be out for lunch surely. He'll be back in an hour or so."

"He'll be damned lucky," I said, "if he's back in twenty years."

"Twenty years? Where the hell is he? In Mars?"

"He wishes he were. He's in the can."

"For what?"

"Murder."

Sackler stared at me for a moment. Then that damnable grin came back over his face. He rubbed his hands together like an Armenian rug merchant who has spotted a fat, virginal Iowa school teacher disembarking at Port Said.

"Good," he said. "That's fine, Joey. You should be happy."

"Me? Why?"

"We'll get him to retain us. Part of the fee will be the remitting of the rent raise. Joey, you're saving fifteen dollars a month. You're a very lucky man."

"Wonderful," I said ironically. "Suppose he's guilty?"

"Of murder, Joey? Don't be silly. No one's ever guilty of murder. Of course the fee won't be contingent. We'll just offer to do our best for so much."

He was already standing up, jamming a hat which looked as if it had been worn in the blizzard of '88, upon his head. I watched him, reflecting that with a fee in sight, he moved with all the alacrity of a volunteer fireman.

I said, "Where to?"

"Headquarters, Joey. Let's find out something about this murder before we interview Christie. I like to know the facts before I figure just how much I should charge him."

2

Who's the Client?

DUBIOUSLY, I FOLLOWED him. Brooding about the fact that I was quite likely to lose fifteen dollars a month on this deal, I was less alert than I should have been. Sackler was already halfway through the door of police headquarters before I was out of our taxicab. I paid the amount showing on the meter, reflecting that Sackler would tell me to put it on the expense account—an account which was already eight months old. Disgruntled and sullen I walked with Sackler into the office of Inspector Wooley of Homicide.

Wooley's affection for Sackler was only equalled by Sackler's affection for him. Wooley contemplated Sackler's bank account with the envy of a professional copper whose salary totalled a bare ten per cent of Sackler's income. They had been clashing for years—a fact which probably accounted for Wooley's raised eyebrows and air of suspicion as we entered his office.

"Well," he said with no cordiality whatever, "what reward have you vultures come to claim?"

Sackler clucked like an old hen and turned on an oily charm.

"Come, come, Inspector," he said. "After all we both represent law and order. We should work shoulder to shoulder. If a crime is committed we should spare no effort to convict the criminal. If an innocent man is in jail we should spare no effort to vindicate him."

The expression of suspicion on Wooley's face grew and flourished. "Behind that beautiful gossamer sentiment," he said, "I see that you are pursuing another dollar or two. Come clean, Rex, what is it?"

"I'll be absolutely frank with you," said Sackler, which was big of him considering he couldn't, under the circumstances, be anything else. "It's this Christie case. Give me what you've got on it and I'll do you a favor."

Wooley looked at him with the warmth of a dead halibut.

"What's the favor?"

"I shall save the department from disgrace. I shall save you, personally, from making a fool of yourself."

"How?"

"By showing you that Christie is innocent. I know he is. Play with me and I'll cut you in on what information I pick up. Otherwise you'll bring an innocent man to trial and look like an utter idiot when I break my case."

Wooley remained dubious but not quite so much so. Sackler, he knew, was no man's fool. Sackler had been disconcertingly right on many occasions when the department had been uncomfortably wrong. Wooley tapped a thick finger on his desk top. He drew a deep breath. He said, finally, "What is it you want to know?"

"Everything you have on this murder Christie's accused of. I'm representing him."

I blinked at him. That last statement not only was news to me, it would have been news to Christie, himself.

"If you're representing him," said Wooley reasonably, "you must be familiar with the case. What do you want me to talk for?"

"I want to see if it checks," lied Sackler shamelessly. "If you have anything I haven't."

Wooley spent the next forty seconds in deep thought. "All right," he said at last. "But if Christie's innocent and you can prove it, you've got to promise you'll cut me in on the pinch."

"I give you my word," said Sackler proudly, and I was reminded vaguely of a hophead giving away an imaginary million.

WOOLEY PICKED UP an onionskin report from his desk. He ran his eyes over it quickly and proceeded to give us the gist of the murder for which Doctor Christie was languishing in the can across the Bridge of Sighs.

"The corpse," said Wooley, "is Mrs. Eleanor Harte, wife of Julian Harte. Textile manufacturer. Know him?"

Sackler whose mind was a volume of Dun and Bradstreet nodded. "Blankets. Dabbles in stocks, too. Worth about a million and a half."

"Right," said Wooley. "Last night a guy registered at the Park Hotel under the name of Frank Corn. He also registered for his wife, announcing that she would join him later. Shortly afterwards, Eleanor Harte went up to the room. About a half-hour later this Christie mug comes in."

Wooley broke off as Sackler's hand snaked across his desk and snatched a cigarette from his package. He opened his mouth as if to protest, then sighed as if realizing the utter futility of it all. He continued: "Someone phones the desk that this Corn's room is being broken into. The house dick and the clerk gallop upstairs. They find Christie in Corn's room with Harte's corpse. Apparently, she's been strangled with a hotel towel."

Sackler inhaled luxuriously upon the free cigarette. "That's all?" he asked. "No clues? No hints? No motive?"

"There was a fireplace in the room," Wooley told him. "In it were a few charred rags. In the room was the stench of burning cloth. Christie refuses to talk about that or anything else."

"That's all?"

"So far," admitted Wooley. "But we're working on motive now. I think we have something. With what we've got plus a motive, it doesn't look so well for your client."

Sackler grunted. "What about this Corn guy? What became of him?"

"Disappeared. The way we figure it was he had a date with this Harte dame. When he found out what happened, he took it on the lam. Undoubtedly, he wasn't using his right name at the hotel, anyway."

Sackler put out his cigarette. He glanced over at Wooley's pack. Wooley moved it carefully beyond the danger zone of Sackler's reach. Sackler shrugged his shoulders resignedly and stood up.

"All right," he said, "thanks. Now can you fix it so I can have a personal interview with my client."

Wooley picked up the phone and spoke to the Tombs next door. "All right," he said. "It's fixed. Go ahead. But remember, whatever you find out you tell me first."

"Naturally," said Sackler with an inflection that made it sound something like go to hell.

The iron door clanged behind us and we sat on the hard bed in Christie's cell. Christie peered at us through the crepuscular light. He was a short, pudgy man, with tiny blue eyes, several chins and the neck of a bull moose. It seemed to me that he looked at us without enthusiasm. If Sackler imagined we were going to be greeted as a couple of white-horsed deliverers, Christie's first words dispelled that illusion.

"I understood I was permitted no visitors save my lawyer," he said sharply. "May I ask just what you're doing here, Sackler?"

"Well," said Sackler, "I heard you were in trouble. Since we're old acquaintances, since my business is getting people out of trouble, I thought I'd come over and offer my services."

"Offer them?" said Christie. "For how much?"

There were times when I believed that Sackler's reputation had reached Mars.

"Well," he said, "naturally, business is business, Doctor. You have a healthy medical practice. You own a lot of real estate. I thought perhaps, I should ask fifteen hundred dollars, plus of course, the remittance of that ridiculous rent raise you've pinned on me."

CHRISTIE DREW A deep breath. He turned to me. He said, in a tone of utter disbelief: "Mr. Graham, is he real? Does he actually exist? I sit here in the shadow of the electric chair and he drops in to haggle about a fifteen dollar a month rent raise. Is it possible?"

"Absolutely," I said. "It's a wonder he didn't bring in a carton of cigarettes for you, sell them to you at a neat profit."

Sackler glared at me. However, he kept his temper. He permitted no emotions to interfere when he was engaged in the delicate business of setting a fee.

"Of course, Doctor," he said, "I realize you are upset. However, it's only natural that you'd want to retain me. I have the best deductive brain in the city. If anyone can spring you, I can. If I investigate the case the truth shall be uncovered. What's fifteen hundred dollars, what's a lousy rent raise compared with your life, your freedom?"

Christie lit a cigarette and rested his back against the solid wall of the cell. "Will you go away," he said wearily. "Will you get the hell out of here? Or do you make a charge for that, too?"

Sackler shook his head. He disliked close fisted clients. "Good God, man," he said, "you can't count money at a time like this. Though, I might shave the fee a little. I—"

Christie stood up. Even in that dim light, I saw that he was enraged. His voice was thick and angry.

"If your fee was six cents I wouldn't retain you. I don't care to get sprung as you call it. I'm innocent and I'll prove it at the right time. Now get the hell out of here."

Sackler, seeing his fee vanishing before his eyes, became desperate.

"Now, Doctor," he said, talking quickly as if he was uttering his last words on the scaffold, "I won't haggle with you. I'll give you a bargain price. I'll—"

Christie pushed past him. He thrust his face up against the bars of the cell door. He yelled at the top of his voice for the guard. The guard, certain that nefarious doings were under way, came racing down the cell block, his drawn gun in his hand. He thrust the muzzle through the bars. He said excitedly, "Stop it. Whatever you're doing, stop it, or I'll shoot."

"You see," said Christie. "He says to stop it."

"Stop what?" snapped Sackler. "We're not doing anything."

"You're annoying me," said Christie. Then to the guard, "Get them out of here."

The guard unlocked the door and escorted us out. Sackler was glowering as we walked into the street. I looked at him and grinned. The grin grew to a chuckle. He swung his head around and glared at me.

"And what the devil are you laughing at?"

"We've been thrown out of a jail," I told him. "That marks a new low in our penurious career. Besides, you've failed to arrange a fifteen hundred dollar fee." I gave out with a fresh peel of laughter.

"And you," said Sackler savagely, "have just laughed yourself into a fifteen dollar a month salary cut. So I again inquire what the devil you're laughing at?"

What indeed? I stopped laughing immediately. I fell into step at his side. Glumly the pair of us retraced our steps toward the office.

Sackler puffed at one of his home made cigarettes. I wondered how I was going to make up that fifteen bucks a month. I looked up as Sackler spoke.

"There's something very funny about that guy, Joey."

"You mean Christie?"

"Yeah. It looks as if he doesn't care about facing a murder rap. Most of them are putty in my hands once they're in jail. How do you figure it?"

"Maybe he believes that his life is cheap compared to what you'd rook him out of if he retained you."

"YOU ARE A very comical fellow," said Sackler. "You are an uproarious comedian. You are—click!"

"I am what?"

"Not you. I have an idea. Harte."

"The corpse or the manufacturer?"

"The manufacturer, you idiot. The guy whose wife was killed."

"What about him?"

"He'd like to know who killed her, wouldn't he? Apparently,

Christie is a pretty dubious pinch. Wooley said they have no motive. They can't develop a murder case without a motive. Maybe if we get to Harte before the coppers find a motive, he'll retain us."

"To do what?"

"Dig up a motive that'll burn Christie."

"I thought you said Christie appeared innocent."

"So what? Even if he is, a motive shouldn't be hard to cook up, if the fee's right."

"A moment ago you were going to save Christie from the chair. Now you're going to send him there."

"Well, why not? He raised my rent, didn't he? He had me thrown out of the Tombs, didn't he? A character like that is capable of murder, Joey."

He pursed his lips righteously and I reflected how wonderful it was that his noble rationalizations were always on the side of the most money. Now he had his battered hat on again.

"We're going to call on Harte, Joey. I should've thought of that before. He's a much better type of client than Christie anyway."

I followed him into the street, a single thought in my mind. I climbed into the taxi and sat close to the door, my hand on the door handle. I had made up my mind to one thing. I was *not* going to get stuck with the cab fare this time.

Sackler apparently realized what was in my mind. Anyway, shortly before we reached Harte's Madison Avenue apartment, he reached into his pocket, withdrew a leather change purse and groped reluctantly into its depths. He pulled out some change. A coin fell to the floor of the cab. I bent my head looking for it.

"Pish," said Sackler, "a dime, that is all, Joey. You constantly imply I'm cheap. I am not cheap enough to bend down for a dime. If you are, it is yours, Joey. I spurn it."

Well, if he was bent on making a magnificent gesture it was all right with me. I ran my hand across the floor of the cab until I found the coin. A dime was a dime in my book. It was at least a free glass of beer. I straightened up, the coin in my hand, then cursed myself for the little father of all the suckers in the world.

The cab had stopped. I looked out the window just in time to see Sackler's figure disappearing through the revolving doors of a huge apartment house. I was alone in the hack, a dime clutched in my cold indignant fingers. The meter registered forty-five cents. Sackler had played me for John Fall again. The taxi was costing him one thin dime.

I paid off the taxi driver and joined Sackler in the elevator. I did not speak to him on the way upstairs.

Julian Harte had a butler and the sort of apartment that went with one. The butler, elegant as something out of Hollywood, escorted us through a tremendous foyer into a luxurious living-room. The shades were pulled almost completely and the room was dim. However, even in that dimness I could plainly see that the furniture was of a caliber I would never afford as long as I was employed and paid by Rex Sackler.

3

Joey Chisels In

JULIAN HARTE, GRAY, emaciated and looking older than the forty-odd Wooley had told us he was, sat in an upholstered chair against the rear wall. On a divan opposite him was a woman. She had a magnificent crown of flaming red hair and eyes that held little flecks of green in them. She sat with crossed legs and I was aware that my pulse picked up a beat as I looked at her.

Both she and Harte stood up as the butler, reading Sackler's name off his card, announced us with suitable disdain.

Mr. Harte, who appeared affable enough, inclined his head and said: "Well, gentlemen—and what can I do for you?"

The redhead said imperiously: "Sit down, Julian. I'll tell you what you can do for them. You can offer them money to tell us a lot of things that we already know."

The antagonism of her tone took even Sackler aback for a moment. However, the thought of Harte's bank balance enabled him to recover quickly.

"Madam," he said, "you misjudge us. True, in our business fees are not unimportant. But our prime aim is to see justice done."

"It'll be done all right," said the redhead. "The criminal is in jail isn't he? I hardly think your professional services are needed, Mr. Sackler."

Julian Harte ran a hand over a furrowed brow and sighed.

"Let Mr. Sackler state his business, Theresa. By the way, this is my sister. She came in from Chicago the night that my wife— my wife—was killed."

Sackler made a noise of sympathetic understanding. It was quite convincing. Only I knew that the sound of silver was clinking in his ears.

"I have been at police headquarters," he said. "Everything indicates that Christie killed your wife. However, they'll never convict him without motive. Inspector Wooley is worried about that. I thought that, with my help, we could establish a motive in order that justice be done."

All this noble talk about justice was beginning to pall on me. I stopped listening to Sackler's sententiousness, and paid strict and carnal attention to Theresa Harte. I thought that if Sackler didn't antagonize her too much, I might ask her for a date.

"The motive," said Theresa Harte, "is simple enough. My brother and I intend to inform Inspector Wooley of it shortly."

Sackler's face fell like a bomb. If there was a motive to pin on Christie, Christie was as good as fried. In that event there was no fee here. Since Christie himself refused to play ball, there was obviously no fee to be had anywhere.

Harte lifted his head. It seemed to me that there was a great and enervating weariness upon him.

"Perhaps, Theresa," he said gently. "Perhaps that motive won't hold up. I hope to God it won't anyway."

Sackler's head thrust itself forward on his shoulders. He looked like a setter spotting a quail.

"Maybe," he said, "if there's any doubt we could look into it. Maybe we could even break it down if that's what you want, Mr. Harte."

Harte's sister looked at him with a bitter contempt that would have caused the most brazen courtesan to blush. Not so Rex Sackler.

She said: "It doesn't matter which side you're on, does it? As long as there's a fee involved."

Sackler inhaled deeply, preparatory to delivering a short homily on his own noble motives. But before he could speak, Harte addressed us.

"I may as well be frank with you. My sister here and my wife have been cool to each other for years. The reason, Theresa tells me, is that my wife made a practice of being unfaithful to me. My heart is reluctant to believe it. Unfortunately, my intelligence tells me it is true."

SACKLER PICKED THAT one up quickly. "The idea is, then, that Christie was her lover. He found her in this room with Frank Corn. So he killed her. Is that it?"

"Of course, that's it," snapped Theresa. "Corn was a new paramour. Christie found it out. He killed her. There's your motive."

Sackler nodded. "Where did she meet Christie?"

"Right here," said Theresa. "He's been my brother's physician for years. So there's the case, Mr. Sackler, open and shut. I'm afraid there's no money in it for you."

Sackler looked like a child whose lollypop has been rudely snatched away. Julian Harte stirred again in his chair.

"Wait a moment," he said. "I think we owe it to Eleanor's memory, also to Doctor Christie to look as deeply into this as possible. Mr. Sackler, I'm prepared to retain you."

Sackler's smile was the smile of a saint who has been in direct communication with heaven for the first time. I looked at him in disgust. The luck that fell about him was most depressing to me. I transferred my gaze to Theresa. The sight of her aphrodisiac beauty was more pleasant. I decided she would look even better if there was more light.

I said: "It's a bit dark in here, isn't it?"

Harte pulled a bell rope behind his chair. The butler appeared.

"Will you raise the shades?" said Harte. "And in the meantime—" He rose, crossed half the room, picked up a hammered silver box of cigars, offered them to Sackler and myself. I took one. Sackler snatched his as if afraid the offer might be withdrawn. The shades went up and I knew my theory of the effect of light upon Theresa Harte had been sound.

The butler was walking to the door as Harte put down the cigar box and returned to his chair. I heard a sudden thud, and swung my eyes away from their hot blooded contemplation of Theresa Harte. Then, to my utter astonishment I saw Julian Harte reposing upon his posterior on the floor. There was an expression of bewilderment on his face. The butler's hand was on the back of his chair and I was willing to swear that that chair had been moved back a good foot from its former position.

Theresa's laughter swept the room. The butler grinned. A smile, not too natural, crossed Julian Harte's face.

"Wentworth," said Theresa, "you're the limit. I think you should let up on this horseplay while Mr. Julian is upset."

I blinked and looked at Sackler. He said quizzically, "Horseplay?"

Theresa nodded as the butler helped her brother to his feet. "Wentworth is incorrigible," she said. "He's been with Julian for years. They're more like pals than master and servant. He's always playing tricks on Julian. Trying to embarrass him before guests. But I must say he hasn't done anything as old as that chair-pulling act for a long time. Has he, Julian?"

Julian Harte had picked himself up and was now seated in his chair. He smiled weakly. "No," he said, "not for some time. Wentworth, you're overdoing it. Now go out to the pantry and stay there. I'm in no mood for fooling."

The butler left the room. I still stared at Sackler. God knew, I wasn't very familiar with the customs of the upper classes, but if butlers were in the habit of jerking chairs from under the descending backsides of their masters, all I could say was, that Hollywood had completely misinformed me regarding the *haute monde*.

Sackler registered with a bland dead pan. He was permitting nothing to divert him from the principal issue at stake.

"You were saying, Mr. Harte, that you were about to retain me?"

"Right," said Harte. "I want you to look into two things. First the guilt or innocence of Doctor Christie. Second, I want to be certain of these reports about my wife. If she was untrue to me, I would like to be sure of it. If not, I owe it to her to find out. For a flat fee of one thousand dollars, will you accept the commission?"

Would he accept the commission? Would a horse eat hay? Would the Japanese regret Pearl Harbor? Would I snap up a date with Theresa Harte?

WHILE SACKLER WAS yessing Julian Harte, implying that the matter of the fee was unimportant as long as justice was done, Theresa spoke angrily. "Julian, you're wasting money. Surely you take my word for it. I could have told you about Eleanor and Christie a long time ago. I told her I knew of it. I hoped she would tell you herself. Since she didn't I hardly thought it my place to. However, that was the reason we never got along together."

Harte sighed wearily. "I know," he said. "I know, Theresa. However, I'll feel better if I have incontrovertible evidence. I prefer Mr. Sackler to work on the matter."

Sackler stood up and beamed like a man who has made a very good deal for himself, which as a matter of fact he had.

We returned to the office in a bus. This time I was taking no chances.

"That Theresa," I remarked to Sackler. "Quite something, isn't she?"

"I didn't notice," he said loftily. "When I'm making a business call, I don't bother with women."

His tone nettled me. "You never bother with women," I told him. "It might cost you a dollar."

"Very well," he said. "It's a fair enough deal. You drink in Theresa's beauty. I shall siphon profits from Julian's bank account. You the butterfly and I, the ant, Joey. You are a low, loose character with an eye for a trollop."

I became unreasonably angry. "She's not a trollop."

"She is a tramp," said Sackler cheerfully. "As long as you care for women like that Joey, you will never make a nickel. You will never grow intelligent. You shall never solve a murder case and set up business for yourself. You are a ne'er-do-well, Joey, despite all I do for you, despite all the money I have showered upon you."

I retorted shortly that all the money he had ever given me could be comfortably stored in his shallow heart. Then for the second time in one day, I ceased speaking to him.

The following day Sackler left the office about ten o'clock. I assumed he was about to do some routine checking on Christie and the amours of Eleanor Harte. Normally, he would have assigned such prosaic tasks to me, however, since yesterday relations between us had been somewhat strained.

I read all the papers, completed the crossword puzzle in the *Mirror* and foundered on the one in the *Tribune*. I ate a leisurely lunch, returned to the office about two, to find Sackler still missing.

A few moments later the telephone rang. An excited voice asked for Sackler. I announced he was out and asked for a message. The voice came staccato into my ear over the wires.

"My name is Corn. Frank Corn. I don't want to get mixed up with the police. I got some information about that Harte killing."

My heart picked up a beat. "Frank Corn," I said, "wait a minute," as I thought I heard the outer door open. I listened for a moment, decided I had been mistaken.

"Listen," I said. "This is Sackler's assistant. I don't know when he'll be back. So I'd better come over and see you myself. Where are you?"

"The Melton Hotel. Room 414."

I scribbled it on a piece of paper and hung up. The blood was surging through my veins and I was more excited than I had been for months. I was quite conscious of Sackler's insulting behavior of yesterday. I remembered that among other contumely, he had said that I lacked the intelligence to break a murder case.

Well, perhaps, with the fortuitous aid of Frank Corn, I would break one under his avaricious nose. Anyway it was worth a try. For once I was in that position Sackler always strove for. I had absolutely nothing to lose.

I JAMMED MY hat on, went downstairs and took a taxi. At least this time I didn't have to expend effort trying to jockey out of paying the bill. I got out at the dilapidated marquee of the Melton Hotel and went inside.

I didn't bother to announce myself. The Melton was the sort of place where the clerk didn't bother about it either. I went up to the fourth floor and hammered on the panel of 414.

The voice that had spoken to me on the telephone invited me in. I entered a cheap hotel room, replete with brass bed and dolorous wall paper. Sitting in a rachitic chair was a tall, gaunt man. His cheeks were hollow and his eyes were sunken. His fingers were long, thin and tapering. They reminded me of the fingers of a violinist. He stood up.

"I'm Corn," he said. "Frank Corn."

"I'm Rex Sackler's assistant. Joey Graham. What's on your mind?"

Corn plucked a speck of dust from his sleeve and I noted that his suit was well cut and of expensive material. I figured he could well afford a better hotel. This doubtless was a hideout.

"I'm in a jam," he said. "I know who killed that Harte dame even better than the police. They're going to need my testimony to convict. I want to do the right thing. But I don't want to get into trouble."

"*You* didn't kill her, did you?"

Corn looked as if I'd suggested he was a Japanese spy. "Good God, no!"

"Then what are you worried about?"

"I'd be a damned important witness. I'm afraid they'd hold me in the can. Material witness. High bail. My business affairs won't permit that at this time."

I looked at him appraisingly. I asked: "How did you happen to call *our* office?"

"Damn it," he said impatiently, "I've just told you. I don't want to sit in the can as a material witness. I want a private detective to represent me, to look after my interests. I asked about town and was told that Rex Sackler was the best man in the business."

"All right. What exactly is it you want us to do?"

"I want to tell you fellows what I know. I'll let you know where I am. You can tell the coppers what I've got. Produce me in time for the trial. Not until then."

"All right," I said. "What *have* you got?"

"I was in that hotel room when Christie came in that night. He was waiting for the Harte woman."

I lit a cigarette and hoped my fingers were not trembling with excitement. It looked as if the star witness in the Harte case was being dropped squarely into my lap. Armed with Frank Corn's testimony I might be able to do a spot of fee manipulating on my own hook.

"I'll keep you out of the coppers' hands," I told him. "What have you got?"

"I picked up that Harte woman a few days before she was killed. I had a date with her at that hotel. I was up there waiting for her when this guy Christie comes in. He's sore as hell. He tells me he knows what's going on. He swears he's going to kill her, tells me I'm lucky he's not killing me. He tells me to lam, that he'll wait for her."

A tiny suspicion crawled into my brain. "So you left merely because a stranger told you to?"

"Hell, I figured he was her husband. How the devil was I to know all about her?"

"O.K.," I said. "You're prepared to offer this testimony at Christie's trial if I promise to keep you out of the can until then?"

Corn nodded. "I'll be right here. I'm using the name of Wilson. Call me when you want me. I'm due back in Chi, but I guess I'll have to stick around until this is over."

I DREW A deep breath. This was even better than I had expected. Wooley had no motive. True, Theresa Harte offered to provide one. But for her to know Eleanor Harte had been untrue to her husband and for her to prove it were two entirely different things. With Frank Corn as my own personal witness, I could prove it. For the first time in my life, it seemed that I was in the driver's seat while Sackler struggled between the shafts.

Frank Corn groped in his pocket. "There's this, too," he said. "This is evidence and I guess it keeps my nose clean."

He handed me a piece of scented writing paper. I read the writing on it in a happy murmur.

Darling,

Take a room under the same name at the Park Hotel. I'll join you a little after eight.

Love,

E.

"That," I said, standing up and putting on my hat, "seems to clinch it. You stay here where I can get in touch with you. And I'll keep the coppers off your trail. I—"

A blast that sounded like an attack on Hickman Field filled the room. I saw a hand and a gun show suddenly over the transom. Two bullets smashed into the wall over Corn's head. My hat flicked off my head as if snatched by an invisible hand. It fell to the floor, a scorched hole in the top of the crown.

I flattened myself against the wall. Corn raced into the bathroom as if eighteen devils were on his tail. The shooting ceased as suddenly as it had begun. The hand disappeared. I heard footfalls diminuendo down the corridor. I whipped my own revolver from its shoulder holster and rushed to the door. There was no one in sight as I gained the corridor.

There were, I knew, at least three exits from the Melton Hotel. Pursuit at this moment was futile. I returned to Corn's room. Corn emerged from the bathroom, his thin, gaunt face paler than usual.

"My God," he said. "My God, to think—"

"To think what?" I said sharply. "Who was that? Who is interested in taking a pot shot at you?"

He shook his head. "No one. That is—" His voice faded into a mumble. And I could get no more out of him. I took my departure, leaving Corn a very worried man.

I stopped off on the way back to the office and spent a reluctant three dollars for a new hat. The hole in the old one would have merely invited a cross examination from Sackler. And I was by no means prepared to tell him about my own private witness at this point.

A thought came to me then. I got into a taxi and went back

to Julian Harte's apartment. To my delight it was his sister who opened the door. I showed her the letter Corn had given me. I said: "Sackler wanted to ask you if this is your sister-in-law's handwriting."

She held it up to the light and studied it with her green-flecked eyes.

"Undoubtedly," she said. "Where did you get it?"

"That," I said, "will all come out at Christie's trial."

She smiled at me and I was aware of a very odd sensation at the pit of my stomach. Convicting Christie, I thought, wasn't going to cause her any qualms. Proving that the sister-in-law she had never liked was a tramp wasn't going to do me any harm with Theresa, either.

Sackler was at his desk when I returned. He remarked the new hat and inquired as to the business of the day. I replied shortly that there hadn't been any. I stowed the letter Corn had given me in the top drawer of my desk and sat down to smoke and read the evening papers.

Once I looked up to see Sackler gazing at me, an odd expression on his face.

He said: "I've already spoken to Wooley. He's getting Christie out of the can long enough to bring him up to Harte's tomorrow. May I request your presence?"

I was aware of a warm glow. "You shall have it," I said. I did not add that I would bring along a friend myself. Frank Corn was going to be with me. I would bide my time and when Sackler got his case all mixed up, I would step in with Frank Corn and confound him.

I whistled happily as I skimmed through the comics.

4

The Payoff

AT HARTE'S IT seemed that each representative of law and order had brought a friend. Christie sat on the sofa, Wooley hovering over him as if he expected the doctor to essay a rush-out at any moment. I clung to Frank Corn's arm as if he were a twenty-dollar bill. It was Sackler's guest that startled me.

He had brought a girl, young, attractive and possessed of a deferential manner, whom he had introduced as Miss Grey. She sat demurely in a straight-backed Windsor chair and stared at the far wall. One thing about her puzzled me. She apparently knew Christie. She had spoken to him when she'd come in.

Julian Harte lounged back in his chair against the wall; beside him stood his sister looking shrewdly about the room as if to take the measure of the company. Christie had aged several years. He looked as if he didn't care whether or not the chair lay at the end of the trail.

For that matter, my own witness didn't seem any too happy. He stared down at the carpet with the air of a man who would prefer to be somewhere else. Julian Harte cleared his throat. He said: "I take it, Mr. Sackler, that you have succeeded in the task I set you."

Sackler looked at me, then at Harte. There was a depressed expression on his face. "I'm afraid I haven't got much."

Wooley chewed his dead cigar as if it were his bitterest enemy. He glared at Sackler.

"You haven't got much!" he roared. "Do you think I take a murderer out of the Tombs for exercise? You told me to bring Christie here. For what? Fun?"

Sackler's expression was positively dolorous. "I'm sorry," he said.

"Sorry!" howled Wooley. "What's the D.A. going to say? He only released Christie because I told him it would clean up the case. Are you trying to make a fool out of me?"

Theresa Harte's green eyes met mine. I beamed. I tightened my grip on Corn's arm. For the first time in my life I was about to play the star role while Sackler did straight man. I made the most of it. "Tarry a while," I said, playing it to the hilt. "Sackler may have fallen down. I haven't."

Everyone's eyes were upon me. Sackler appeared mildly surprised. Wooley said impatiently, "Well, what is it, Joey? What have you got?"

"I have worked with Rex Sackler far too long to divulge such information until I find out who's paying me," I announced.

"If you have any information of value, you needn't worry about that," said Theresa. Our eyes held again and I thought I noted a touch of puzzlement in her gaze. It annoyed me slightly. I was damned if I saw why it was so out of the ordinary for Joey Graham to reveal a modicum of intelligence. After all, Sackler wasn't Einstein.

"Damn it, Joey," snapped Wooley. "It's bad enough to hear Rex haggling without you too. Now what have you?"

"Watch your tone," I told him. "You'll be thanking me in a moment. First, I have definite proof against Christie, second, even more definite proof of the infidelity of Mrs. Harte."

Harte stirred uneasily in his chair. Christie looked at me

blankly. Miss Grey still stared demurely at the wall, while Sackler, helping himself to one of Harte's cigars, ignored me.

I PUSHED CORN out into the center of the room. "This man had a date with Mrs. Harte the night of the murder. Christie came into the hotel room where they had their rendezvous. He kicked Corn out, said he'd wait for Eleanor Harte himself and threatened to kill her."

For the first time since his arrest Christie made a statement. He rose to his feet, stared at Corn and shouted: "That's a lie. That's a damned lie!"

Wooley pushed him back into his chair. Sackler said blandly: "Is that a fact, Joey?"

Theresa glanced at Corn, then at Sackler. Corn said to me: "Doesn't he know? Didn't you tell—"

I knew what he was going to ask. I shut him off before Sackler realized I'd been holding out on him completely.

"Here's a letter," I said, "from Eleanor Harte arranging the meeting. The whole thing is obvious now. Christie was one of her lovers. He discovered her with Corn and killed her. There, Wooley, is your case. There, Mr. Harte, is indisputable evidence of your wife's unfaithfulness."

An expression of pain flickered across the face of Julian Harte. "All right," he said, "I asked for it. You were right Theresa. As for you, young man, I'll see that you get a check."

With great effort I refrained from sticking out my tongue at Sackler. Wooley took the cigar from his mouth and slapped me on the back.

"Good work, Joey," he said. "I guess you caught Rex napping this time."

I stood in the center of the floor, bowing like a producer who has received the Academy Award. Then suddenly Doctor Christie sprang to his feet again.

"No!" he cried. "The whole thing is ridiculous. Theresa, for God's sake—"

He sat down again—this time without waiting for Wooley to push him. He buried his face in his hands and wept silently. Sackler blew cigar smoke toward the ceiling.

"Joey," he said, "you are a louse."

I looked at him. The phrase was in character, yet there was something about his manner I didn't like. First, he wasn't sore—and he certainly figured to be. Second, there was a bland calm about him that made me very suspicious.

"You held out on me, Joey," he went on. "I am very much ashamed of you."

He met my eye and grinned maliciously. I was aware of a sudden emptiness at the pit of my stomach. Was it possible I hadn't brought it off, after all?

"O.K.," said Wooley. "I guess I can take my prisoner back to the can. I better take that Corn along as a material witness, too."

Corn opened his mouth to protest. But before he could speak, Sackler said: "Wait a minute. I want absolute silence in this room for the next three minutes. I also want Miss Harte to turn around and face the wall until I tell her to turn around again."

With the exception of Miss Grey who still gazed at the wall as if it were Robert Taylor, we all stared at him.

"Why?" said Wooley.

"A whim," said Sackler.

Wooley looked at him for a long moment. "All right, Miss Harte."

Theresa Harte executed a gesture of impatience. She spun around on her spike heels and faced the wall. The rest of us regarded Sackler expectantly. Sackler drew a deep breath. He thrust his right hand in his hip pocket and brought it out again, clutching an automatic.

He leveled the gun muzzle squarely at the breast of Julian Harte.

He said, quietly: "Mr. Harte, you will hand over your wallet to me. Then you will go to your desk and deliver to me any letters you may have from your wife. Early love letters, everything."

A PUZZLED FROWN crawled across Harte's brow. He said, a note of annoyance in his tone: "This is absurd. I shall do no such thing."

I glanced from Sackler to Harte. Was it possible Sackler was going to accuse Harte of killing his own wife? It didn't seem possible to me. Besides, what about my witness? I took a firmer grip on Frank Corn's arm. As long as I had his testimony there seemed to be little danger of Sackler knocking this case out of my hands.

"I am very serious," said Sackler. "I am prepared to go to grim and obvious lengths if you don't obey me."

"You are a fool," said Harte testily. "There is nothing in my wallet, there are no letters of my wife's which could throw any light upon the murder. I refuse."

I bit my lips. If Harte was refusing to perform what seemed a harmless and simple request, with a gun aimed at his heart there must be a damned good reason for it. Sackler inhaled again.

"All right," he said, "you asked for it."

He stood up, gun in hand, a menacing expression upon his face. Harte staring death in the face remained absolutely unmoved. Not a facial muscle changed expression. His eyes were fixed, unblinking on Sackler. Wooley took a step forward.

"Rex," he said, "are you crazy? You can't kill a man in cold blood. Put up that gun! Put—"

Theresa Harte swung around and stared at Sackler, horror in her green-decked eyes. She uttered a sharp little cry. "Julian! He's got a gun. He's—"

The metamorphosis of Julian Harte's face was a remarkable thing. An instant before he had been calm and unruffled as a corpse. Now, he was suddenly pale. Fear had been stamped on his face by an invisible die. He moved halfway out of his chair and said in a voice that quavered, "Disarm him, Inspector. My God—"

Wooley took a second step toward Sackler. Sackler sat down again and restored the gun to his hip pocket. He waved a languid hand and said, "There. See?"

With the removal of the gun's threat, we relaxed with two exceptions. Theresa Harte glared at Sackler, her teeth set firmly in her lower lip. Her brother remained on the edge of his chair. He said: "Put that gun away. Inspector—"

"He's put it away, Julian," said Theresa. I stared at her for a moment, then the brain cells began to function.

"He can't see!" I said breathlessly. "Harte's blind."

Sackler nodded complacently. "Almost, Joey. Not quite. He can make figures out dimly, can't you, Mr. Harte?"

Harte sighed, closed his eyes and sat back in his chair. Sackler looked as smug as Heinrich Himmler after a pogrom. My brain cells continued to function.

"That chair," I said to Sackler. "The last time we were here. Harte sat on the floor not because the butler was clowning but because he didn't see the chair."

"Very good, Joey," said Sackler and there was a note in his voice I didn't like. "Harte knows this room well enough to get around in it. That day he rose to hand out the cigars just as the butler was pulling up the window shades. The butler inadvertently moved the chair out of the way as he passed. Harte sat where the chair was *supposed* to be and finished on the floor."

"But why?" I asked. "Why is Harte's blindness kept undercover? Why did they tell that ridiculous lie about the butler with the comical spirit?"

"There were two very good reasons," said Sackler. "One is that Harte's a sensitive man and he didn't want his ailment generally known. The butler knew, of course. So did his sister. So, as a matter of fact, did his wife. The second reason is that it suited Miss Harte's purpose to keep it from me."

"Why should Miss Harte want to keep it from you?"

HE SMILED HIS most unpleasant smile at me. "I am about to disillusion you, Joey. Miss Harte's lovely face hides a blackened soul."

Christie drew in his breath with an odd hissing sound. Theresa Harte kept her fascinating eyes glued on Sackler. I glanced around at Corn. As long as he was there I had tangible evidence that my case had not yet broken down.

I said: "Tell me about Miss Harte's soul."

"It is an avaricious soul, Joey. Coupled with a mind which informed her that since her brother has a brain tumor which has almost blinded him, since he can live only a short while, that she will inherit all the Harte wealth if Mrs. Harte dies before her husband."

Julian Harte shook his head again. "I don't know exactly what you're driving at," he said, "but, if by any chance, you are accusing my sister of murder, I call attention to the fact that her train from Chicago arrived in town at 8:45. Under those circumstances it would have been impossible for her to have been at the Park Hotel at the time of the tragedy."

I'd forgotten that. Now, it seemed to me that whatever Sackler was aiming at he was going to miss.

However, he still retained his air of infuriating smug calm.

"I'm glad you mentioned that," he said to Harte. "You were informed that your sister would arrive at 8:45. With your butler you went to the station. You met her there. At precisely what time?"

"What does it matter?" said Harte testily. "At 8:45, or a few minutes later. Why?"

Sackler fixed Theresa Harte with his dark smoldering eyes. "Because," he said, "the 8:45 from Chicago didn't get in at 8:45 that night. It was twenty two minutes late."

Harte stiffened in his chair. I said, "Elaborate."

"Miss Harte arrived in town much earlier. She told her brother she'd arrive on the 8:45 just in case something went wrong with her plans and she was suspected. She returned to the station after she'd left the Park Hotel, pretending she'd just arrived. She neglected to check on the train."

I turned it all over in my brain. What Sackler argued now

contained a modicum of sense. But if he was right Corn was wrong. I couldn't see any percentage in Corn's lying.

Julian Harte licked dry lips. "Are you saying that my sister killed my wife in order to inherit my money?"

Oddly enough it was Christie who spoke next. "My God," he said. "No. You're all wrong, Sackler. I killed Eleanor Harte. I did it. I did!"

Well, that was all right with me. But I knew Sackler wasn't kidding either. I said quickly: "It doesn't seem to matter what Rex has, does it, Inspector? After all with my witness here, with Christie's confession, the case is cold, isn't it?"

"Of course it is," said Corn quickly—too damned disturbingly quickly for me. Why the devil was he so suddenly interested?

"Christie fries," said Wooley with finality. "We have motive, a witness and, by God, a confession. I'll take Corn along as a material witness."

To my complete surprise, Sackler said, "Oh no, you won't."

"Why not?" demanded Wooley.

Sackler sighed. "For heaven's sake, use your head. Christie's confession doesn't mean anything. He's crazy in love with Theresa Harte and has been for years. He's still uncertain as to whether she killed her sister or not. But if she did he's bent on dying for a mad sentimental reason. He had nothing to do with it. Except for the purchase of a scarf."

"Damn you," said Wooley, "will you make a little sense?"

SACKLER WAVED A hand in the direction of the silent Miss Grey. "This is Christie's secretary. By dint of threat, bribery, and charm, I managed to get some valuable information from her. First, I learned from her the secret of Christie's unrequited passion for Miss Harte. Second, she showed me the X-rays on Harte. I don't know a hell of a lot about X-rays. But I believed it was a brain tumor. I recalled that chair episode and assumed he was probably going blind. I pulled that gun on him to prove it."

"You've told us all this," I said.

"Patience, Joey," he said and there was a wicked glint in his eye. "I have also learned that Christie has sent one hell of a lot of presents to Miss Harte in the past few years. His secretary would buy them, mail them for him. Once he sent her a scarf. Didn't he, Miss Grey?"

The Grey girl spoke for the first time. She said, "Yes," in a thin, frightened voice.

"You'll recall," said Sackler, "there was some burned fabric in the fireplace of the room where Eleanor Harte was killed? I wondered what the devil it was Christie could have burned. Obviously something incriminating. When I learned of the presents he had sent Theresa, I searched the list for something made of cloth. There were stockings and this scarf. Then of course, it came to me."

"What came to you?" snarled Wooley.

"The fact that a scarf had been used to strangle Mrs. Harte. Christie found the scarf about the corpse's neck. He knew it would throw immediate suspicion on Theresa. Hence he burned it and planted the hotel towel around Mrs. Harte's neck. That scarf business was a bad bungle, eh, Pogany?"

Corn started. He looked at Sackler for a moment, then quickly averted his gaze. I began to worry.

Wooley said: "What the devil is this all about? What scarf? Who's Pogany?"

"I shall sum it up in a paragraph," said Sackler. He took another free cigar, lit it and proceeded to do so.

"Theresa Harte, hating her sister-in-law, avid for money, learns that her brother will not live long. She plans to kill her brother's wife. To this end she comes from Chicago with a notorious thug named Pogany, alias Frank Corn. She tells her brother she will arrive at 8:45. She arrives much earlier, has Pogany check into a hotel room and tells her sister-in-law to meet her there. Then she arranges a rendezvous with Christie in the same hotel room. Pogany meets Mrs. Harte in that room. He strangles her. Christie arrives in time to have the killing pinned on him. Simple, isn't it?"

"No," I said.

"I can make it slightly clearer, Joey," said Sackler, "but not much. When Theresa Harte made whatever excuse she *did* make for leaving her sister-in-law alone in that room, she inadvertently left her scarf behind. Pogany enters, probably with the intention of strangling Eleanor Harte with a towel. He sees a scarf which he naturally assumes belongs to his victim. He kills her with that, gets out of the room before Christie enters. Christie recognizes the scarf as one he once gave Theresa. Fearful she will be arrested for the murder, he burns it and substitutes a towel around the neck of the corpse. Now is it clear?"

I BLINKED. A lot of it was crystal clear. I jerked a thumb in Pogany's direction. "But what about him? Why should he—"

"He played you for a sucker, Joey. When I took the job from Julian Harte, Theresa worried a little. She wanted to plant a sure motive on Christie. So Pogany called to tell you he saw Christie in that room, to show you that forged letter. Those two items would insure Christie burning. That along with his own attitude."

"Well," said Wooley, "what was his attitude? If he was innocent, why didn't he say so?"

"He was bewildered. He wasn't sure whether or not Theresa was the criminal. He was in love with her. He was even prepared, perhaps, to take the rap to save her. He just didn't know what to do. He was still mulling it over in his mind."

Theresa Harte was glaring at Sackler. There was a vibrant huskiness in her voice as she spoke.

"It's a lovely theory," she said. "I can't imagine much of it coming under the heading of admissible evidence in court."

"The confession will," said Sackler confidently.

"What confession?" said Wooley. "For God's sake, you mean Miss Harte is going to confess?"

"No," said Sackler. "Pogany."

"Don't be a fool," snapped Theresa Harte. "If what you say is true, why should he confess?"

"To ease his own rap. To get even with you for trying to kill him. You decided he knew too much. If he also were dead, you'd be in the clear."

Pogany's eyes flashed. He spat out an obscene epithet at the girl. "It was you!" he yelled. "It was you who fired those shots. I told you you did it!"

"And I told you I didn't!" Theresa screamed back at him. "I knew nothing about it. I—"

"That is a lie," said Sackler blandly. "I saw you."

We all looked at him again. "I came into the office, my fine Judas," he said to me, "just as you were taking that phone call from Pogany. I was interested to know how you'd handle it so I retired discreetly. I followed you. I was concealed in the hallway when you had your treacherous interview with Pogany. I saw Miss Harte climb on a chair and shoot through the transom."

Pogany threw a barrage of oaths at the Harte girl. Then he calmed down somewhat and said: "All right. I'll play it your way. But I'm a state's witness. I'm entitled to clemency."

Sackler waved an insouciant hand toward Wooley. "Take them away," he said. "It's now your department. Now, Mr. Harte, I believe I have established reasonable proof of your wife's honor. May I have my money?"

With a trembling hand Julian Harte wrote out a check. Christie rose from his chair. He stood with bowed head before Sackler.

"I don't know whether to thank you or not," he said. "I didn't know what to do. I was morally certain Theresa had something to do with the murder. But I loved—I loved her so much, I didn't know whether I should defend myself, thus implicating her or not. And, of course, Mr. Sackler, you'll forget about that rent raise."

Sackler took the check from Julian Harte. He said: "Forget the rent raise? Certainly not, Doctor. Prices are going up. Inflation has begun. You are entitled to that raise. You shall have it."

WITH WHICH STUNNING and magnificent statement, he strode from the room with me at his heels.

In the taxicab downstairs, I asked the three questions that were burning in my mind.

"First," I said. "How did you know Corn was Pogany?"

Sackler puffed luxuriously on Harte's cigar. "Easy, Joey. I eavesdropped during your interview. I knew you had that letter.

I simply took it out of your desk and had the coppers examine the prints on it."

"All right. But what about the rent? Why are you suddenly willing to pay an extra fifteen bucks a month?"

"Me, Joey? I'm not paying an extra fifteen a month."

My heart sank at that. "Why?" I said, deathly afraid that I already knew the answer.

"It's coming out of your salary, Joey. It is the reward of treachery. You deliberately held out on me, Joey. You are a Benedict Arnold, though, of course, you're not getting his prices."

I kept my rage to myself and my mouth shut. I hastened on to my third question.

"When you saw Theresa taking those pot shots at Pogany, why didn't you pinch her right there?"

"Oh. I would have, Joey, if I'd seen her."

"If you'd seen her?"

"Yes. She didn't fire those shots, Joey. You see, I knew I needed Pogany's evidence even before I knew he was Pogany. I figured if he thought she'd shot at him he'd be a more tractable witness. So I fired them."

Panic rose up in me.

"You fired them?"

"Yes, Joey. Of course I didn't intend to hit anyone, it was simply to cause a rift between the two accomplices."

I said, "Oh, my God," and clapped a hand to my temple. Sackler was the world's worst shot. When I thought of his firing a gun into a room where I sat, I shuddered.

"Do you realize you might have killed me?" I demanded indignantly. "You're the lousiest marksman in the entire solar system."

"Oh," he said complacently, "I'm not so bad."

"Not bad? Do you know you shot my hat off? Do you know if that bullet had been six inches lower, I'd be a corpse?"

"Oh, well," he said, "it was that chair. It was a rickety old chair that I stood on. It really wasn't my fault."

He puffed easily at his cigar while I stared at him. A sense of baffled outrage overwhelmed me. I thought that never could I feel more indignant, until he said, blandly, "Besides, it was an old hat, Joey," and then I knew I had been wrong.

Killer, Can You Spare a Dime?

What a day for Sackler! A corpse spilling a fortune in gems across his desk—a fee-dodger tracked down after nine years—and Joey, his own assistant, getting into such a jam that he has to kick back $2,500 in future wages in exchange for his penny-pinching boss's help!

1

Out Cold

I DROVE THE old coupé slowly uptown from the office to the dreary street of brownstone houses where I dwelt in my solitary furnished room as befitted one who drew his weekly paycheck from Rex Sackler. A long dull night stretched before me. Tomorrow was payday. Hence, I could afford no date, no movie and was forced to economize in the essential matters of buying my dinner, the evening newspaper and such.

The prospect was bleak.

During the afternoon I had been considering asking for an advance. But after listening to Sackler lift an agonized voice to heaven as he made out his state income tax I discarded that mad idea. Getting an advance from Sackler was rather in the nature of negotiating an unsecured loan from a Glasgow bank.

Discontent mantled me as I turned into the shabby street. The newspapers informed me that a war boom was in progress, that labor was collecting more cash than ever before in history. That fact applied to me as a eulogy applies to Hirohito. I still drew my meager salary from Rex Sackler and Armageddon, itself, wasn't going to lift my salary one single mill.

I brought the creaking coupé to a halt before my house. I opened the door and slid out from behind the wheel. I bent over to lock the door. I turned my head slightly as I heard a scraping footfall behind me. An arm encircled my neck. A hand reopened the door of the coupé. I was pushed violently back into the car.

By the number of hands that grabbed me I knew there were two of them. I lashed out wildly and essayed to reach for the Police Special in my shoulder holster. Something wet, humid and quite nauseating was jammed up against my face. I felt as if my nose had been pushed into a most unpleasant marsh.

I tried to hold my breath to keep the fumes of the chloroform from my lungs. I felt as if my chest were bursting. Desperately I tore at the hands which held me. I was aware of the strength evanescing from my muscles. There was a sickening grayness before my eyes, the smell of all the hospitals in Manhattan in my nostrils and a revolving clamminess at the pit of my stomach.

Then suddenly I was in another world, filled with gaunt shadows and horrifying pastel dreams. I was out cold.

I STIRRED AND opened my eyes to find myself cramped once again behind my own steering wheel. I had a headache which spread across every muscle of my body. I shook my head and peered out the window of the car. It was parked before my own house.

I blinked, stepped out of the coupé and my knees buckled. I grabbed the door handle to prevent myself from falling. I blinked again and looked up and down the block for a copper. Then my stomach turned slowly over. I felt a violent nausea. I raced up the brownstone steps and reached for my key-ring at the same time.

A moment later I was violently ill in my own bathroom. When that was over I was in no mood to search for a copper. I was in no mood for revenge upon the guys who had snatched me. More than anything else in the world I wanted a pillow.

"For you," Hans nodded. "But get those men who killed my friend."

I reeled from the bathroom to the bed and fell heavily upon my face. It was bright sunlight when I opened my eyes the next time.

The chloroform had left me pretty shaky and the whole damned procedure had left me completely baffled. Why anyone in this town had wanted to put the snatch—even temporarily—on Joey Graham was utterly beyond me.

I went through my wallet and my pockets. Nothing was missing. I dressed slowly and meditatively. Maybe Rex Sackler's talents could pull the answer to my odd adventure out of the sky. I certainly couldn't.

As I reached for my coat something prickly and sharp bit into my finger, drawing blood. I looked closely at the sleeve. A cockleburr had attached itself to the fabric of the jacket. I blinked and thought that one over.

The last time I'd been in the country was when the ward leader gave a Staten Island outing three months ago. Certainly, I'd never picked up anything as bucolic as a cockleburr on Manhattan Island. I removed the prickly ball from my coat and went downstairs to the car. As I drove downtown I resolutely decided to thrust last night's affair from my mind.

Sackler had announced often and loudly that he was the brain in our office. I decided to toss the problem into his own shifty lap. Since I was out nothing more than the slight shock to my nervous system, he could handle it for me. I left the car before the antique building on Madison Avenue that housed our office and went upstairs.

Rex Sackler was already at his desk. He looked at me severely as I entered. He consulted his watch elaborately. He ran thin fingers through black hair and shook his head. The register upon his sharp face was that of a man sorely put upon.

"Joey," he said, "you take advantage of my benign nature. Punctuality is a virtue. You are fat from easy living. I overpay you. I tolerate your laziness. I—"

I was not listening to his speech. My eyes, startled and aching, regarded the suit he was wearing. It was the color of dying grass—green turning wearily to brown. Its cut had been smart back in '28. It sported four brave buttons on each cuff and the trousers were as tight as a sailor on Sand Street.

I blinked. I forgot my own tale of kidnapping. This suit was nothing for me to gaze upon in my chloroform hangover condition. I averted my gaze and inquired as to its origin.

"My suit?" said Sackler. "You envy me, Joey? You envy my taste."

He stood up and pirouetted like a fashion model. "A neat

little number," he said with satisfaction. "A bargain, too."

"Where in the name of God did you get it? Did you snatch it from the corpse of a bookmaker?"

"It was paid for," said Sackler, "by the Bijou Theater. They gave me a check when I threatened to sue them."

"Sue them? For what?"

"Damages. It was a matter of wet paint in the men's room. It ruined my good suit."

His good suit! In all the time I had known him he had possessed but two suits, both of which had been new when Andrew Volstead had been a household name. I turned my head about cautiously so that the green atrocity he wore would not slam into my vision too abruptly.

"You must be slipping," I told him, "if you could only get enough dough from the Bijou to pay for that verdant shroud you're wearing."

SACKLER SAT DOWN again. His arm stretched forth like a starving boa constrictor and snatched a cigarette from the package on my desk. He exhaled a mouthful of smoke. He said: "The theater awarded me a check for one hundred dollars."

"My God," I said, "you actually made them believe the rag you were wearing was worth that much? Moreover don't tell me you laid out a hundred bucks for that number you've got on now."

"This garment," said Sackler, "cost twelve dollars. Second hand."

I searched my vocabulary to tell him precisely what sort of a cheap thus and so I thought he was. I found no words effective enough. He had picked up a spot of paint on a ten year old suit. He had collected one hundred dollars' damages. He had paid twelve bucks for another outfit and, doubtless, deposited the remaining eighty-eight in one of his several Postal Savings accounts.

I sighed and sat down. Rex Sackler's passion for money made a mother's love for her first born a pale and nebulous thing. Sackler piled up dollars with an avidity equaled only by his reluctance at disgorging them.

He dwelt in a draughty furnished room where the discomfort was commensurate with the rent. He drank alcoholic beverages only when he had carefully figured that the free lunch he could consume was worth three times the cost of his beer. He rolled his own cigarettes and wrote violent letters to Robert LaFollette each time a new tax was mentioned in the House.

I sighed, lit a cigarette and moved the deck out of Sackler's reach.

"Listen," I said, "I have a problem for your mighty mind. A matter of kidnapping. Last night, I—"

He looked up from the letter he had just opened and interrupted me with a sound blended of crowing triumph and a gurgle of delight.

"Joey," he said, "they've found Maxwell."

"I hope he is broke," I said. "Moreover, I hope he is out of a job."

Sackler grinned so happily I knew that none of my hopes were coming true.

"On the contrary, Joey. He has an important defense job. With a firm who frowns on its employees becoming involved in law suits. This epistle from the collection agency informs me he has capitulated. He will drop in here shortly and do the right thing."

I shook my head in disgust. Morty Maxwell had a single claim to fame, one distinction that lifted him above all his fellowmen. He was Sackler's only debtor. He was the only person, living or dead, who owed Sackler a fee which had never been collected.

The debt was some years old and for almost a decade Sackler had bombarded Maxwell with letters, threats and tearful pleas. To utterly no avail. This horrible condition had eaten away at Sackler's soul for many moons. It had given me no little delight.

But now he was apparently about to collect. I felt as morose about it as if I were actually paying the debt myself.

"All right," I said. "That makes your record absolutely perfect. Nobody owes Rex Sackler. But as I was saying I have a little case for you. A kidnapping. Last night when I drove home, I was jumped by—"

This time the slamming of the outer door interrupted me. Inspector Wooley of headquarters entered the room. Upon his weather-beaten face he wore the expression of a cat who has just spotted a sleeping bird with a broken wing half a block away. In his hand was an official-looking document with a very legal red seal pasted prominently in its corner.

He sat down in the chair before Sackler's desk, lit a cigar and raised his eyes toward the ceiling. Sackler, whose affection for the inspector was quite similar to the inspector's affection for him, said, irritatedly: "What the devil are you doing?"

"Praying," said Wooley.

"It's as effective a way as any for you to solve cases," snapped Sackler.

"It's not that," said Wooley sweetly. "I am merely praying that you borrowed Joey's car last night. Did he, Joey?"

I WAS AWARE of a tiny emptiness at the pit of my stomach. There was a touch of dryness in my mouth. Sackler stared at Wooley blankly.

"Your ridiculous prayer remains unanswered," he said. "I did not borrow Joey's car last night. I spent the evening at the Bijou Theater."

"A pass, undoubtedly," said Wooley. "Well, Rex, next to putting *you* under arrest and informing *you* that you're about to be sued for a small fortune, I'd prefer to do it to Joey than anyone else in the world. I was sort of hoping that you'd borrowed his car. But I suppose we can't have everything. Come along, Joey."

By now I was frankly scared. At least a glimmer of what had occurred came to me.

"Wait a minute," I said. "What do you want me for?"

Wooley lifted his shaggy eyebrows.

"Too drunk to remember, Joey? Then I'll tell you. Leaving the scene of an accident. After, of course, hitting a woman and a child and wrecking a parked car. Two pedestrians got your license number."

I stared at him stunned.

"You'll probably get a two-year rap," went on Wooley cheerfully. "Not to mention the civil suit which should tie up every penny you can earn in the next twenty years." He stood up. "Well, come along, Joey. I have a nice cool cell waiting for you."

"Wait," snapped Sackler. "Joey, did you hit anything with your car last night?"

I took a deep breath, I said, "No."

Wooley looked troubled. "You mean someone borrowed it?" He thought of something and brightened a little. "As owner you're liable on the suit anyway, you know."

Sackler waved him to silence. "Who used your car last night, Joey?"

"I don't know."

Both Sackler and Wooley stared at me, incredulous. I hastened to explain.

"I was trying to tell you when the inspector came in. I was kidnapped last night. I was doped. While I was out the snatchers must have used my car. See?"

Even to my ears it sounded a trifle thin. Wooley looked as if he were listening to a hophead. Sackler shook his head as if to say: "Can't you do any better than that, Joey?"

"I tell you I'm leveling," I said loudly, as if to make up for the little conviction in my story. "I was snatched. I had just arrived home with the car when a couple of guys jumped me." I gave them the entire story and as I went on I realized that its Mother Goose qualities became more and more pronounced.

I concluded lamely, glanced at Wooley anxiously. He drew a deep breath.

"So," he said, "Joey Graham was snatched. You did not, of course, notify the police, when you returned home."

"No. I got sick suddenly from the chloroform. This morning I thought I'd talk it over with Rex first."

"So," said Wooley again. "And they didn't request that you raise any ransom, did they?"

"They didn't speak to me at all."

"Ah. Was anything missing from your pockets? Money, papers, anything at all?"

I felt like a guy in the basement of the Ninth Precinct house with a rubber hose suspended above his head.

"Nope. Nothing. But I tell you—"

"You tell me one damned incredible story," said Wooley. "You claim you were kidnapped by two thugs who asked nothing of you. Who robbed you of nothing. Who, according to your tale, chloroformed you and took you for a jaunt in your own car, finally returning both your body and the coupé to your own front door. I trust, Joey, that you find a jury more gullible than I am."

SACKLER LOOKED AT me shrewdly as if he were examining the change from a five dollar bill. There was a peculiar glint in his eye which I didn't like. It seemed to me that I was in enough trouble already without Sackler taking a hand.

"Joey," he stated sententiously, "you are in a jam."

That much I knew. I had heard stronger alibis than mine disbelieved by the police department.

"You need help, Joey. You need my brains. If we could actually prove you were kidnapped you're clean. You can't hold him responsible, even civilly, Inspector, for damage done by his car while that car was held illegally."

"That we can't," said Wooley. "Can you prove he was actually kidnapped?"

Sackler shrugged. "Perhaps. I've solved some difficult cases in my time. I'm sure Joey will trust me with this matter. Won't you, Joey?"

"Of course," I said. "I need all the help I can get. I probably need bail, as well."

Sackler sighed deeply. He turned to Wooley. "Considering the several favors I've done the department, considering the solutions I've dropped in your lap, would you agree to releasing Joey in my custody if he becomes my client?"

Wooley thought this over. The inspector envied sorely the fact that Sackler's income was at least five times his own. Moreover he strongly resented Sackler's constant trumpeting of his superior talents. However, there was a wide streak of fairness in him. Sackler had, more than once, tossed a solution in the inspector's lap, permitted him to garner all the credit. Sackler, of course, had picked up all the cash.

"All right," he said reluctantly. "I can fix it with the D.A. However, you must tell me officially that Joey's your client. That you're working to prove that ridiculous story of his is really true."

I lit a cigarette and sighed with relief. For a moment the sound of the tumbril's wheels had been sounding in my ears. True, I was in a jam. But Sackler, despite his frugal faults, was no man's dope when it came to cleaning up something like this. Moreover, he had obviously kept me out of a cell. For that I was reluctantly grateful.

"Thanks, Rex," I said. "I—"

Wooley, standing in the doorway, repeated: "Then, officially, Joey *is* your client?"

"Well," said Sackler, "that, of course, is up to Joey."

"Naturally," I said. "Naturally, I'm your client. Under the circumstances I'm glad to be. Further, I want to thank you—"

I broke off suddenly, clapped a hand to my head as the awful thought came to me. When, since that day when cosmos was created, had Rex Sackler ever done anything for nothing? When, since the firmament first came to order at divine command, had Sackler ever accepted a client free? I groaned and wondered how I could have been such a simple-souled sucker.

Sackler tapped a forefinger on the desk top. There was an expression on his face all too familiar to me. I had seen it there often when he was estimating exactly how much cash he could siphon from a client's wallet. He was, I knew, figuring with Dun and Bradstreet accuracy, precisely how much he could hold me up for.

Sackler assumed a pious expression and rolled his eyeballs toward the ceiling. "Friendship and business do not mix," he announced. "There is the minor matter of the fee."

I drew a deep breath and wondered if it was cheaper to go along quietly with Wooley.

"How much?" I asked like a kidnapee inquiring the ransom.

SACKLER STROKED HIS jaw with his thin fingers. There was a glint in his eyes that caused me to tremble and I could almost feel the flutter of my pocketbook in my breast pocket.

"Joey," he said, and Hitler would have coveted the oil in his voice, "Joey, we've been together a long, long time. As a personal favor to you, I'll take the case for, say, twenty-five hundred dollars. How does that strike you?"

"Like a hammer," I said. "Where in the name of God would I get twenty-five hundred dollars?"

"I won't press you," said Sackler with the air of a man endowing an orphanage. "I'll charge no interest. We'll take it out of your salary. Say thirty per cent of your salary until it's paid."

I glared at him like a searchlight. Wooley stood grinning by the doorway. "When thieves fall out," he murmured *sotto*.

"Are you mad?" I said. "Thirty per cent of my salary? Of course, I'd sooner take my chances in court. I've no record.

I'll draw a suspended sentence. Not more than ninety days anyway."

Sackler pursed his lips and looked at me blandly.

"Possibly," he said. "You may, Joey. But how do you beat the civil rap?"

"What civil rap?"

"The law suits of the injured people, of the owner of the damaged car? They have you cold, Joey. From what little I have heard it seems like a simple twenty grand at least. They'll collect, too, Joey. They'll take a cut of your salary for the rest of your life. My fee only touches you for a few short years."

I scratched my head and suffered from nausea. For years I had stood silently by as Sackler gently put clients over a barrel. Now I found myself in the same unenviable position.

This was Hobson's choice, indeed. Unless I could prove positively that the coupé had been stolen I most certainly was stuck cold with a damage suit, not to mention what jail sentence I might undergo for hit and run driving.

On the other hand if I retained Sackler to look after my interests I was taking a thirty per cent salary cut for a long time to come. A prospect which appealed to me like cafeteria stew to a gourmet.

I sighed heavily and looked up. Wooley was grinning like a more obnoxious species of ape in the doorway. Sackler watched me with quivering nostrils. The smell of money was being breathed luxuriously into his lungs.

"Suppose I lose both ways," I said. "Suppose I agree to your terms and you fail to clear me?"

"I don't usually take contingency fees, Joey," said Sackler nobly. "But because of our association I'll make an exception for you. I'll draw up a contract. Thirty per cent of your salary until the twenty-five hundred is paid. Payable only if I demonstrate to the satisfaction of all concerned that your car was illegally out of your possession when the accident occurred."

I closed my eyes and shuddered. I felt like a small-time bank in the fall of '29.

"Very well," I said, "I'll pay it."

I sat down, defeated as a Georgia Republican. Wooley chuckled audibly and strode from the office. I stared broodingly out the window. I did not dare look around. I knew the gloating in Rex Sackler's face would turn my stomach over.

2

Hot Ice

FOR A LONG time I sat alone with my sorrow. Sackler had gone to work immediately on the contract. He had drawn it up air-tight. If he extricated me from the mess I was in he was to withhold thirty per cent of my salary to the total of twenty-five hundred bucks. If he failed he would take nothing at all.

An instant after I had signed it I realized what a wonderful little sucker I was. For if Sackler failed I would go to the can where I'd draw no money at all. And when I got out my little suing friends would rob me of anything I ever should earn in the future.

I felt sick and weary. The sudden slamming of the outer door caused me to lift my head. A man entered.

He was thick, squat and blond. A single glance at him revealed his German nationality. His face was pale and there was pain stamped in his blue eyes.

He walked bent over, his hands held to the lapels of his topcoat. He fell into the chair on the near side of Sackler's desk. He said, with a heavy accent: "I am Hans Drager. You Rex Sackler?"

Sackler nodded. "Yes, I'm Sackler."

Hans took off his homburg and put it on the desk. His hair was stiff as if starch had been applied to it. A closer examination showed me that it was dry blood that caused the odd bristling.

The front of his coat fell open. His collar was unbuttoned and the front of his white shirt was dark red. Blood stained the hair of his exposed chest.

He plunged a hand into his pocket. He withdrew it, held it over Sackler's desk and opened it. A dozen glittering objects fell upon the battered wood. Sackler's eyes lit up like a blasted ammunition dump. I sprang out of my chair and stared over Hans Drager's shoulder.

I am no lapidarian. I can estimate within ten dollars one way or the other what a wrist watch will hock for. Beyond that I'm a layman. But even a layman would have known that the gems Hans had dropped so casually on Sackler's desk had never reposed on a tray in Woolworth's.

"What's this?" asked Sackler, and his voice was thick. "Are these—these for me?"

Hans nodded. "For you," he said. "But get those men. Those men who killed my friend, Hein—"

The last syllable died away like the final whisper of a discouraged breeze. Hans slumped forward in his chair. He would have slipped onto the floor had I not held him. I straightened him up in the seat and dropped my fingers to his pulse. I felt no answering beat.

Sackler looked at me inquiringly. I shook my head. I examined Hans Drager's body cursorily. I shook my head again.

"He must've got here with his last ounce of strength. I don't know how he did it. Obviously he got a crease in his skull and a couple of bullets through his chest, damned near the heart. He's dead, all right."

Sackler looked from the body to the gleaming pile of jewels upon the desk.

He regarded me anxiously. "You heard what he said, Joey? Just before he died."

"What did he say?"

"That this stuff was mine. That's what he intended and I've always been a great believer in carrying out the wishes of the dead."

I looked at him with distaste. "You are a very noble character," I told him. "You've just taken me for a fortune, now you want to snatch these gems from a corpse. You're a commercial ghoul."

"Now, Joey, be reasonable. Don't be petty merely because you're about to pay a legitimate fee. You heard him say that these baubles were for me."

"Conditionally. He said you were first to find the men who killed someone. He was offering you a fee. Provided you did something. Do it and they're yours."

"But he mentioned no names, Joey. He never told us who it was that—"

Again the outer door opened. Two men walked in. The first was a tall, emaciated individual with black seething eyes which darted about the room as if he were casing the joint. His companion who walked behind him was middle-aged, ruddy-faced, and possessed of a pair of blue eyes which were entirely too ingenuous for one of my suspicious nature.

THE TALL MAN looked at the body of Hans, motionless in the chair. He lifted his gaze to Sackler.

"When did he get here?" he asked in an authoritative tone. "How long's he been dead?"

There was a degree of arrogance in his manner and that, I

knew, nettled Sackler. Arrogance was a virtue on which he believed he held a monopoly.

"Who the devil are you?" he demanded. "A corpse in my office is between me, God and the local police. I hardly think you represent either of the latter two."

The tall man glared at him. He took a deep breath as if to utter an explosive epithet. Then he exhaled the air hissingly as if he had thought better of it.

"I'm Sheriff Donald of Webley County. This is the town constable of Permeten. His name is Nelson."

"I am unimpressed," said Sackler. "What the devil do you want here?"

The sheriff looked as if he wanted very badly to put Sackler in his place. The constable touched his arm as if to remind Donald that perhaps diplomacy in this instance was the better policy.

"This man," said the sheriff, "is Hans Drager. He's from my county. I traced him here to arrest him."

"On what charge?"

"Murder."

Sackler's eyes glittered. "Whose?" he said quickly.

"A fellow called Heinrich. A German refugee. This Drager killed him last night. Robbed him of a mess of cached jewelry. I see some of it on your desk right now."

Sackler had forgotten about the gems. He stared down at them now and panic was in his face. If the stuff was stolen, whether or not Drager's dying wish had been for Sackler to keep it, it was going to be snatched from his avaricious grasp in short order.

His annoyance at the sheriff's manner vanished. In its place there came an oily smile and a fulsome presence. His terror at losing the gems forced him into an ingratiating role. Now there was money at stake and no sacrifice, no humiliation, was too great for Rex Sackler.

"Now, now, Sheriff," he said. "Let us not be too hasty. Perhaps these aren't the gems that were stolen. Perhaps this man you speak of—this Heinrich—wasn't killed by our dead friend here, after all. Just before he died he said something about giving me these jewels to solve a murder. He must have meant the murder of Heinrich. We shall look into the case together, Sheriff."

The ruddy-faced constable sighed heavily. "The case is open and shut," he said. "I'm sure we don't need your help, Mr. Sackler."

"You're damned right we don't," snapped Donald. "I see quite clearly what the game is. He wants to keep his greedy hands on those gems. Well, he can't. They're stolen property. The murder and the robbery happened in my jurisdiction. You, Sackler, will keep your snatching fingers out of this."

I giggled and Sackler flushed. Apparently our reputation had traveled far beyond the county line.

Sackler glared at the sheriff. "Your jurisdiction, hell!" he exploded. "Perhaps Heinrich's killing was. But that's all. This corpse"—he indicated Drager—"happens to be in my office. In New York County. These jewels are here, too. If it's out of my hands, it's also out of yours. It's a matter for the New York coppers. Joey, get Wooley on the wire."

The sheriff looked at the constable. It appeared to me that they were both concerned and angry.

I picked up the phone and put the call through to headquarters. Constable Nelson said: "Why all this red tape? We are both interested in the maintenance of law and order. Just hand the jewels over to us, and send the body to the morgue."

Sackler shook his head righteously. "This may be an important case. Something too big for a couple of hayseed town marshals."

The sheriff took a deep breath and blew up. He hurled a magnificent vocabulary at Sackler with specially ornate adjectives regarding the inevitable fate of those who hoarded nickels and dimes. Sackler replied in kind.

THEY WERE STILL at it hammer and tongs when Wooley arrived. The inspector shut them up, called the meat wagon to remove Drager and took the gems from Sackler's desk, dropped them into his own pocket. Sackler watched them disappear like a kid whose mother has just snatched his last lollipop.

I heard a footfall in the outer office and a moment later Maxwell entered. He walked up to Sackler's desk and took a wallet from his pocket. He sighed and shook his head.

"You're a damned persistent creditor," he said. "I thought I was the only living guy who'd ever beat you out of anything. I guess I have to forego that distinction now."

Sackler forgot about the insulting words of the sheriff. He grinned like a Cheshire cat loose in an aviary. He held out his hands.

"Fifty-three dollars, I believe."

Morty Maxwell nodded. He counted the money out of his wallet. "Well," he said, "I guess I lose. Though it *did* take you nine years to catch up with me."

Sheriff Donald evinced interest. "Nine years?" he said. "You mean you've owed Sackler this debt for nine years?"

"About that," said Maxwell. "I'd never pay it off now except that I don't want to have a lawsuit plastered on me at my new job."

Sackler reached his hand out for the bills. The sheriff's hand shot out and fastened itself about Maxwell's wrist.

"Wait," he said, "you'll get no lawsuit. That debt's outlawed. After nine years he can't collect. The statute of limitations on debt runs only seven. You don't have to pay him at all."

Sackler's face turned white. He snatched at the money in Maxwell's hand. Maxwell removed it from his reach. He looked gratefully at the sheriff.

"Is that true?"

"Sure, it's true," boomed Wooley happily. "You don't have to pay him."

The laughter echoed through the room. Maxwell happily returned the bills to his wallet, bowed to the sheriff.

"I'm exceedingly grateful," he said. "Good-day, gentlemen."

He turned on his heel and left the room. The sheriff grinned wolfishly at Sackler. Sackler's face resembled an overripe tomato.

"Get out!" he yelled. "Get out of my office before I murder you. You rat, you swindled me out of a legitimate fee. I ought to strangle you. I ought to—"

He stopped, for once in his life speechless. The sheriff followed by the constable, left the room. Wooley's meat wagon man came in and picked up Drager's corpse. Wooley, smiling broadly, rattled the jewels in his pocket, and slammed the door behind him.

Sackler looked utterly desolate. He had been swindled out of Maxwell's money. He had lost a hatful of precious stones.

He had been insulted in his own domain by a county sheriff. I threw back my head and howled with laughter.

He jerked his head up and glared at me. "May I call your attention to a certain fact?" he said acidly. "If I find out who swiped your car last night I draw thirty per cent of your salary for a considerable period. If I don't, you'll lose a twenty thousand dollar law suit. Now may I inquire what the hell you're laughing about?"

My risible muscles became dead-pan in nothing flat. Under the circumstances what the hell *was* I laughing at?

Sackler stood up. He looked outside the window. A light rain beat against the pane. He sighed deeply. He said: "Joey, let's take a ride out to Webley County."

He took a shabby raincoat from its hook and donned it. "I better drive, Joey. It seems you can't be trusted with a car."

I wished to heaven he'd stop harping on that. Every time I thought of what was going to happen to me financially, an egg beater started spinning in my stomach.

We went downstairs to the coupé. Sackler climbed in behind the wheel. We set out, moving conservatively, toward the Queensborough Bridge.

3

Red Light

THE RAIN BEAT down on the windshield. Sackler drove like a maiden aunt, peering through the glass and moving like a snail who is very much afraid of trucks. At Madison and Fifty-sixth he halted.

I paid little attention to him. I felt like Wall Street on a well-known day in 1929. Whatever happened I was out dough. I feared that as usual Sackler would profit.

He said in my ear: "How's that light, Joey? I can't see it from here."

I peeped out the window. The light was red against us and a water-proofed copper stood on the sidewalk three yards away from it. I took a meager revenge.

"Green," I said. "Go ahead."

Sackler put the coupé in gear and we moved forward gingerly. Halfway across the street the copper's whistle blasted in our ears. Sackler stopped the car. I studied a grocery store window with intense interest. The copper loomed up on Sackler's side.

"Are you blind?" he roared. "Going right through a red light? Give me your license."

I felt Sackler's eyes upon me though I did not turn around. He muttered something savage about Judas and dove into his raincoat pocket for his license. I turned around to see his face turn white.

"It's not here," he said. "I'd swear I left my license in this coat. You remember it was raining the last time I drove, Joey. I—"

The copper regarded him with satisfaction.

"Driving without a license, eh? I'll have to take you in."

"Look," said Sackler desperately. "I'm Rex Sackler. You know damned well I have a license. I just can't find it, that's all."

The copper's expression became positively beatific.

"Rex Sackler?" he said. "It's a pleasure. We just go down to the precinct house and you stay in a cell while someone goes and checks the license for you."

Sackler's glance at me held cobra's venom.

"Wait a minute," he said. "Isn't there any way we can fix this up?"

The copper nodded happily. "Of course," he said.

Their eyes met. Sackler looked at me. The three of us knew perfectly well what way there was to fix it up. Sackler's sigh sounded like a dry wind over a graveyard. He fished into his wallet and produced a ten dollar bill. The copper took it very smoothly. The car moved on.

"Joey," said Sackler, "you are a miserable hound. You deliberately told me that light was green to cost me money. I shall remember this."

I didn't answer him. I was too concerned with my own troubles. We drove in silence until we were almost at the Webley County line. Then Sackler murmured: "A missing license, Joey. Do you see its significance?"

I saw nothing and said so. We drove through the village of Permeten and came to a halt at the secluded cottage where Drager and Heinrich had lived.

WE WERE GREETED by an old gnarled man who was raking leaves. He introduced himself as Joe Turner, the gardener. Sackler, lying glibly, announced that we were state detectives come to look into the matter of Heinrich's demise.

"He was a funny feller," said Turner. "I guess all foreigners are funny. Beat it out of Germany with those Hitler guys on his tail. Kept himself locked in the house. Never talked to no one. I only saw him two or three times. Never spoke to him at all."

Sackler grunted. "How did you get your instructions about your work and so forth?"

"Through this Drager feller. He didn't speak English so good. But you could understand him."

Sackler nodded. "Have you the keys to the house?"

Turner produced a bunch of keys and led us to the front door. He ushered us into the foyer, then returned to his raking.

"Well," I asked, "what now?"

Sackler shrugged. "Let's look around."

We did without finding much. In the bedroom we found a trunk whose lock had been forced. It was without any significance at all to me, but Sackler studied it for a long and thoughtful moment. He then busied himself at the closets. A number of well-cut suits hung there.

After a short search he came over to me at the window. "Look, Joey," he said, "I found a number of these in the vest pockets of several suits."

I looked at several penciled slips of paper containing short sentences written in a language I judged to be German.

"Probably inconsequential notes," I said. "Can you read any of them?"

"I can make out a few. For instance, one reads: 'Can we get any pumpernickel in the village?' Below it, in different handwriting is an answer, reading: 'Possibly. I'll try.'"

"Very powerful clues," I said ironically.

"Quite," said Sackler. "I didn't think you'd see it."

He put the paper in his pocket. He said suddenly: "Joey, look through the desks. See if you can find any lawyer's letterheads. Any notation with the address of attorneys."

I shrugged and didn't ask why. After a few minutes' rummaging I came across a few letters from the firm of Albany and Danewright, counsellors at law. I handed them over. Sackler was genuinely elated.

"Wonderful, Joey. Things get better every minute. Now let's get out of here and pay a visit to the sheriff and constable. Do you think they have a dial phone, Joey?"

I neither knew nor cared. I was busily engaged in beating my breast mentally about the financial crucifixion I was about to undergo.

THE SHERIFF AND Constable Nelson shared the same office. As we entered they were about as cordial as a pair of awakened lions. Sackler glanced immediately at the telephone. It had, I observed, no dial.

Sackler said, "Good-day," in his most honeyed accents and it got him precisely nowhere.

The constable stood up, blinked his blue eyes, and said: "You have neither authority nor jurisdiction in this county. If you're here regarding the Heinrich murder you can get the hell right back to New York."

Sackler elevated his eyebrows.

"Gentlemen," he said, "after all, we're all only interested in seeing justice done. Let's not bicker."

Sheriff Donald took his pipe from his mouth and regarded

Sackler antagonistically.

"Look here," he said, "there's no fee in this for you. Drager killed Heinrich. There's no doubt about it. He was a drunken bum. Why, only just before the murder we picked him up drunk, booked him on a D.O. charge and during the night he broke out of jail."

"Sure," echoed Nelson. "Besides, I've heard Heinrich say he was afraid of him. Afraid to trust him with all that jewelry around. Only kept him around because he was sorry for him. They'd gone through hell together in Germany."

Sackler brazenly helped himself to a cigarette from the constable's desk.

"You heard Heinrich say that?"

"With my own ears. More than once, too."

Sackler grunted. "This," he said, "is all very interesting, gentlemen. I'll bother you no longer. Come, Joey."

I followed him out of the office. The hostile glares of the sheriff and the constable followed us both.

Outside, I said: "This is all very fine and a magnificent example of scientific detection, I suppose, but what about me?"

Sackler halted outside the Western Union office by the railroad station.

"You, Joey?"

"Me. I'm in danger of being sued for millions on account of my car hit somebody. I engaged you to get me out of that jam. Would you mind deferring this murder and looking after my interests?"

"Of course not, Joey. That's exactly what I'm about to do right now. Wait here for me a moment."

He disappeared into the Western Union office. I saw him

in whispered conclave with the clerk. A moment later he emerged, beaming.

"Relax, Joey," he said. "Drive me back to town in silence. My brain cells are functioning."

I drove him back to town unhappily. I saw no out for myself. Little Joey Graham was due for a financial beating either way. I was a most despondent assistant at that moment.

At the office, Sackler said: "Tomorrow, Joey, is the day. Tomorrow in the late afternoon. Now make a few appointments. Ask Wooley if he would kindly put in an appearance at Heinrich's house. Call the sheriff and the constable and make the same request of them. We'll meet them there, say at six o'clock."

I picked up the phone. "What about me?" I asked again. "When do you get around to my problem?"

"All in good time, Joey. All in good time. Never will I let a pal down. You should know that."

"Not for twenty-five hundred bucks you won't," I said bitterly, as I put the call through to headquarters for Inspector Wooley.

THE NEXT DAY we arrived in Webley County a good half-hour before the time we were supposed to meet Wooley. I parked the coupé in the garage. We passed the time of day with Turner, the gardener, who was again engaged in raking leaves off the lawn. Sackler lit a cigarette and stretched his arms expansively.

"It's great out here in the hills, Joey. We should get out of town more often. Let's take a short stroll while we're waiting."

He walked out into the grounds at the rear of the house.

Having nothing better to do, I followed.

We walked aimlessly along a gravel path, bordered by weary rose bushes. In the distance stood a weather-beaten summerhouse.

As we approached it leisurely we heard voices. We were too far off to distinguish the words. However, from the tone it was apparent they were being uttered by an angry man.

Sackler screwed up his brow thoughtfully. He adjured me to silence with a gesture. We drew near to the summerhouse silently. Now we could hear the wrathful dialogue from within clearly. We stood less than six yards beyond the glassless window when we heard the shot. I sprang forward, but Sackler's hand restrained me. Gripping my arm firmly he moved up closer to the window.

I stared inside and drew a deep breath. I struggled to loose myself from Sackler's grip, but he only held me tighter. We waited, silent and motionless, staring through the window for a full minute.

Then Sackler turned around and moved off swiftly into the gathering dusk, dragging me along with him as if in a hurry.

We were almost back at the house when he released me. I turned on him angrily.

I said: "Are you crazy? Are you going to let that pass? It may well be—"

He shushed me in his most superior manner. "Everything is working out beautifully, Joey. I assure you I am earning my fee."

The reference nettled me. "You fool," I said, "suppose he lams? Suppose it's mur—"

"Joey," said Sackler, "you are paying the bill—or part of it. You are buying my talents. For God's sake, permit me to use them."

"What the devil are you talking about? What's this got to do with my case? What's it got to do with my car being swiped?"

"If you could understand that," said Sackler, "you wouldn't have to retain me to answer it for you. Relax, Joey. Lean on my brain. You're paying for it, aren't you?"

By this time I was so annoyed I wasn't looking where I walked. With the result that my foot slammed clumsily against a decorative rock at the border of the lawn and I fell gawkily upon my face. A small stone ground into my temple and drew blood. I got up cursing.

Sackler, completely indifferent to pain other than his own, walked on to the porch.

"Too bad, Joey."

I wiped the blood away with my handkerchief as Wooley drove up, chauffeured by a uniformed copper.

The inspector, with a copper three paces behind, came toward us. He was chewing on an unlit cigar.

"Well," he said, none too cordially, "I don't know what the devil you're dragging me out here for, Rex. It's beyond my jurisdiction."

Sackler lifted his eyebrows. "Is it? Drager died in New York County, didn't he?"

"So what? Drager was killed by a law officer in pursuit of his duty. Heinrich's death is the only one to be questioned and from what the sheriff said that's clear enough, too."

Sackler's eyebrows lifted another millimeter. "Is it?" he said again.

4

Double Amnesia

ALL OF US looked around as we heard the sound of running feet coming toward us. Constable Nelson arrived breathless upon the porch.

"The sheriff," he said, panting. "Dead. Shot himself. Just found him in the summerhouse. His gun in his hand. God, I never thought he'd do it."

Wooley looked at Sackler. So, for that matter, did I. Sackler remained very calm. He said to Nelson: "Can you imagine why he would do that?"

"Yes," said Nelson. "He was short in some of his office accounts. He'd told me about it. But I never dreamed he'd do a thing like this."

"Didn't you?" said Sackler quietly.

These two-word questions of his were beginning to get on my nerves. "Damn it," I said, "I may as well say that—"

Sackler said, "Shut up, Joey," and glared at me. Wooley chewed his cigar as if it were spearmint.

"Why have I been brought here?" he demanded. "If there's a suicide in the summerhouse let the county constable take care of it. If there's any mystery about Heinrich's death, let the local authorities look after it."

"And," said Sackler, "if Hans Drager was murdered in New York County, what then?"

"He was killed by a sheriff while resisting arrest," said Wooley, shouting now. "That's not murder."

I felt that I would scream if Sackler said, "Isn't it?" again. He did.

"Heinrich, a refugee, who took his wealth out of Germany in jewels was murdered for those jewels," said Sackler. "Drager was murdered for another reason."

Constable Nelson coughed. "We know Heinrich was murdered," he said. "And we know Drager murdered him."

Sackler looked at him coldly. "Your principal evidence of that is that you overheard Heinrich say that he feared Drager. Is that right?"

"Sure it's right," said Nelson. "The sheriff and I heard him say it with our own ears."

"You are a Japanese diplomat," said Sackler.

Nelson and Wooley stared at him blankly. I translated. "He means you're a liar."

Nelson bridled. "What the devil do you mean? How could you possibly prove what I heard or didn't hear Heinrich say?"

"Easily," said Sackler. "Heinrich never said anything. He was dumb. He was a deaf mute."

"I," said Wooley, "am a monkey's uncle if I can figure how you figure that."

"It was very simple," said Sackler. "First, several slips of paper I found in his pockets. They're in German and concerned with the most simple matters. For instance, there's one which freely translated tells Drager to ask the gardener to mow the front lawn. There's another, inquiring what time Drager is going to the village. There's an answer below it in another handwriting, obviously Drager's. There are a number of others. There can be no reason in the world for such communication, save with a deaf mute."

We digested this. Nelson said: "Did you find many of those notes? Could you read them all?"

"Yes," said Sackler. "And no. I found plenty. I couldn't read them all. But a German professor is translating them for me now. They should prove interesting."

"Wait a minute," said Wooley. "Those notes might be anything. They indicate he was dumb. They don't prove it."

"Coupled with the fact that Heinrich didn't telephone me," said Sackler, "it's strong enough evidence."

Wooley almost bit his cigar in two. "Why the devil should he telephone you?"

"He distrusted the police," said Sackler. "Perhaps because he knew you are such notorious bunglers. Perhaps because of unpleasant experiences with the Gestapo."

WOOLEY SAT DOWN on the porch rail. Constable Nelson sighed and looked at me. I scratched my head and wondered what this all had to do with establishing the fact that my car had been swiped. Again I thought of the financial threat hanging over my head. Again I was aware of that nauseous sensation at the pit of my stomach.

"Look," said Sackler, "I'll make it as simple as possible. Heinrich has a fortune in gems. This fact is learned in town. Suppose a couple of law enforcement officers wanted to cut themselves in? So they pinch Drager, Heinrich's right-hand man, on a D.O. rap. They try to bribe him into revealing the jewel cache. He won't bribe. So they threaten him."

"So," I said, picking it up, "they lock him up and he escapes, warning Heinrich."

"Right. Heinrich is panicky. He's afraid to get in touch with any coppers because he figures they'd merely refer it back to the sheriff's office here and where will that get him? What he needs is a private operative who is trustworthy, talented, lion-hearted, understanding—"

"For God's sake," snapped Wooley, "cut out the advertising matter and get on with it."

"All right," said Sackler. "So he found me in the Red Book, or perhaps he'd heard of me. I do get my name in the columns, you know. So because he's dumb he can't phone and Drager doesn't speak English well enough to do it for him. He wires."

I blinked at that. "We got no wire from him."

"We certainly did not," said Sackler. "However, I'll come to that in a moment. As soon as our villains find out about that wire, they decide to waste no more time. They come out here, kill Heinrich, shoot Drager, believing they've killed him too. They search the place for the jewels and find most of them. Drager however is not dead. Concentration camps had made him incredibly tough. He makes his way to my office—bring-ing along a handful of gems missed by the thieves—and dies there. Because of a telegram which I'll explain later, the sheriff figures that Drager has come to me, so he follows him there, hoping he can arrive in time to keep Drager's mouth shut."

There was a long silence. Sackler coughed loudly and took a piece of paper from his pocket. "This," he said, "is a note I found in Heinrich's house the other day. A letterhead of a law firm. I assumed that they were Heinrich's lawyers. I phoned them. They were."

"So?" said Wooley.

"I assumed further that they might have a will executed by Heinrich."

"So?" said Wooley again.

"So," said Sackler, "they did. A will in which Heinrich left all he owned to his friend and protege, Drager."

Nelson shook his head, puzzled. "What's this got to do with the rest of it?"

"A great deal," said Sackler. "If Heinrich left all he owned to Drager and if he died before Drager, as we know he did, then logically those gems Drager gave to me are mine legally. You understand, inspector?"

Nelson's face grew red. "By God," he said, "*I* see it all right. You've invented an ingenious theory to enable you to keep that jewelry. You'd sell your soul for a dollar and a half. Everyone knows that."

Wooley gazed at Sackler with an unfriendly look in his eye. "Well?" he said challengingly.

Sackler donned his expression of outraged innocence, the misunderstood civic fighter.

"Gentlemen," he said, "gentlemen. Ah, well, the righteous must suffer on this earth. What I have told you is true."

"It might be provable," said Nelson, "if you'd ever received a telegram from Heinrich."

"And the money order which accompanied it," said Sackler, meeting his eyes squarely. "Now, I shall proceed to earn the second part of my fee. Attention, Joey—you are paying for my next words. You may as well hear them."

I listened without enthusiasm. Whatever he said was going to cost me money.

"The telegram theory," he began, "was something I'd pretty well figured before I ever came out here. I am no believer in coincidence. I hardly believed that two thugs who just wanted a car, any car, would happen to pick out Joey's. I thought there was some reason for it. Then when I found my driver's license was missing, I had the answer."

"Look," said Wooley, "if it kills you, will you make a straightforward statement."

"Sure," said Sackler amiably. "This is a small town. After Drager sends his wire, the sheriff hears of it. Fearing my interference, he realizes the wire must be intercepted. It is early evening. The chances are I'm not in my office. If not, the wire will be delivered early in the morning. The sheriff springs to the telephone."

I WRINKLED MY brow. "Is that why you asked if it was a dial phone?"

"Precisely, Joey. If it wasn't a dial the call could be traced, which it was. The sheriff calls a couple of thugs in town. He gives them instructions. Whereupon they hijack Joey. They choloroform him and one of them holds him in Central Park while the other takes his keys and car and drives to my office. The car was incidental; the keys were important."

"And signs for the telegram," I said.

"Signs for the telegram, Joey. But it is a money order. Heinrich, hearing of my fondness for—ah—businesslike procedure, enclosed a retainer. Our thug needed some identification to cash the order at Western Union. He looked around, found my driving license in my coat and swiped it."

I saw a little light. "And while in my car he had that accident and scrammed, replaced my keys and left me parked before my own house."

"Exactly, Joey. A piece of information which will cost you

twenty-five hundred dollars. A bargain, I may add."

I shuddered. I felt as if I had just gulped a Mickey Finn. "You can prove this?" said Wooley quietly.

"Of course. I told you I had the call traced. The thugs are at this moment in the gentle hands of Captain Guelph of your own department. With the aid of a rubber hose and the fact that there's a murder involved, I'm certain they'll break down. Moreover, there's the check, endorsed with my forged signature in Western Union's files. These facts, I believe, clear Joey here and clean up everything else."

Wooley threw his cigar away, put another between his teeth and began chewing viciously. Constable Nelson came suddenly to life.

"You're accusing the sheriff of all these things?" he asked.

"Partly," said Sackler. "The sheriff and his accomplice."

"Accomplice? Who was his accomplice?"

"You," said Sackler.

Nelson drew a deep breath. He remained silent for a long moment, then he said explosively: "You may have a case against the sheriff, purely circumstantial, of course. Your case against me is even flimsier. It's all circumstantial. It's your word against mine. Juries usually believe law officers. You'll never pin Heinrich's death on me."

Sackler shrugged. "It doesn't matter to me why you burn," he said. "Beat the Heinrich case and you fry for killing the sheriff."

"What does that mean?" snapped Wooley.

"Nelson and the sheriff quarreled about the division of the loot. In the summerhouse a little while ago. Nelson snatched the gun from the sheriff's holster and killed him, planted the gun in his hand and came here later howling suicide. You'll recall, Nelson said something about the sheriff being short in his accounts. Well, as soon as he left here you can bet Nelson was going to the office they share jointly and fix things so that the sheriff *was* short."

"This time," said Wooley, "can you prove it?"

"Sure," said Sackler, "I got here early. I saw it happen. I heard them quarrel and saw the sheriff murdered by Nelson."

Nelson licked dry lips with a nervous tongue. He stared at Sackler and his blue eyes glittered hotly.

"*You* saw me?" he said. "That's fine. Suppose I swore I saw you kill the sheriff. It's still your word against mine before any jury."

Sackler didn't bother answering that. He was looking at me and there was a dreamy expression in his eyes. He was thinking, I knew, of all the money he would save on my salary for the next few years.

"Sure," shouted Nelson. "It's your word against mine. You had a motive. There are witnesses who heard you threaten to kill the sheriff because he told Maxwell not to pay you that fifty-three bucks. Everyone knows you'd murder your own mother for dough. Suppose I swear I saw you kill the sheriff?"

For an instant Sackler looked startled. Wooley eyed him speculatively, dreaming a happy dream of seeing Sackler arraigned for murder. Even if he beat the case, the embarrassing fact of his coming to trial would be an occasion for celebration among his enemies whose name was John Q. Legion.

I could tell by watching his usually impassive face that these thoughts flickered through his brain. Then he smiled and recovered. "That's a very pretty thought," he said easily. "But it so happens that there were two eyewitnesses to your dispatch of the sheriff. Joey saw it, too. He was with me."

I thought I saw a shadow of disappointment come into Wooley's eyes. Nelson still stared at Sackler, wondering if he were bluffing, or if I had actually been along. I turned my head around, opened my mouth to corroborate Sackler's statement, when the idea hit me with the force of a baseball bat.

"Well," said Nelson hopefully, "if he was with you, if he was a witness, too, why doesn't he say so?"

"Yes," said Wooley, interested, "were you there, Joey?"

I INCLINED MY head slightly and gazed vacantly out over the lawn. I uttered a minor key groan and clapped my hand to my temple. Out of the corner of my eye, watching me, I observed Sackler, suspicion welling up in him like erupting lava.

"Joey!" he said sharply.

I did not move.

"Joey!" he said again. "Damn it, don't you know your own name?"

I shook my head slowly. "No."

They all stared at me. Wooley and Nelson registered surprise. Sackler was very close to panic.

"Don't be an idiot," he snarled. "What do you mean you don't know your own name?"

"That fall I had a little while ago," I explained. "When I smacked my skull against that stone in the garden. It's done something to me. I can't remember anything. Amnesia, I guess they call it. The pain is frightful. I remember nothing up to the time I fell. It's terrible," I said, playing it to the hilt, "not knowing who you are!"

"Joey!" shrieked Sackler, beside himself. "Stop this clowning!

It's untimely and unfunny. Tell this man you saw him shoot the sheriff. Tell him, Joey."

I dropped my head into my hands.

Nelson stared at me, his mouth twisting in triumph. "See," he said, "it'll be my word against yours, Sackler. I'll swear I saw you shoot him because of that fifty-three bucks. If you have me pinched, Inspector, you'll have to take him along, too."

Wooley looked very pleased indeed.

"Well, Rex," he said, grinning, "if Nelson insists he saw you kill the sheriff, I'll have to hand you over to the proper authorities. Both of you can go to the can together."

Sackler glared at me.

"Joey," he roared, "tell the inspector what you saw at the summerhouse. And stop this nonsense."

I lifted my head, looked around the room, wild-eyed and uttered a shriek.

"Amnesia," I howled. "I'd always laughed at it. Never quite believed such a thing could happen. Now it comes to me. Alas! Oh, God, oh—"

"Oh, hell!" yelled Sackler. He took a deep breath and showered me with muddy words. "Amnesia," he said, "you filthy, money-grubbing fake. You can't remember, eh? Well, there's one thing you'll remember well enough. That piece of paper I have in my pocket authorizing me to deduct twenty-five hundred dollars from your salary, provided, I proved your car was stolen when it was involved in those accidents. You remember that, don't you?"

I merely moaned again. Wooley's grin grew more expansive. "You'll probably beat it, Rex," he said with phoney assurance, "at the trial you'll probably be acquitted, you know."

Sackler gritted his teeth. "All right," he said, defeated. "All right, Joey. Suppose I get amnesia, too. Suppose *I* tear up this little document I have in my pocket. Suppose I forget it was ever executed. *Then* could you recall having seen Nelson kill the sheriff in the summerhouse?"

I took my hand away from my head and blinked. "A glimmer comes to me now," I said. "My name, I think, my first name is—Joey. Isn't it? I'm beginning to remember faintly."

Sackler took his wallet from his pocket and withdrew a piece of paper from it. He waved it before my eyes. Then he folded it into four pieces and tore it into fragments.

"Well?" he said bitterly.

"Ah," I said briskly, "it all comes back to me now. I'm Joey Graham. You're Rex Sackler. That's Constable Nelson, the man I saw shoot Sheriff Donald in the summerhouse. And that man, of course, is our old pal, Inspector Wooley. It's all clear now. My memory is fresh, bright and green."

"Your soul," said Sackler, "is black, moldy and mud-caked."

Wooley threw away his cigar. "You'll swear to that, Joey?"

"Sure," I said, "it's true. Thank God, I recovered my memory in time to see justice done."

I DROVE THE coupé back to town, Sackler sitting beside me slumped in his seat, staring with dark brooding eyes, through the windshield.

As we approached the Queensborough Bridge he lifted his fist and hammered it against his chest.

"I beat my breast," he explained dolorously. "I have done a thing I have never done before in all my life."

"Which is?"

"I have solved a case for nothing. Free, gratis, without cost."

"I don't see it," I told him. "When Heinrich's will is probated you'll get those jewels. They're worth plenty."

"Fool," he said, "That is my fee for solving Heinrich's murder. I get nothing at all for finding out who stole your car. Joey, how could you do this thing to me?"

He turned his head and looked at me reproachfully. I will swear a teardrop glistened in his eye.

Murder By the Ears

The World's Champion Nickel-nurser is back to defend his title against all-comers—including the greedy refugee who smuggled a pair of diamond earrings into the country which gave him sanctuary, and the blackmailer whose itching palm reached out once too often.

1

The Sackler Luck

REX SACKLER SNATCHED up the pencil, seized the gin rummy score pad and laid down his cards with the air of a man slapping a cashier's check in front of a paying teller.

"With a hundred point bonus for game, Joey, that makes two hundred and eighty points net. At two cents per, it'll be five sixty. And I can change any bill up to a hundred."

Disconsolately, I pushed my chair away from the table. After playing cards with Sackler I felt like a horse who was always running against Sea Biscuit. I reached for my wallet with no enthusiasm whatever and extracted a ten dollar bill. I handed it to him sourly.

He took it with a grin as broad as a chorus girl's mind. He withdrew his own wallet which looked as if he had ringed it at the St. Louis World's Fair in 1900 and plucked out four bills which were a thin decimal point away from complete disintegration.

He laid these on the desk and groped in his coat pocket for a leather change purse. He unclipped this and fingered out forty cents in change. He pushed the whole amount across the desk to me and said with dripping con-man affability: "Well, that's the way it is, Joey. I win today. You win tomorrow."

I stuffed the change bitterly in my pocket. "You mean you win today, *you* win tomorrow," I said, crossed the room and stared morosely out the window to the Madison Avenue traffic below.

The body had been dragged across the study floor.

There was a three minute silence behind me. Then Sackler said: "Joey, I've been doing a little figuring."

I knew I was supposed to ask what he had been figuring. But I didn't. Whatever it was it would only result in my being taken for even more of my salary. Thus far, this week, Sackler had won back about thirty per cent of what he had paid me last Wednesday.

"Yes, sir," said Sackler. "On my figures, Joey, I make it that during the last two weeks seventeen men have come into this office and only two women."

I turned around and looked at him. "Startling intelligence, indeed," I said. "So what?"

"So," said Sackler, "working out the odds on past performances there are two chances in nineteen that our next visitor will be a woman. In other words it is seventeen to two against. Phrased differently, it is eight and a half to one that the next person to enter this office will be male."

I STARED AT him coldly. "My wallet," I said, "is locked. My money is buried in my pocket deeper than the bullion at Fort Knox. I decline to bet you that night will fall. I have ceased to be a gambler."

Sackler sighed. He ran thin, sensitive fingers through hair as black as the raven's wing. He stared at me with dark and avaricious eyes. His nostrils quivered as they invariably did when the scent of money was in the air.

"Joey," he said, "if you don't speculate you can't accumulate. However since you're a little behind I'll give you a break."

"A Greek," I murmured, "with a gift."

He ignored that. "I'll offer you a price," he said. "I'll be a golden-hearted fool and give you a price even you can't afford to refuse. I have already stated that the odds are eight and a half to one that our next visitor will be a man. Joey, I throw money at you. I toss it in your lap. Instead of eight and a half, give me six and a half and I'll bet you the next person to cross this threshold is of the feminine gender."

I considered this. I checked back in my mind to make sure his figures were correct. As far as I could remember the deal seemed all right. Certainly less than 15 per cent of our visitors were women. Certainly the odds were, for once, in my favor. Certainly, I was due to win a bet from Sackler.

"I am weak," I said. "I should be confined. I take you. I'll give you thirteen dollars to two."

I crossed the room and opened the door which led to the outer office. Then I returned to my desk. From where we sat we could see the frosted glass panel of the outside door which opened into the office. Now we sat in tense silence watching it for a silhouette which would decide whether I collected two dollars or paid out thirteen.

Unfortunately, experience was a teacher to whom I rarely listened. By now I should have known better than to bet Rex Sackler on anything at all. Each Wednesday he paid me a totally inadequate salary and devoted the remainder of the week to winning it back again. He was usually successful.

Sackler loved money as Abe Lincoln loved the common people. He fought for a dollar as a bull buffalo fights for its mate. The clink of silver in his ears was finer music than Beethoven's Fifth and the rustle of folding money was to him a gentle, perfume-laden spring zephyr.

And once a buck finally reached Sackler's grasping fist it could safely figure it was home. He spent with all the whole-hearted enthusiasm of an Italian soldier laying down his life for Mussolini. He had a fortune stashed away in War Bonds and I fear his motive was security and the interest rather than undiluted patriotism.

His room rent ran about four dollars a week and his meals were bought on a meal ticket plan which gave five fifty in calories for five dollars. The cash he spent for clothes would hardly have decently garbed a Hottentot. And as far as I had observed his sole expense for amusement was whatever he won gambling with me.

I stared at the frosted panel of the door and my lips moved in silent prayer. Sackler leaned back in his chair and his gaze, directed at the same point as mine was the gaze of a man watching a horse race in which he had several potatoes invested.

My watch ticked off four tense minutes. A shadow loomed up on the other side of the door. It was quite obviously the figure of a man in shirt-sleeves and my heart picked up a beat. I glanced over at Sackler. His brow was corrugated in a black frown and he ran his hand furiously through his hair.

The knob turned and the door opened. Across the threshold stood a man with a bucket in one hand and an assortment of cleaning apparatus in the other. He peered at us inquiringly. He said: "Want your windows cleaned?"

One certain fact came to both Sackler and myself simultaneously. If our answer was affirmative he would enter the office and I would win the bet. If negative, he would go away and Sackler would get a second chance.

At exactly the same moment, I said "Yes," and Sackler said "No."

THE WINDOW CLEANER stared at us uncertainly but did not move. "Come on in," I said hastily. "I'll pay you out of my own pocket."

"Stay out of here!" roared Sackler. "This is my office and I'm partial to dirty windows."

"Damn you," I yelled, "you're cheating! He'd come in if you'd let him and I'd win."

"He shouldn't count anyway," shouted Sackler. "He's neither a client nor a bill collector. Window cleaners shouldn't count."

The window cleaner still stared at us, blank wonderment in his eyes. An idea came to me and I stood up. So did Sackler. He seized my arm.

"Oh, no, Joey," he said. "I know what you're up to. You're going to pull him over the threshold."

We stood there struggling angrily, while the window cleaner goggled at us as if we were insane. Then Fate and Miss Madeline Draper tossed my thirteen dollars into Sackler's bursting coffers.

She strode past the dazed window cleaner who still held the door ajar. She was tall, long-legged and brunette. Her face reminded me of one of the better jobs of Perc Westmore and her figure convinced me that perhaps that stuff in Esquire wasn't so exaggerated as I had thought.

Sackler said "Scram" to the window cleaner, "That's thirteen dollars, Joey," to me, and "Sit down, Madam," to the girl.

He sank into his swivel chair, relaxed, with a benign grin on his face. He had won thirteen bucks from me; he had saved the window cleaning fee, and it was quite in the cards that he had a client. The girl came to the point like a setter.

"I'm Madeline Draper," she announced. "My brother was killed yesterday."

Sackler breathed deeply and his eyes lit up with that odd glitter which invariably came to them when he smelled money. He looked Madeline Draper over like a guy casing the First National Bank of Peoria, which, in a manner of speaking, he was.

He noted her expensive suit with satisfaction. He remarked

mentally the gleaming wrist watch on her arm. He observed the brilliant ring upon her finger and he actually drew his breath in sharply when his eyes fell upon her earrings.

Their perimeter was diamonds set in platinum around a dark green emerald. That center stone was so big I failed to understand why her lobes didn't droop. I essayed a fast calculation as to their cost, then gave it up. Anything over two hundred bucks was calculus to me.

I knew from the ecstatic glow on Sackler's face that he, too, had appraised those earrings nicely. I knew, further, that he was engaged at the moment in figuring precisely how much the traffic would bear. Even before he knew what a client wanted he almost always knew the amount of his fee.

He bowed his head with disgusting servility and said in the accents of a society doctor at the bedside of a decaying plutocrat: "Miss Draper, you have my sympathy in this hour of sorrow. I read about your brother's death in the papers. My heart goes out to you. If there is anything I can do, command me."

He did not add that her command was going to cost her a pretty penny. The girl took a handkerchief from her bag and dabbed it at her huge black eyes.

"I want you to find out who killed him," she said. "If you succeed money is no object."

I winced perceptibly. Sackler grinned like a dragon.

"But," he said, "I understand from the papers that the police have—"

Madeline Draper forgot her sorrow for an instant while she achieved a magnificent sneer. "The police!" she said.

Sackler nodded again. "My sentiments exactly," he said.

They certainly were getting along beautifully together. I watched them morosely. I was thinking of two very depressing items. First, I had lost my bet; second, it looked as if Sackler was once again going to collect a juicy fee from a client. I relished these things as Tokyo relishes a bomb.

"Anyway," said Sackler, "according to the report I read, the police believe that a burglar entered your brother's study, shot him, broke open a safe, took several thousand dollars in cash and some jewelry. Is that right?"

"It's right that the police believe that," said the girl brittlely. "It isn't right that it's true."

Sackler's eyebrows lifted. "You have evidence contrary to the official theory?"

"Some evidence and a great deal of suspicion."

"Of whom?"

MADELINE DRAPER LOOKED at him steadily for a long moment. "It's hardly my place to tell you," she said. "There are reasons why I shouldn't, reasons why I won't. Now let us understand each other. First, I want my visit here, our relationship as client and investigator, kept absolutely secret."

"With us," cooed Sackler slimily, "discretion is only surpassed by efficiency, eh, Joey?"

"You've left out fee collecting," I told him. "We're not so bad at that."

He glared at me. But the girl smiled.

"I'm glad you mentioned that," she said. "Mr. Sackler, I've followed your career in the newspapers for a long time. I admire you. You like money; so do I. You work for money; so do I. I want a man who wants a fee and will work for it. Frankly, I'm suspicious of those who prate of justice and nobility. If you're working for profit we know just where we stand."

Well, that was laying it on the line. Sackler blinked at her thoughtfully and did not answer.

"I think my brother was killed by someone other than ordinary robbers," she went on. "I do not think the motive was burglary. I shall write you a check for five hundred dollars as a retainer. If you can prove that the police theory is wrong you shall have forty-five hundred more. If not, nothing. Will you take it?"

Would he take it? Will the Air Corps fly over Japan? Will a duck enter a natatorium? I lit a cigarette and sighed unhappily. Sackler held out a fountain pen while the girl groped in a capacious bag for a checkbook.

She said, as she wrote: "I like your methods, Mr. Sackler. I've been a vocal and loud partisan of yours for years. I think we'll get along very well together."

And why not? For five hundred dollars Sackler would get along very well with the man who murdered his mother for the rubber in her girdle.

He folded the check with the tender care of a mother folding the diaper of her first-born and stowed it away in the depths of his wallet.

He said: "If you'll leave the details, addresses, et cetera, with my assistant there, I'll get to work on the case within the hour."

I scribbled down what data she gave me while Sackler, quite pleased with himself, leaned back in his chair and rolled himself a cigarette.

I finished jotting down the details. Madeline Draper smiled a farewell at Sackler, tossed her head entrancingly and walked toward the door. Sackler stared after her, his eyes focused on those fabulous earrings.

As the door slammed behind her he turned his head and stared at me. I returned his gaze blandly, pretending I didn't have the slightest idea of what was on his mind. He scratched his palm with the subtlety of a bass drum solo and said primly: "It is a virtue to pay one's debts promptly."

"Really?" I said. "The landlord would be delighted to hear that sentiment."

But now he was too financially elated to be downcast at the mention of the overdue rent. He held his hand out and his fingers twitched.

"Thirteen dollars, Joey. Won fairly and squarely. Pay me."

I took out my wallet and paid him. I said: "You are in league with Satan. You always win. You take thirteen bucks from me and five hundred from that girl. Is there no end to your cursed golden luck?"

As if in answer to my question the outer door opened. An elderly man thrust his head through the doorway and said in guttural accents: "Mr. Sackler, could you take another client?"

I clapped my hand to my head. The joint was raining clients. Sackler stood up, beamed and bowed.

"By all means. Come in, come in."

"And bring your checkbook with you," I added bitterly.

2

One Case—Two Fees

OUR VISITOR WAS gray-haired, of medium height and clad in an oddly cut suit. He wore glasses and a professorial air. He seated himself on the far side of Sackler's desk and sighed heavily.

"Mr. Sackler," he said, "I am an Austrian. I do not know much about your American private detectives. However I am here to put myself in your hands."

Through a cloud of disgust, I watched Sackler grin. While I starved slowly to death on the meager salary he paid me, it seemed as if absolute strangers came up to him and handed over their watches and pocketbooks.

"My name," went on the elderly man, "is Fritz Kruger. I have heard of you often through a friend of mine who thinks you are the greatest detective in the world. So I have come here. I am prepared to pay you any reasonable fee if you can do what I ask."

Sackler promised heartily to perform whatever task was desired.

"Of course," continued Kruger, "this task must be absolutely confidential. Moreover anything I tell you here today must be absolutely secret."

"Of course, of course," said Sackler impatiently. He disliked dialogue which held up the first installment of his stipend.

"I escaped from Europe," said Kruger, "with great difficulty.

I was forced to leave all my cash and nearly all my property behind. I did, however, salvage my wife's jewels. They are worth a great deal of money."

"Yes, yes," said Sackler. "Go on."

"I got those gems into this country." Here Kruger hesitated, glanced with some embarrassment over toward me.

"Continue," said Sackler. "That is Mr. Graham, my trusted assistant."

"Well," said Kruger, "I'm afraid I brought those gems into this country without the formality of paying duty on them."

With an effort Sackler forced away the expression of serene joy which lighted his face and substituted in its place sanctimonious horror.

"Mr. Kruger!" he exclaimed in shocked accents. "That is a serious offense. How could you commit a crime against the country which offers you shelter and sanctuary?"

I glared at him, annoyed. Despite the noble sentiments that fell from his hypocritical lips, I knew damned well that mentally he had jacked up the fee. He could add a little subtle blackmail to the amount he would ask now that Kruger had confessed he had broken the law.

Kruger averted his gaze before Sackler's righteousness. "I shouldn't have done it," he said. "It was my wife's idea. I regret it now but I'm afraid to offer to pay. I've had enough of prison in Austria. But anyway I want you to help me, Mr. Sackler. I want to tell you what I want and discuss the matter of your compensation."

The last word struck a responsive chord in Sackler's mind. He groped in his pocket and produced his wallet. Already he had held Madeline Draper's check for the better part of an hour and that was strictly against all his principles.

The moment he obtained a check he converted it into cash. This time he had forgotten that procedure. But now he remembered.

"Joey," he said, "take this down to the Federated Bank. Get it cashed. Hurry."

I took the check from him, donned my hat and coat and left him to the solitary pleasure of extracting a fee from old man Kruger.

I returned with five crisp one hundred dollar bills in my pocket. They burned my fingers as I handed them over to Sackler. His grin split his face in two. His eyes were alight with a happy flame. He actually hazarded an awful off-key fragment of song as he stowed the cash away in his wallet.

"Well," I said sourly, looking around the room, "where is it? Don't tell me you have it in your pocket?"

"What's that, Joey?"

"Kruger's shirt. Don't tell me you didn't get it?"

He didn't get sore. "In a figurative manner of speaking, you might say I did, Joey. Don't take off your hat. We're going."

"Going where?"

"To the residence of Mrs. Draper, the widow of the man who was killed."

"Oh, we're doing the Draper case first, eh? I thought maybe Kruger was more important."

"We're doing them both together, Joey. As I figure it, it's practically the same case."

More than that he would not vouchsafe as we went downstairs, climbed into our ancient coupé and drove through traffic uptown.

IT WAS OBVIOUS as I looked at the Draper estate that Robert Draper, the murdered man, had money. About a hundred green well-tended acres surrounded a huge colonial house set in the center of a smooth lawn.

I parked the car and we disembarked. I rang the bell and adjusted my tie to look well before the scrutinizing eye of the butler whom I expected to open the door. A moment later I got the scrutinizing eye all right. But no butler. Inspector Wooley of police headquarters stared at us from the threshold.

There was little warmth in his gaze. His suspicion and dislike of Rex Sackler was equaled only by Sackler's suspicion and dislike of him.

"Well," he said, "and what do you two mugs want?"

Sackler came to the fore. "There has been murder done," he said dramatically. "Naturally in the interests of justice I am here to see that the culprit is apprehended."

"In the interest of what?" snapped Wooley. "How much dough are you making this time?"

"A pittance," said Sackler with the phoniest sigh I have ever heard. "Times are hard in my profession. It must be wonderful to have a regular job like you, Inspector. Paycheck laid on the line twice a month whether there's any crime or not."

A red flush crawled into Wooley's face. He knew damned well that Sackler made eight times as much money as he did. This was a fact which invariably nettled him.

He opened the door wider with marked reluctance and stood aside.

"Well," he said, "if the family's retained you I suppose you'll have to come in. But I tell you, Rex, this is no spot for a mastermind. The case is open and shut."

Sackler lifted his eyebrows.

"You mean you have the killer?"

The flush on Wooley's face became deeper. "No, not that. But it was simple robbery. Draper was at his safe when a thug came in the window. Draper dove at him and the thug shot. Then he rifled the safe and made away with the loot. We're picking up every known crook in the vicinity. We'll have him before forty-eight hours have passed."

A voice in the hallway behind Wooley said: "Come in, Mr. Sackler. I'm glad you wasted no time."

It was Madeline Draper. Wooley stood aside with ill grace and the girl escorted us down a long, magnificent hallway to a broad living-room. As we entered the first person I saw was Fritz Kruger.

I looked indignantly at Sackler who avoided my eye. Kruger's presence indicated that he, too, was paying Sackler to find out who had killed Robert Draper. In short, this time he was collecting two fees for the same work.

Kruger stood up. Seated near him was a small blond woman of about thirty. Her face was swollen and in her hand she held a handkerchief. It was apparent that she had been crying.

Madeline Draper introduced the woman as Helga Draper, her brother's widow. Then she proceeded to introduce Kruger. Neither he nor Sackler gave any indication of having met before. Rather bewildered I picked up the cue and played it the same way.

"Now," said Sackler, "may I have what facts there are in this case?"

"The facts are simple," shouted Wooley. "And I already gave them to you. Robbery. Armed robbery. We'll have our hands on the killer within—"

"Forty-eight hours," said Sackler. "Sure, I know. Miss Draper, will you tell me what happened?"

She nodded her head and those damned earrings rattled like gold coins. I stared at them fascinated.

"Certainly," she said. "Come along to the study. I'll tell you what I can."

She led the way from the drawing-room with Sackler and myself following her. Wooley brought up the disgruntled rear.

THE STUDY WAS a room lined with bookshelves. A huge French window opened out on to the lawn and against the far wall was a square steel safe.

"Helga discovered the body," said Madeline Draper. "She didn't hear the shot as she was in her room in a distant part of the house. Looking for Robert later, she came here and found him with a bullet in his head. The safe door was open and it had been rifled."

Sackler grunted. "What was missing?"

"A little over eight thousand dollars in cash. Some jewelry and several bonds. To the value of about twenty-five thousand dollars."

"What about the window? Was it open?"

Madeline Draper nodded. "Helga says it was. But she closed it while waiting for the police to arrive."

Sackler scratched his head. Tremendous fee or no tremendous fee there was very little to go on here. True, Inspector Wooley was marvelously consistent at being wrong but I found myself hoping to heaven that this time he was right.

"Anything else?" asked Sackler hopefully.

Madeline Draper shook her head and smiled intimately at

him. "Nothing I can tell you," she said. "But doubtless there's lots you can discover for yourself. Why don't you look around?"

This time Wooley grunted. "What can he find that we haven't found?" he demanded. "Although if you know this much, Rex, you may as well know about the body. Not that it means anything."

"The body?" said Sackler alertly. "What about it?"

"It was moved after the killing," said Wooley. "As we figured it from the bloodstains the shot must have been fired while Draper was directly in front of the safe. Then it was dragged away all across the room behind the table there. But we figure the murderer did that to make it easier to get to the safe. Draper's body was in the way where it fell."

Sackler's brow corrugated. "Interesting," he said. "At last we have something to work on."

Wooley and I regarded him with frank skepticism. We were both of the unspoken opinion that the last observation came under the general heading of impressing the client. For the life of me I couldn't see anything particularly illuminating in the fact that the body had been pulled out of the way of the safe door after the murder had been committed.

"All right," said Sackler, "if that's all you have we'll pick up from there. We'll need no more help. Joey and I will just wander around the house looking about. Come on, Joey."

He strode from the room with me at his heels and Wooley glaring after us.

An hour later it seemed to me that there were several hundred rooms in the mansion. Sackler and I went carefully through each one. Why, I didn't know. We looked in drawers, desks and closets. After twenty minutes of this, I said: "Don't you think I could look more thoroughly if I knew *what* we were looking for?"

"I don't know myself, Joey."

"Then why—"

"There's something about this case," said Sackler, "that gives off an odor of halibut. Something very odd. I don't know just what it is but I sense it. I'm looking for anything that may help me. But I don't know what specifically."

We continued our futile hunt for nothing and my temper mounted. Then at least three hours later, while we were in the rooms of Mrs. Draper, Sackler, who was in the bathroom, uttered a low piercing whistle.

Like an obedient hound I trotted into the lavatory and stood at his side. He was standing over the toilet. He had lifted the china lid off the water tank and was peering inside.

"Joey," he said, "roll up your sleeve."

"For what? I—"

"Joey, look!"

I peered over his shoulder into the tank. There, at the bottom beneath the water was a rectangular metal box.

"Get it, Joey," said Sackler.

I plunged my hand into the water and brought up the dripping box. I handed it to Sackler.

HE EXAMINED ITS exterior carefully. It was obviously watertight. Yet when he tried its lid it opened easily. It had not been locked.

"Odd," said Rex Sackler.

I stared at the currency in the box and the shining jewels, at the gilded bonds within and echoed, "Odd, indeed."

"I don't mean the loot," said Sackler testily. "I mean the fact of its being unlocked."

I shook my head. "You," I said bitterly, "are one lucky thus and thus."

He turned and looked at me in mild surprise. "Why, Joey?"

"First," I said, "you have been promised two fees for solving one case. Second you stumble on to this which breaks it for you as easily as breaking an egg."

"Really, Joey? And how do you figure that?"

"Obvious," I said. "Even to Wooley. His wife knocks him off. Rifles the safe and stashes the stuff here. Then gives out a tale about robbers. God, you're lucky."

Sackler shook his head. "Joey," he said, "you have a very simple soul. You are several miles away from the truth. It isn't quite as easy as you think. Even your theory about the two fees isn't quite accurate. However, come along and let us interview Mrs. Draper."

Downstairs in the hall, Sackler put the metal box in the pocket of his overcoat which hung in the closet. Then he went back to the drawing-room. Mrs. Draper was there alone. She was staring into the glowing embers on the open fireplace. There was morbid melancholy in her eyes.

Sackler cleared his throat and she looked up at him.

"Mrs. Draper," he said, "if I may I'd like to ask you a few questions."

She bowed her head in assent.

"First," said Sackler, "do you know accurately exactly how much money your husband had in his safe?"

She shook her head. "I'm afraid only my husband knew that. He was accustomed to keeping large sums of money and other property in the house."

"But you don't know exactly how much?" persisted Sackler.

Helga Draper shook her head. "Only his secretary would know that. You can find him at Mr. Draper's office."

Sackler thanked her and left the room. I trailed along behind him.

"What are you doing?" I asked. "The cat and the mouse? Or are you pretending to work for the fee to make the high price look more reasonable. It's obvious she killed him and hid that stuff to make it look like robbery."

He looked at me and clucked like an old hen. "Joey," he said, "you should've been a copper. You've one of those leap-at-conclusion minds which is convenient when you don't know what the hell is going on. Now, take a short walk for yourself. I wish to think."

With no reluctance I left him. I idled through the tremendous house and made my way to the enclosed sun porch on the east side of the house. While strolling down a vast corridor I saw Madeline Draper emerge from a side door and walk hastily along ahead of me.

She passed beneath two hanging portieres and over the clacking of her spike heels on polished wood I heard a tiny tinkling sound. As I reached the curtains I noticed something gleaming on the floor. I picked it up and gasped.

It was an earring. One of those two earrings which must have been worth a small fortune. I stood for a long time staring at it. Mentally I translated it into terms of cash. I had a glorious picture of myself telling Rex Sackler to go to some frugal hell, resigning and setting myself up in a neat bungalow on the Pacific Coast.

It was a pleasant dream but a short one and I am constrained to say that it was not honesty alone that made the decision to return it necessary. Of course the girl would miss it. There would be a search. The servants were quite probably trusted and since Sackler knew he didn't have it he would naturally believe that I had. Wooley would probably demand that we all be searched and I would get stuck.

I dropped the earring in my pocket and followed Madeline out into the grounds. When I caught up with her I would give it back. She seemed lavish enough with money where Sackler was concerned. At least I could expect a reward.

However as I wandered aimlessly about the estate I saw no sign of her. I was not particularly concerned. The grounds were large enough to account for that and doubtless I would meet her again at the house before Sackler decided he had acted impressively enough to break the case and collect his dough.

3

Murder Note

I MUST HAVE strolled about for the better part of an hour before returning. Then as I reached the house I heard a shrill and terrifying feminine scream from somewhere inside.

I galloped along the corridor in the direction of the yell and came, finally, to the butler's pantry. Helga Draper stood in the doorway looking very panicky indeed. Doubtless, it had been she who had uttered that awful shriek. At her side, holding her hand, was Fritz Kruger.

Sackler stood in the center of the room.

I pushed my way inside and came up at Sackler's side. I stared down at the floor. Lying there was Madeline Draper. There was an ugly hole in the side of her head and a thirty-eight clutched in her inert fingers.

Blood ran in a crazy rivulet along the slick linoleum of the floor. The girl's black eyes stared blankly at the ceiling and her left hand was twisted in an odd position behind her head. In the fingers of that hand was a slip of paper.

Footfalls, heavy and authoritative sounded behind me and Inspector Wooley, wearing his hat and coat, burst into the room.

"What's this?" he said. "I was just going home when one of the servants told me—"

He caught sight of the body and said: "Good God, what's this, Rex? What happened?"

Sackler turned to him. "This?" he said with soft irony. "It's easy, Inspector. A thug came in the window, killed Miss Draper and rifled the butler's pantry."

Wooley glared at him. "Damn you," he said. "Stop clowning."

He knelt down at the side of the corpse. From the doorway, I heard the gentle sobbing of Draper's wife. I heard the consoling voice of Kruger as he essayed to calm his sister.

"She's dead, all right," said Wooley. "A young, handsome girl like that. It's—"

He broke off as Sackler suddenly clapped his hand to his head. There was an expression of a lost soul upon his face. His eyes were wide with horror.

"What's wrong?" I asked. "Have you lost a nickel?"

"A nickel?" echoed Sackler and his voice was a quivering tragic vibration. "I've lost a client. My God, she'd only paid me a retainer. Who's going to pay the rest of my fee?"

Wooley stood up and looked at Sackler in horror. I grinned happily. Sackler's expression was agonized and it would not have surprised me in the least had he suddenly begun to beat his breast and wail like a banshee.

I walked around the body and bent over. As yet, it appeared neither Sackler nor Wooley had seen the paper in the dead girl's hand. I bent over to pick it up and as I did so my heart picked up a beat. The second earring was missing!

WITH AN EFFORT I retained my dead pan. There was an angle to be figured here but I had no time to figure it now. I took the paper from the cooling fingers of the girl. I held it out. I said: "Did you guys notice this?"

Wooley snatched it from my fingers as if it held the murderer's name. It appeared, as he read it aloud, that it did.

I killed my brother (it read) *for personal reasons. Then my conscience compelled me to kill myself.*

"The signature," said Wooley, "is Madeline Draper's." He breathed a sigh of relief. "Well, that explains that all right. For a moment I thought—"

Sackler who had been looking over his shoulder interrupted. "That note's typewritten, Wooley. It doesn't mean a thing."

"Why not?" snapped Wooley. "It's just as likely she'd type it as write it in longhand."

"Maybe," said Sackler. "But since her signature isn't written in her own hand it proves absolutely nothing."

They bickered back and forth. I didn't listen to them. I had a weighty problem on my mind. Where in hell had that other earring gone to? It seemed most unlikely that she dropped the second one accidentally as well as the first.

Had it been Sackler who had discovered the body I wouldn't have given the matter another thought. I would have known damned well that the valuable bauble was reposing in his wallet. Sackler would easily become a ghoul for the amount which that earring would bring.

The question was, then, where had it gone? Who had taken it? And what should I do with its mate which was at the moment burning a hole in my vest pocket?

I thought once again of what I could do with a neat little bundle of cash. Of course I would have to deal with a rat-faced little fence I knew in Harlem and he would, in the manner of his kind, chisel me out of a good fifty per cent. Nevertheless there should be enough left over to keep Joey Graham for some time in a manner to which he was completely unaccustomed.

Then, after the fashion of a congressman, who six months

ago claimed we couldn't be attacked, I proceeded to a beautiful blinding rationalization.

Suppose I turned the earring in? Who'd get it? From what I'd learned about the Draper family there weren't any relatives left save the widow. Helga would certainly be picking up enough from her husband's estate to keep her in luxury for the rest of her life. So I really wouldn't be taking anything from anyone who couldn't well afford it.

Three more minutes of this sort of thinking and I was thoroughly convinced that selling the earring and keeping the cash was not only honorable and right but the only possible course for a thinking civilized man.

I returned to reality as Wooley, hurling an epithet at Sackler, stalked angrily from the room to the telephone in the outer hall. Sackler sighed heavily and walked over to me.

"Come on, Joey," he said. "Let's go back to the office. There's nothing more to be done here."

As we got into our coats in the foyer Kruger came out of the drawing-room. He shook his head sadly.

"A bad two days for my sister," he said. "These killings have upset her terribly. But at least everything's explained now. Inspector Wooley tells me that he is sure Madeline killed her brother, then remorsefully killed herself. At least the mystery is cleared up."

Rather to my surprise Sackler didn't argue with him as he had with Wooley.

"Yes," he said, "it's a comfort to have the mystery solved anyway. Of course, that other deal of ours goes, doesn't it?" Kruger looked at him oddly, then nodded his head. "Yes," he said, "of course. If you care to deliver now, I'll settle." Sackler appeared nettled. "Not just yet," he said. "I'm not quite prepared to deliver."

Kruger seemed somewhat puzzled. "Oh, I thought you were. I believed you were ready now. However, I'll wait. You'll get in touch with me?"

"Sure," said Sackler, "probably tomorrow."

We left the house and clambered into the battered coupé. As I put it in first and pulled out of the driveway, I said: "What's this deal you have with Kruger? It looks funny to me."

Sackler was staring broodingly through the windshield. He said, "Does it, Joey?" and nothing more all the way into town.

WE SAT IN the office for two days while Sackler registered heavy and profound thought. I saw by the papers that Inspector Wooley, despite Sackler's protest, had accepted the obvious theory, which, incidentally, I was inclined to believe myself.

Sackler however was worried. I was certain now that Kruger had also promised to pay him for the solution of the murder. It wasn't like Sackler to concern himself with a case when the client who had retained him was dead, incapable of signing any more checks.

Then, too, I had a problem of my own. I still had the earring in my vest pocket. I had decided to wait a little while until the Draper killings had been forgotten before I tried to get rid of it. Besides, another point worried me. Who the devil had swiped my earring's mate?

Sackler still had the waterproof box he had taken from the toilet tank, in the bottom drawer of his desk. It puzzled me that he had not turned it over to the police. I did not believe he intended keeping it. It would be a little too raw.

At least no one knew that I had the earring. But I knew Sackler had that box and Mrs. Draper could probably make a damned shrewd guess that he had. So keeping it came under the general heading of professional suicide.

So exactly what went on in his head I didn't know. Withholding the evidence that he had was going to get Wooley very sore. So when he did expose it he'd better have a good story to go along with it.

Midday of the second day we had spent in silent brooding, Sackler got up, sighed and reached for his hat.

"Joey," he said, "I'm going over to Draper's office. There are a couple of questions I want to ask. Then I think I'll know all the answers."

I regarded him quizzically.

"Then you still don't accept the story Wooley has given out to the papers?"

"Why should I? There's no money in that theory."

The door slammed behind him and I was alone. I had been alone for the better part of an hour when a uniformed messenger entered, handed me a small package and a receipt and said: "Sign here. It's for Rex Sackler."

I signed and he left me alone again staring at the name on the little box in my hand. It was a familiar name and, under the circumstances, one that disturbed me a little—that of a well-known firm of jewelers.

I turned the package over in my hand dubiously. I calculated mentally the time it would take Sackler to reach Draper's office and return. I decided there was enough to enable me to open the box and tie it up again before he came back.

I picked at the string which fastened it. I carefully removed the paper. I lifted the lid of the blue plush box and stared with wide eyes at the missing earring.

I blinked at it for a long time. I figured all the angles. I glanced at my wrist watch again to see how much time I had left before Sackler returned, then I sprang to the classified directory and thumbed rapidly through the A's.

In less than three minutes I found what I was looking for. I snatched up the plush box and raced out to the elevator. Twenty minutes later I was back at my desk with the earring rewrapped neatly and placed on Sackler's desk.

I was reading the afternoon paper and looking as innocent as a choir boy when Sackler came in.

His eyes lit up as he saw the package. "Ah, Joey," he said, "and when did this arrive?"

"A little while ago," I said guilelessly. "What is it?"

Sackler waved the question aside airily. "Oh, nothing. Just an inconsequential gadget, Joey. Now get your hat on. We're going out to Draper's at once."

"Draper's? For what?"

"To earn an honest penny. And incidentally to tell that moron, Wooley, who killed Robert and Madeline Draper."

He opened the desk drawer and withdrew the box he had taken from Helga Draper's bathroom. He tucked it under his arm, dropped the package containing the earring in his pocket and said: "Are you ready, Joey?"

"For anything," I said and I meant it literally.

4

A Thousand Apiece

AS I DROVE the coupé out to the Draper house I was aware that Sackler was fumbling in his pocket. I heard the rustle of paper and realized that he was taking the earring from its package. I grinned happily to myself. I wasn't quite sure what turn events would take when we arrived but the way I saw it there should be an honest dollar in it for little Joey Graham.

Wooley, whom Sackler had phoned, was already at the house when we arrived. He stood in his favorite position, leaning against the mantel-piece in the drawing-room. Helga Draper, white-faced and nervous, sat in a rocking chair whose movement never ceased.

Kruger munched an unlit cigar. He looked oddly at Sackler as he shook his hand.

"I thought I'd hear from you before this on that other matter," he said.

"Relax," said Sackler, "I'm prepared to take that up now as well as a couple of minor matters. Murders, to be precise."

Wooley looked daggers at him. "Damn you," he said. "You're a money-grubbing louse. We have this case neatly wrapped up. Explained to everyone's satisfaction. Now, just for money you're going to wreck our theory."

Sackler spread his palms in a gesture which implied helplessness. "Justice," he said. "Justice makes her demands, Inspector, what else can I do?"

"Well, go ahead," said Wooley. "Go ahead and get it over."

Sackler helped himself to a free cigarette from a silver box on a taboret. He drew a deep breath and said: "First, I wish to consummate a private business deal with Mr. Kruger. For the return of certain property of yours, Mr. Kruger, you promised me a sum of money in cash. Is that right?"

Kruger nodded. Sackler plunged a hand into his coat pocket. He withdrew a pair of earrings. He held them out and they shimmered in his palm.

"Are these they, Mr. Kruger?"

Kruger nodded again. Wooley craned his neck forward. "Wait a minute," he said, "aren't those the gadgets I saw this Madeline Draper wearing the other day?"

"True," said Sackler, "but Mr. Kruger will have no difficulty in proving ownership, will you, Mr. Kruger?"

Kruger glared at him. "Well," said Sackler, "I'm waiting."

"For what?" said Wooley. "What's going on here anyway?"

I said nothing but I knew I was vastly more interested than the inspector.

"For my fee," said Sackler. "Here are the earrings, Kruger, as per contract. Pay up."

Kruger took the earrings. He sighed heavily and reached for his wallet. He counted out a number of bills and I counted silently with him. He handed two thousand dollars to Sackler and I hastily divided that sum by two and my grin was as wide as Sackler's when he took the money.

"One minute," I said, "do I understand that when Kruger came to the office that day he offered you a fee to produce those earrings for him?"

"Right," said Sackler. "And, as usual, I have come through.

The job is done, the fee collected. Everything is neatly consummated."

"Not quite," I said grimly. "There is something I would like to say. I—"

"My God," said Wooley, clapping a hand to his forehead, "I came here to listen to the solution of a murder case. I'm not interested in how much dough you guys collect. Get started talking, Rex."

"Wait," I said, "I—"

Sackler waved me to silence. "The inspector is right, Joey. Whatever you have to say will keep."

I shrugged. That last statement was true enough. The longer I waited the louder I could laugh.

"Now," said Sackler, "I state categorically that Robert Draper was killed by his sister Madeline."

Both Wooley and I blinked at him. "Now how do you figure that?" asked Wooley. "My burglary theory is sounder."

"Your burglary theory," said Sackler, "gives off a ghastly odor."

"Why?"

"Primarily because the body was moved, dragged halfway across the study floor and parked behind the table."

"What does that prove?"

"That the killer was an amateur with a weak stomach for corpses. A thug would have shot Draper, rifled the safe and that's all. If an amateur, particularly a relative who would object to having a pair of dead eyes staring at her while she robbed the safe, had done it she would move the corpse where she couldn't see it."

I THOUGHT THAT one over. It seemed logical. "You're

arguing, then," I said, "that Madeline shot her brother. She rifled the safe to make it look like a hold-up but couldn't stand the sight of the body while so engaged. Hence she dragged the corpse behind the table where she couldn't see it."

"Right," said Sackler.

Kruger nodded with what seemed to me, enthusiasm.

"That's reasonable," he said. "It makes that suicide note she left understandable."

Wooley scratched his head. "Maybe," he said slowly, giving up his thug theory with utmost reluctance. "Have you anything else?"

"Sure," said Sackler. "Both Mrs. Draper and Draper's secretary assure me that the exact amount of money and deeds kept in Draper's safe was known to no one but Draper. Yet Madeline mentioned numbers. She said eight thousand dollars in cash, which was correct and twenty-five thousand dollars in bonds which was also correct."

"How the devil do you know it was correct?"

Sackler pulled the tin box he had found in Mrs. Draper's bathroom from his pocket, laid it on the table and said, "Count it."

Wooley opened the box and stared at the contents. Kruger peered over his shoulder. I glanced across the room toward Mrs. Draper. She looked no more upset than before. She appeared neither surprised nor concerned at the appearance of the box.

"Where'd you get this?" snapped Wooley.

"All in good time," said Sackler. "The point is that Madeline Draper was something of a tramp. She had few scruples. She decided that if her brother was dead she would get the estate."

"How could she?" I asked. "Naturally, the dough would go to the widow."

"If she was here, it would," said Sackler.

Wooley took a cigar from his vest pocket, bit off the end and put it in his mouth. He chewed it savagely and glared at Sackler.

"What the devil are you talking about? Say it in simple English, will you?"

"If Mrs. Draper killed her husband, she couldn't get the estate, could she?" asked Sackler. "The law won't permit a killer to benefit by his crime. She would get neither the estate nor the insurance, if any."

I was beginning to get it now. "And then the dough would, of course, go to the next of kin which was Madeline."

"That's right, Joey."

"What's right?" howled Wooley. "What the devil are you talking about? First you say Madeline killed Draper, then you announce that if Mrs. Draper killed him she wouldn't inherit the estate. What is this? Choctaw?"

Sackler sighed the sigh he reserved to indicate that the stupidity of the police department was a heavy cross for him to bear.

He said: "You're not very bright, are you? The point I'm making is that Madeline killed her brother, then, after thinking things over planted the evidence on Mrs. Draper."

Kruger inhaled sharply. His sister sat on the edge of her chair and looked at Sackler with terror-filled eyes.

"You see," said Sackler, "Madeline, wanting dough, knocks her brother off. She makes it look like robbery. Then she plants the stolen stuff on Mrs. Draper. She expects the coppers to find it, to believe that Helga Draper pulled the phoney robbery and killed her husband. The coppers pinch Helga, send her away, maybe to the chair, and Madeline collects, get it?"

Wooley frowned and grappled with the theory. Sackler, enjoying himself, continued: "However, the cops were dumber than usual. They looked over the house casually never thinking to peep inside the toilet tank in Mrs. Draper's bathroom. Hence they never found the stuff that Madeline had planted."

"So," I put in, "since she couldn't very well find it herself she called us in."

"Me," said Sackler arrogantly, "not us."

I didn't retort. I would make him pay for that in a little while. I licked my lips in anticipation.

"All right," said Wooley, "so then she got the horrors about what she'd done and killed herself, is that it?"

Sackler took another free cigarette from the box. He said, "No."

"Well, damn it," snapped Wooley testily. "So what did happen?"

"Recall that note?" asked Sackler. "That typed suicide note? The last sentence in it read: 'My conscience *compelled* me to kill myself? Note that word compelled. It's the past tense. Would someone who is not yet dead, who intends killing himself write 'compelled'? No, she would have written 'compels.' On the other hand, someone faking it, someone already thinking of Madeline as dead *would* use the past tense."

"Who killed her then?" said Wooley.

Sackler glanced at Kruger. He pointed a finger at him and said, "He did."

THERE WAS A long silence. Helga Draper uttered a little gasp. Wooley stared at Kruger as did I. Kruger stood absolutely still, staring at the opposite wall. He did not speak.

"Get this," said Sackler. "Kruger is greatly attached to his sister. He disliked Madeline who, as I remarked, was something of a tramp. She mentioned my name several times in front of Kruger, because I am not entirely without fame and she thought I was good.

"She came to me, engaged me to look into this case—actually to find the evidence she'd planted and your coppers had overlooked. On the same day Kruger came to me. He wanted me to get back for him a pair of valuable earrings that Madeline had swiped from him."

"Why didn't he call the cops?" said Wooley. "Why did he have to pay you for a job like that?"

"Because," said Sackler, "he'd smuggled the earrings in from Europe. The cops would ask questions and he'd get pinched. He—"

Kruger uttered a cry. "This is unfair," he shouted. "This is unethical. What I told you was confidential. You promised that you wouldn't mention it. You—"

Sackler lifted a silencing hand. "It won't matter," he said. "It won't make any difference to you."

"The hell it won't," said Wooley. "If he's a smuggler, I'll turn him in. He'll serve time for this."

"He may even burn," said Sackler.

Kruger's face paled.

"Let me tell it in my own way," said Sackler. "As I told you, Madeline, knowing Kruger couldn't squawk because the stuff had no duty paid on it, calmly helped herself to those earrings. Kruger offered me two grand to get them back from her. I accepted the offer. But when I told him that Madeline had already engaged me on the murder case, Kruger looked quite worried."

"Why should that worry him?" demanded Wooley.

"He didn't trust Madeline and he loved his sister. He was afraid that Madeline had done exactly what she did do. He spoke to her about it. She laughed at him. She told him that it was possible his sister killed Draper, that if that could be proved she would inherit the estate. Then he realized that she had engaged me to try to pin the killing on Helga. Kruger, a neurotic sort of gent after his experiences in Europe, shot her, typed out that note and planted it in her hand. He figured that would clear up everything."

Kruger bit his lip. "All right," he said, "I was certain Madeline killed her brother. Your theory about that is correct. But you can't prove I killed her. You have nothing that would hold up in a court of law."

Wooley looked worried again. "No, Rex," he said. "You haven't."

"True," said Sackler, "that's why we need a confession."

Kruger laughed and there was a touch of hysteria in his tone. "Confession?" he said. "From me? I've stood the tortures of a concentration camp. Do you think your third degree methods will make me confess?"

"Yes," said Sackler. "Look here. If you don't admit the killing, I'll keep my mouth shut about Madeline killing her brother. We'll simply announce that we found this box and where we found it. You will go free, but your sister will be charged and doubtless convicted of murdering her husband."

Kruger was silent for a long time. Across the room I heard his sister sob quietly. Then Kruger nodded his head. "All right," he said. "I killed her. I hated her. Not only did she steal my wife's earrings but she blackmailed me, too. Threatened to tell the authorities about my smuggling. All right, Inspector, I'll go along with you."

I took a step forward. I said: "Wait a minute."

They all looked at me. "Those earrings," I said. "May I see them?"

KRUGER TOOK THEM from his pocket and handed them to me. I took a penknife from my pocket. I opened it and ran its blade over the face of the diamonds on one earring. It left no mark. I did it again on the second earring. It left a visible scratch.

"Look," I said. "One of these is phoney. You're entitled to your money back, Mr. Kruger."

For the first time in my life I saw Rex Sackler reduced to absolute speechlessness. Wooley said: "Are you trying to run a fast one, Rex?"

Then Kruger uttered the most awful words that Sackler had ever heard. He said: "I demand my money back."

Wooley grinned delightedly.

"You said something about justice a little while ago," he said. "Very well, I shall see it done now. Either return that dough or I'll take you in for swindling this man."

Sackler opened his eyes and glared at me. He put his hand in his pocket and withdrew his wallet. He said from the side of his mouth, "Judas!"

"One moment," I said. "Naturally, Mr. Kruger, you want to retrieve those earrings. Naturally if it took two of us to produce the pair of them you would pay the fee and split it between us. Right?"

Kruger nodded slowly. I whipped the second earring' from my vest pocket.

"This is genuine," I announced. "I will submit it to any test at all."

I scraped it with the knife, which left no mark. I handed it to Kruger. "Now," I said, "I believe I get one thousand dollars and Mr. Sackler the other."

WE SAT SILENTLY in the coupé as we drove out to the main highway. We had gone eight miles when Sackler spoke.

"You are a wicked, iniquitous louse, Joey," he said vehemently. "Where the devil did you get that earring?"

I told of Madeline Draper's dropping it, of my picking it up in the hall. He looked at me with accusing eyes.

"Why didn't you return it at once?" he said. "Don't answer me. I know. You were working on some scheme to keep it. To sell it and retain the tainted proceeds. Joey, you are a thief as well as a traitor."

"You," I said, "are a ghoul. You found Madeline's body. You took the remaining earring. Then you went away and kept your mouth shut waiting for someone else to find the corpse. You were afraid that someone might miss the earring and if it had been you who found the body they'd believe you took it."

"You are mad!" roared Sackler. "It was my job to recover the earring. What if I did take it from the corpse? You have stolen one thousand dollars from me as surely as if you had used a gun."

"Sure," I said. "I'm a wicked character. As I figure it you must have come along right after Kruger killed her. He left the earring figuring that if he took it you'd think he'd killed Madeline. He left it for you to pick up. Only finding one you searched for the second. When you couldn't find that you took the original to a jeweler and had a phoney made in order to collect the fee."

"How did you know it was phoney?"

"Because I had the real one. Besides I took it across the street to an appraiser while you were down at Draper's office."

He clapped his hand to his head again. He lifted his eyes to heaven. He cried in tortured accents: "What perfidy! I have nurtured a serpent in my bosom."

I didn't answer. I hummed happily as I drove along.

"It's the work of a maniac!" said Memberson, war-industry tycoon. "The killer is an escaped lunatic—my son!" So Sackler, the penny-pinching private op, sets to work at Memberson's country estate following the riddle-strewn trail of club-footprints and smoke-signals—and finally tapping out a message in Morse to a living corpse, imploring it to—

Come Out of the Grave

1

Murder Makes Money

THE INDUSTRIAL SECTION of Newark moved stolidly past the train window and disappeared silently into the morning mist. The day was unusually gray and for me, unusually early. Sackler's phone call had routed me from a warm bed at dawn's crack and now, at eight o'clock in the morning I found myself lolling in a private compartment of a crack train roaring down to Washington.

Rex Sackler sat uncomfortably on the edge of his seat as if he feared there would be an extra charge if he leaned back.

There was an expression of stern disapproval in his black eyes. I looked at him inquiringly. He had given me no details at all regarding this trip.

I said, with the air of a man who announces two and two are four: "Of course, you're not paying for this compartment out of your own pocket?"

"I am not," said Sackler as if he were denying a treason charge. "The expenses are being covered by Henry L. Memberson."

I made no effort to mask the envy I felt. Henry Memberson built bombers for the Army. He was industry's miracle man. His publicity was equaled only by his competence.

If he was Rex Sackler's current client I greatly feared that the Sackler bulging bank account was about to be considerably fattened.

I said unhappily: "What's it all about?"

*Behind the Negro came an apparition
with a smudged face and blazing eyes.*

"I have no details, Joey. Memberson called me long distance at four this morning. Told me to take this train to Washington, to grab whatever accommodation I could get. He's joining the train at Philly. We'll pick up the details then." He added thoughtfully: "We'll also pick up the train fare I've paid out."

"I have no doubt of that," I told him. "Does this expense account include breakfast? I'm hungry."

"Nothing was said about food. Memberson merely

announced that I would be compensated for the train fare."

I sighed. "Well, how about a trip to the diner at our own expense? I need some coffee."

Sackler ran his long thin fingers through hair black as a raven's wing.

"I'm not hungry, Joey. Couldn't eat a thing, really."

I looked at him appraisingly. Dining car coffee was fifteen cents a cup; toast ran at least a quarter. And Rex Sackler was not one to let go of a nickel without a struggle.

"Look," I said, "are you willing to run the risk of rickets? Are you willing to suffer the gnawing pangs of hunger at your stomach lining, rather than invest a buck for breakfast?"

Sackler looked at me reproachfully. He made a clucking sound like a commiserating old hen. There was a note of injury in his voice as he spoke. "Joey, your ideas of my penury are ridiculous. Would I ever consider a dollar where health and comfort are concerned? Would I ever consider saving a nickel if I were hungry?"

"Yes," I said flatly. "I guess that last speech indicates that I'll breakfast alone. You can stay here rubbing a five dollar bill against your stomach. Maybe that'll help."

I slammed the door of the compartment and made my way to the rear of the train and the diner. I supposed Sackler would find as much satisfaction contemplating the total amount of his War Bonds and savings accounts as I would in ham and eggs.

For the regard of Rex Sackler for a dollar bill was a beautiful and constant thing.

He spent his money as carefully as a man loading TNT; he saved it as assiduously as a squirrel piling up nuts against a tough winter.

The war had made most people forget that there had been a crash in 1929. But that was a memory to which Rex Sackler clung like a vindictive elephant. He entrusted no money to banks. His huge balance was socked away in several postal savings accounts and the rest of it was in War Bonds, relentlessly earning its three and one third percent per annum.

He dwelt in a tiny furnished room where comfort existed in inverse ratio to the rent. He owned two suits, one of which had been purchased shortly before Herbert Hoover assured us prosperity was hiding itself impishly around the corner, and the other one shortly afterwards.

His hat was a shapeless blob of felt at least three years older than your Aunt Hattie and his shoes had been resoled more often than a hot diamond.

Each week he paid me a totally inadequate salary to act as his strong arm and assistant, then promptly tried to win the money back from me at various gambling games of his own invention. He was, I shudder to say, quite successful at it, too.

I GLANCED OVER the menu the dining-car steward placed before me, studied the prices and ordered a meal the cost of which would have caused Sackler to wince. I ate it happily. In a few moments, replete with food, I would return to the compartment and gloat.

Sackler would still be hungry. I would be full. Those were two circumstances which I would not fail to call to his attention. It wasn't often I found myself in a position to needle him.

We were passing through New Brunswick as I made my way back through the swaying cars. Just as I reached the door of our compartment the Pullman porter passed me.

"I hope the gentleman with you is better, sir," he said solicitously.

"Better? What's the matter with him?"

"I guess it's indigestion. I've taken him in three cups of hot water in the past half hour."

I grunted and suspicion rose up within me like a geyser.

I entered the room and the odor of coffee rose to my nostrils. Sackler's hand closed over a small tin can on the seat at his side and he transferred it to his pocket. But not before I had read the label.

He sipped coffee from the cup in his fingers and I noted that there were some crumbs in his lap. I fixed him with an accusing eye.

"So," I said, "you weren't hungry. You couldn't eat a thing, eh? Where did you get that coffee?"

"Oh, this?" he said with choir-boy innocence, lifting the cup.

"Oh, I ordered it from the diner, Joey. Of course, it meant a tip in addition to the cost. But I prefer to breakfast in privacy."

"You are an iniquitous liar," I said bitterly. "Beside you the Scotch are a prodigal and open-handed race. I know what you did. You ordered three cups of hot water from the porter. You have in your pocket a can of instantaneous coffee. Moreover, judging from the crumbs on the worn fabric of your suit you also brought a sandwich along."

He buried his face in the coffee cup and ignored me.

"Furthermore," I told him, "you are a selfish so-and-so. You could have offered to share your lunch with me. But no. Underpaid as I am I shell out a buck in the diner, while you, wallowing in riches, eat in here like a poverty-stricken day-laborer."

He regarded me blandly, untouched by my diatribe. "Foresight, Joey," he said. "You have none. I have. Why should I share with you? Even though routed from my bed in a dazed condition at 4 A.M., I recalled that the Pullman people charge outrageous prices. Even then I had foresight enough to provide myself with a sandwich and a can of instantaneous coffee. You, improvident Joey, spend a dollar in the diner."

He sighed a slimy, unctuous sigh. "I fear you will finish in the gutter, Joey."

He turned his head and stared, engrossed, out the window at the New Jersey scenery. I was still telling his stony profile what I thought of him when we pulled into North Philadelphia.

Sackler adjusted his tie and his eyes took on the gleam which they invariably wore when he was on the verge of adding another dollar to his bank account. A moment later there was a sharp knock at our door and in response to Sackler's invitation two men entered.

Memberson I recognized from the several million photographs which had been published in the newspapers. He was a short, squat man, gray and wrinkled. His eyes were pale blue behind his spectacles. He was almost bald. He hardly looked like the industrial hope of America to lick the Axis but I knew very well that if anything happened to him the Berlin radio would gloat happily and the stock in a score of enterprises of which he was a director would fall drastically.

The second man was tall, and, it developed, Memberson's lawyer. His name was Heatherington. He carried a briefcase—the lawyer's badge of office, and a pair of shrewd brown eyes twinkled behind a pair of thick tortoiseshell-rimmed lenses.

After introductions had been made all around our two visitors sat down. Memberson removed his glasses and mopped his brow with a silk handkerchief. I noted that his hand was trembling.

"Heatherington," he said, "you're sure they can't do anything to him? You're positive?"

"We've been all over this," said the lawyer patiently. "Legally they can do nothing. He's been insane for years. We'll have no difficulty in proving he's insane now."

"But the police? You know how he is when violent. He may resist them. They'll shoot, of course, and—"

His voice broke and he lapsed to a miserable silence. I watched him with interest. Sackler frowned thoughtfully, engaged, doubtless, in estimating precisely how much fee he would ask.

"Yes," said Heatherington slowly, "there is that risk. But that's why you've called in Mr. Sackler."

"Of course," put in Sackler oleaginously. "Anything at all,

Mr. Memberson. I shall consider it a patriotic duty to aid. If my small help can free you to carry on with greater success in the factory I shall deem it an honor."

"Always provided," I said, "that the price is right."

The three of them ignored me. Heatherington leaned forward in his seat.

"It is a matter of murder, Mr. Sackler."

Sackler received this intelligence as if he were the State executioner who collects a hundred and fifty bucks every time he pulls the switch. His black eyes lit up and he licked his lips. I read his mind like a crystal ball.

Memberson, of course had money. The more important the case, the greater the fee. That was axiomatic. Sackler, too, leaned forward.

"Murder," he said with vast satisfaction. "Well, well, what are the details?"

"My sister," said Memberson hoarsely. "She was killed last night. Shot."

Sackler nodded happily. "And you want me to find out who did it? I think I may say in all modesty that I have been singularly successful in such matters. Naturally, there are certain expenses. However, I am certain that we can come to an agreement. I am equally certain that I shall produce the murderer."

"Wait," said the lawyer. "You don't quite understand, Mr. Sackler. We know who killed Mr. Memberson's sister."

SACKLER'S FACE FELL and I grinned happily. Mentally, he was cutting his fee in half. Catching a killer whose identity was already known rated only half the price he had prepared to ask. The glitter leaked from his eyes and he sighed heavily.

Knowing him as I did I was quite aware that he felt Memberson, personally, had just mulcted him out of several hundred dollars.

Memberson held his hand over his eyes and shuddered. He seemed more upset than Sackler.

"My son," he said. "It's my son, Mr. Sackler. Oh, my God, I—"

"Let me tell it," said Heatherington. "Now Sackler—Memberson, here, has a boy about twenty, whose life has been spent in an asylum. Frankly, he's insane. Has been since he was a child."

Sackler's eyes glowed again. He began to see fresh possibilities.

"And about midnight last night," said Memberson tensely, "Greaves, the butler at my estate in Virginia, called long distance to tell me my sister Alice had been murdered. Shot through the head."

Sackler snatched a cigarette from the package Heatherington had taken from his pocket, assumed an owl-like expression and said, "So?" with the maximum profundity that can be put into a monosyllable.

The lawyer took up the story.

"Richard—that's Mr. Memberson's boy—had always hated his Aunt Alice. You see, his mother had died at his birth and his aunt had raised him. He saw little of his father because of Mr. Memberson's business duties. He blamed his aunt for every disciplinary measure. He was born with a club foot and a terrific sense of inferiority. His mind went when he was thirteen. He was taken away screaming imprecations at Alice Memberson, threatening to return some day to kill her."

"Once three years ago, he escaped," interposed Memberson.

"He actually assaulted his aunt. However we rescued her and sent Richard back to the asylum."

They both looked at Sackler expectantly. Sackler had a faraway expression in his eyes. He was thinking, I knew, of financial matters.

"So," he said slowly, "naturally after you heard from the butler about your sister's death you got in touch with the asylum to check on your son. Is that it?"

Memberson nodded his head slowly and groaned. "That's it, all right. And he was gone. As closely as they could figure it, Richard had escaped some six hours before."

"Well," said Sackler, "obviously you don't want me to find out who killed your sister. What is it I am to do?"

"Find my son. Find him and see that he comes to no harm. No court will convict him. He will be returned to the asylum."

"What Mr. Memberson fears," said the lawyer, "is that the local police, who doubtless are searching for Richard now, may injure him. The boy is mad and angry. He may well resist arrest. He may fight the officers. He will be hurt, perhaps killed. Mr. Memberson wants you to get him before the officers. But see that he comes to no injury."

Sackler blinked and looked unhappy. If his fee was contingent upon his finding a maniac in a country whose area is well in excess of a million square miles—and finding him before anyone else—he was going to earn every penny of it, provided he earned it at all.

Heatherington, apparently, read his mind as easily as had I. "The boy is probably hiding in the woods surrounding the Memberson estate," he said. "He knows them well. It's there you will probably find him. You will go to the estate in Fredericksburg, take the trail from there. It is essential the boy be taken unharmed. Do you accept the commission?"

Rather to my surprise he did not snap it up. It was obvious that he could arrange to collect something whether he succeeded or not. Yet he shook his head thoughtfully.

"Well," he said dubiously, "there are one or two things I'm working on at the moment. It would mean a considerable financial sacrifice. I—"

He saw the accusing look in my eyes and brought his lie up short. He hadn't had a client for two months. But before I could say anything Memberson rushed into the conversation.

"Of course, I am prepared to pay you well, Sackler. Shall we say twenty-five hundred dollars? If you accept, I'll give it to you now. What do you say?"

I CLOSED MY eyes and shuddered. The spectacle of anyone pouring another twenty-five hundred bucks into Sackler's one-way bank account acted like an emetic on me. I opened my lids again to see Memberson patting his pockets like a man who can't find his keys.

"My checkbook," he said impatiently. "I can't find my checkbook. Have you a check, Heatherington?"

The lawyer shook his head. Sackler who never kept a nickel in a bank anyway, of course, couldn't oblige.

"Wait," said Memberson. "There are some stock certificates in your briefcase, Heatherington. Will you accept two shares of stock in the Memberson Enterprises, Mr. Sackler? They're worth a thousand each at par. Their current value is in excess of twenty-eight hundred dollars."

I groaned. Even before Sackler had lifted a finger he was

getting a three hundred dollar raise. Memberson took two certificates from the lawyer, endorsed them and handed them over to Sackler who stuck them away in his breast pocket with an ethereal expression. Beyond the window I saw the drab outlines of the Washington Station.

Heatherington stood up. "We get off here. Unfortunately, it is impossible for Mr. Memberson to accompany you to his farm. However it is in your charge until he arrives three days hence."

Sackler nodded. Memberson gripped his hand and shook it fervently.

"For God's sake look out for my boy. You won't regret it. And I'll see you in a few days."

"One thing more," said Sackler. "What authority have I at your place? Is there anyone there to receive us?"

"I'll phone," said Memberson. "I'll phone Greaves, my butler. There are a couple of research men down there, working on synthetic quinine. But I'll phone, instructing them to give you all possible aid. Good-bye."

He and Heatherington left the compartment. Sackler leaned back against the green cushions and grinned like a jackal. I regarded him with disgust.

"My God," I said, "money pours into you as if you were a vault. Six hours ago you were fast asleep. Now you're twenty-eight hundred dollars richer. What is your secret?"

"Hard work," said Sackler righteously. "And a reputation for competence and integrity. Not to mention— Oh, my God!"

He clapped his hand to his head with such force that it sounded like a claque. His facial muscles sagged in a register of misery. I stared at him, baffled.

"I am puzzled," I announced. "I have never seen you

concerned about anything save money. Since you have a small fortune in your pocket, that you did not have a short while ago, your anxiety cannot be over finances. Yet you look as if you'd dropped a nickel down a subway grating. I am baffled."

Sackler uttered a stifled moan. "Joey," he said in agonized accents, "I forgot to collect the train fare. I laid out over thirty-five dollars in cash!"

I glared at him indignantly. He had picked up twenty-eight hundred bucks yet he was squawking about thirty-five which he would doubtless collect later anyway.

"My heart bleeds," I told him. "Sympathy gushes from me like a fountain and I hope with all my heart that the Memberson Enterprises go bankrupt within the next half hour."

We rode into Fredericksburg in strained silence.

2

Maniac Murders!

LOW-HANGING CLOUDS WERE like great melancholy oysters and the sky was dreary over the State of Virginia. Rain sprinkled down upon the deserted railroad station.

There was no one to meet us and Sackler eschewing the importunities of taxi drivers for the most obvious reason boarded a bus which we were told ran within a few hundred yards of the Memberson estate.

It was an optimistic estimate. The bus let us off at a solitary crossroads that just begged to have Edgar Allen Poe write a sorrowful sonnet about it. We turned our coat collars up against the rain, gripped our valises, and set off on foot.

Off in the gray distance we descried the Memberson mansion. It was vast and colonial. Before it was a tremendous expanse of neatly mowed lawn. At its rear was a tree-covered mountainside. But the fact that interested me most was that it was fully a mile and a half away.

Listening to Rex Sackler's rapid breath helped me ignore my own discomfort. His greatest expenditure of energy in the past decade had been the task of piling one dollar bill on top of the other. He toiled up the hill in front of me like a pack-laden infantryman.

We were within half a mile of the wrought-iron gates which opened into the estate when we suddenly saw a swirl of black smoke rise up toward the sky. Sackler put down his bag, inhaled deeply and stared ahead. I stared with him.

The smoke did not emanate from the house proper. Rather it seemed to rise from the base of the mountain, some distance at the rear of the mansion. We exchanged glances. However, since a constraint still existed between us we did not speak.

Sackler brought a heavy sigh up from the soles of his dusty shoes, heaved on his bag again and marched on with weary resolve. I plodded along behind.

As we turned through the gates, made our way to the glistening white pillars that stood like fluted sentinels at the entrance of the house, Sackler dropped his bag suddenly and whistled. I followed his gaze.

At the edge of the lawn was a border of empty flower beds. Dead centered in the beds were a set of running footprints. Both of us bent down to examine them closely, to see if our first impression was correct.

It was.

Sackler straightened up and spoke to me for the first time in two hours.

"Note the left footprint, Joey. It is larger than the other and sunk in deeper."

I nodded. "Obviously from the heavy shoe that would be worn by a guy with a club foot."

"Right, Joey. And apparently it is fresh. Within a few hours, anyway."

He picked up his bag again and moved up the path. I followed with mixed emotions. If he actually was destined to pick up a pretty fee I would much rather have him work hard for it. Since these footprints indicated that the man for whom we sought was in the immediate vicinity it appeared that Sackler's task was rendered much easier.

I was still brooding about this when we climbed up the steps to the colonial portico and rang the bell. The result of that simple action was overwhelming.

From within the house came the sound of loud voices. I read in them anger, accusation and fear. A moment later racing footsteps grew louder as they came toward us. I saw the crystal doorknob turn and heard a cry of agony.

The doorknob twisted convulsively. The portal was pulled suddenly inward. In the huge foyer was a man—a man with contorted lips and tortured eyes who clung to the edge of the door as if to prevent himself from falling.

His knees were bent and his head sagged on his neck. Again he uttered a frightful groan. Sackler sprang to his side and put an arm about his waist.

From the interior of the house came the sound of excited voices, of running feet. Then suddenly the man who had opened the door fell from Sackler's grasp. He fell forward across the threshold on his knees. He remained in a grotesque prayerful attitude for a moment, then slumped forward with his face upon the doormat.

It was only then that I saw the knife-hilt in his back. It was a smooth black wood and it quivered hideously with the shock of its victim's fall. Blood stained the back of his coat, grew in a widening circle. Sackler stared down at the corpse and shuddered.

"What's the matter?" I snapped. "You've seen a dead man before, haven't you?"

"It's not that. I didn't reckon on two murders. I should have charged him more."

I glared at him indignantly as he stepped carefully across the body and entered the house.

WE ENTERED A vast living-room that looked as if it had been decorated by a moving picture producer. As we dropped our bags on the threshold two men appeared from a doorway leading to a terrace on the opposite side of the chamber from us.

One of them was a tall, lantern-jawed individual, clad in a well-cut blue serge suit. His hair was graying and his eyes were shrewd and intelligent. The second of the pair was of medium height and possessed of the solidest barrel chest I ever gazed at. His face was a pasty white and it seemed to me there was a furtive look about him.

The tall man came into the room first. He stared for a moment at us, thrust out his hand and addressed us in a tone of cordial welcome.

"You're Sackler and Graham, I guess. Memberson phoned that you were coming."

We shook hands and learned that the tall man was Wallace Atherton, an inventor of sorts who was working with his partner in Memberson's cellar where a laboratory had been installed for their research in synthetic quinine. The partner whose name was Westerly was about the house somewhere.

Atherton then brought up the squat man with the shaded eyes. "This is Sammy Blake," he announced. "Sort of a general factotum for Westerly and myself. Does our dirty work. A little tough but invaluable."

We shook hands again. There was something of the quality of freshly caught bluefish in Sammy's handshake. I lit a cigarette and remarked to myself that the atmosphere was extremely casual considering that a corpse lay in the main doorway, that a moment ago the house had been filled with excited shouting.

Sackler helped himself to a cigar from a silver humidor and sat down in a luxuriously cushioned chair. He stretched himself and sighed. "Well, well," he remarked conversationally, "it's good to get in out of the drizzle."

"Sammy," said Atherton, "light the fire."

I stared at them. The attitude of them all, including Sackler, was as free and easy as if they were sitting in the corner pool-room waiting for the first empty table.

I said with heavy irony: "There happens to be a dead man in the doorway. However, I suppose that with a war going on one corpse more or less doesn't matter."

Whereupon I took a cigar myself, sat down and lit it, resolved to be as impervious to the body in the front hall as anyone else.

"Oh my God," said Atherton. "Is he dead?"

"As the dove of peace," said Sackler. "Who is he and who killed him?"

"It's Greaves," said Sammy. "Memberson's butler. The old man will be upset. Greaves has been with him for thirty years."

"I'm glad to hear someone will be upset," I said. "I—"

"Shut up," snapped Sackler. "What happened, Atherton?"

Atherton bit his lip. He looked around the room as if he expected to find a ghost peering over his shoulder.

"He came back," he whispered tensely.

"He?" said Sackler.

Atherton nodded. "Memberson told me on the phone that he had kept nothing from you. Richard Memberson came back. He ran into the house, apparently entering the back door. I was downstairs with Sammy at the time. We heard Greaves cry out. We rushed upstairs in time to see Richard throw a knife."

Sackler inhaled cigar smoke luxuriously. I didn't quite know whether he relished its expensive fragrance most or the fact that it had cost him nothing. He nodded to Atherton to continue.

"He ran out the kitchen door and Sammy and I ran after him. We know how Memberson feels about it. But he eluded us at the edge of the woods there. He's like an animal in that forest. The local coppers have been scouring it all day. Beyond footprints they've found nothing."

"Ah," said Sackler. "Footprints. It's soggy outside now. I suppose there are prints?"

Sammy nodded. "Plain as an elephant's trail," he said. "You want to see them? They run from the kitchen door to the base of the mountain. You can see the mark he makes with that club foot plain as day. Want to look?"

"Not at the moment. You say the local police are on the mountain now?"

"Yes," said Atherton. "He must've eluded them, come down here and killed Greaves, then gone back in hiding again."

"Why should he kill Greaves?"

"He's nuts," said Sammy. "Why should a nut kill anybody?"

Sackler sighed and stood up. His long serious face was graver than usual. He apparently was going to have to work for his twenty-eight hundred dollars after all.

"All right," he said. "Now tell me about Alice Member-son. She was killed late last night. Is that right? Exactly what happened?"

"We'll never know exactly," said Atherton. "We heard a shot.

We rushed to her room. Westerly, my partner, and I got there first. We found Alice blasted through the head lying on the floor. I happened to look up suddenly. I saw a grinning, vaguely familiar face at the window. Of course, it was Richard. But I didn't think of that at the time."

Sackler chewed on his cigar and mulled this over. "Where was Sammy at this time? Where was Greaves?"

"I was in my room," said Sammy. "I heard the shot and a scream. I came down at once. Westerly and Atherton were already in Miss Memberson's bedroom when I arrived."

"Greaves," put in Atherton, "came up just as we were leaving the room to investigate the face at the window. He took one look at Alice and almost collapsed. He was very fond of her."

"So then," said Sackler, "he phoned Memberson. Is that it?"

Sammy nodded. "Right. Memberson said he couldn't make it right away. Had to go to Washington. Of course we had to notify the local cops. Then today Memberson called and said he had hired you."

Sackler puffed furiously at his cigar. A deep frown creased his brow. I was not sure if he was actually thinking or merely impressing the clients.

"Well," he said at last, "you'd better notify the coroner or whoever you're supposed to notify in this county that Greaves is cluttering up the front hall. And I'd like to look at Alice Memberson's body. I imagine I'll have to visit the local undertaker's."

Atherton and Sammy exchanged glances.

"I'm afraid," said Atherton, "that you won't be able to see Alice Memberson's body, Mr. Sackler."

Sackler lifted his eyebrows. "Now look here," he said with heavy authority, "if the local coppers think they're going to stall me they're wrong. I'm Memberson's agent in this thing. I demand to see the body."

HE WAS IRRITATED. Professional policemen hated him, primarily because he made ten times as much money as they did. Invariably the most difficult problem in every case he had was placating the coppers.

"It ain't the coppers," said Sammy. "They'd like to see Alice Memberson's body themselves."

"Well, why the devil don't they?" snapped Sackler.

"They haven't been able to find it," said Atherton softly. "That's one of the things they're searching the mountain for."

Sackler shook his head, sat down and registered complete bewilderment.

"Didn't you just tell me that the body was found on the bedroom floor?"

"Right," said Atherton. "But we closed the door and left it there while Greaves phoned Memberson, while the rest of us went outside to investigate the face at the window."

Sackler slapped his breast pocket as if to make sure his two shares of stock were still there.

"And?" he said.

"And," said Sammy, "when we came back the body was gone. Absolutely no trace of it. No trace of the murder even."

"Except the blood stains on the floor," said Atherton.

Sackler stood up again. He paced the floor and left a cloud of angry smoke behind him.

"Are you telling me that Richard Memberson re-entered

the house while you were all out of the room, snatched up his aunt's body and ran off with it? That's insane."

"Exactly," said Sammy. "Nuts. That's what it is. And that explains everything."

Sackler looked at him as if he suspected Sammy was about to borrow a half dollar.

"What explains what?" he asked coldly.

"Why, like you said. It's insane. Well, Richard Memberson is insane, too. Naturally, everything he does is insane. It explains everything."

I gaped at him. Sackler said icily: "You should be on the Homicide Squad in New York. Your reasoning is similar to theirs."

I grinned, aware that he was thinking of his sworn enemy, Inspector Wooley.

"And now," he continued, "if you'll find what police there are dashing futilely about that mountain top and deliver the corpse of Greaves to them, I'll look over the house to see what I can find. Where is the room where Alice Memberson was killed?"

Atherton sent Sammy to recall the local gendarmerie, then led the way to a room at the rear of the house on the ground floor. It was a bedroom which had obviously been occupied by a woman. The dressing-table was littered with gilded jars of cosmetics. Clothes were flung in disarray about the chairs and bed. A closet door stood ajar revealing a huge wardrobe.

Sackler nodded distantly to Atherton who accepted his nod as dismissal which was a correct interpretation.

Sackler proceeded to nose about the room. He went carefully through the desk. I smoked idly and boredly as he followed up by examining each garment in the closet. Then he returned to the desk and selected a square piece of pink paper from a pigeonhole. He read the writing it contained carefully and stowed it away in his pocket as if it were a dollar bill.

"A clue?" I said, slightly ironical.

"A clue," he said positively. "A bill for a fur coat belonging to Alice Memberson from a storage company."

"Ah," I said, laying it on with a trowel this time, "a most important document."

"It is indeed, Joey. I didn't think you'd see it."

Of course I didn't see it and he knew damned well I didn't but, at the moment, neither of us pressed the point.

We returned to the drawing-room. There we found Atherton and three other men. One of them, Atherton introduced as Westerly, his partner in the quinine research. Westerly was a wispy little man with watery eyes and he wore a continual expression of alarm.

The other pair were Sheriff Desmond and his assistant. The sheriff was built like Gibraltar. He was a huge man, wide and muscular. His face was firm and weatherbeaten. He regarded Sackler as did most professional policemen—with ill-concealed hostility.

"I don't see why we had to have outside talent called up," he remarked to no one in particular. "If anyone can find Dick Memberson on that mountain it'll be folks who know their way around here."

"And if he's not on the mountain?" inquired Sackler.

"Of course he's on the mountain," said Westerly. "We found several footprints."

Sackler shrugged. "My job's to find him and see that he comes to no harm until he is safely in jail—provided it's not too late."

Atherton looked at him oddly. "What do you mean by that?"

Sackler shrugged again. "We'll go to our room," he announced. "We're tired. I shall permit matters to remain in the hands of the sheriff until tomorrow morning."

Desmond glared at us as we left the room. Tact had never been an admirable quality of Sackler's. Now his lack of it had made him another enemy. However, I supposed that since he already had his fee in his pocket he didn't care much about co-operation from the local authorities.

3

Sinister Houseparty

WHEN WE CAME down for dinner the sheriff had left. We ate in company with Sammy Blake and Westerly. Atherton, they told us, was cleaning up some important research in the basement. The meal, served in the grand manner by a couple of colored retainers that I thought had gone out with the Fourteenth Amendment, was dull conversationally.

Sackler, never a social lion, said little. And it seemed that the others didn't feel any heart-warming friendship for either of us.

As we were drinking the coffee I heard the cry. It was a weird eerie sound that seemed to reach up from the bowels of the earth and bounce off a melancholy sounding-board into our eardrums. I shuddered and put down my cup.

Sackler had come to the alert like an air-raid warden. He sat perfectly still, gripping the arms of his chair and listening intently as if he expected to hear the sound again.

He did. It rose, faint and undulating, then fell away leaving a charged silence behind it. Sackler stood up.

"What's the matter?" asked Sammy. "Where are you going?"

"That cry," said Sackler. "Maybe it's Richard. Maybe he's close at hand."

Westerly laughed. A moment later Sammy joined him. Sackler glared at them indignantly.

"I am afraid, Mr. Sackler," said Westerly, "that you've spent most of your life in urban areas. That cry came from the beak of a horned owl. I hate to ruin a detective's theory but it certainly is no clue to the whereabouts of Richard Memberson."

I grinned as I watched the abashed expression on Sackler's face. He drew himself up with dignity and strode from the room to the quarters we had been assigned. I followed along behind.

He slammed the door of our room and said to me: "Joey, what does the cry of an owl sound like?"

I shook my head. "I am strictly Tenth Avenue," I said. "A cop's whistle I can recognize. The roaring of the passing El is a familiar noise to me. But hoot owls—I never even saw one in the Bronx Zoo."

Sackler shook his head and a frown darkened his brow.

"It's odd," he said. "Quite odd. Take this Sammy Blake, for instance. The other two guys may well be chemists. But Sammy's a Brooklyn thug if I ever heard the accent."

"Aren't you building it up a little? With this research stuff, I suppose there's some dirty work to be done. They could have hired a mug like Sammy for that."

"Maybe. But then there's that bill for storage on the fur coat. And another peculiar circumstance."

I saw nothing peculiar about the bill for the coat. I inquired about the second circumstance.

"Those three guys," said Sackler. "Westerly, Atherton, and Sammy Blake. Have you noticed we never see the three of them together?"

"What do you mean?"

"At dinner it was Sammy and Westerly. Before that Atherton and Westerly. When we arrived it was Atherton and Sammy. The three of them are never at the same place at the same time.

There's always one of them missing."

I mulled that one over and decided Sackler was desperately trying to complicate a simple case.

"Coincidence," I said. "I don't see what you're masterminding. Get out on that mountain and find Richard. Turn him in and you're through. Why mess around trying to create mystery where there isn't any?"

"Joey," he said wearily, "you are a fool. Go to bed and leave me alone with my thoughts. You're gullible enough to believe the Berlin radio."

I shrugged and went in to bed. When Sackler was in one of his intellectually superior moods he was utterly impossible. The rain pounced down on the roof and sang me into a sound and restful sleep.

In the morning we ate breakfast with Sammy and Atherton. Sammy looked as if he hadn't slept much. His eyes were ringed and his face was haggard. Sackler ate silently, ignoring the remainder of the company.

When he had finished, he pushed back his chair, and addressed a single question to Atherton.

"You saw Miss Memberson's body after she had been killed. Can you tell me what she was wearing?"

"Well," said Atherton, "I can't give you many details. What with all the excitement, I—"

"Was she wearing a coat?"

Sammy and Atherton exchanged glances. "Why no," said Atherton. "Some sort of a house dress I'd say. Flowered fabric, I—"

"That will do," said Sackler like a schoolteacher and strode from the room.

I followed him to the front door where he hesitated for a moment then plunged out into the rain. He said, "Come along, Joey," just as I was about to turn and re-enter the house.

I plodded resentfully along behind him. "My God," I said. "Are we going to scour the mountain, too? And in this weather? I'm no woodsman, you know. If the sheriff can't find our lunatic, how the devil will we?"

He didn't answer. He marched, purposefully and with bowed head around to the rear of the house. He moved with grim implacability across a landscaped garden. He was headed, I noted, for the base of the mountain where the woods began. My heart sank.

Was he going to be idiotic enough to begin beating his way through that forest? Within the hour we would be as lost as was our quarry. I squished through the mud behind him with no enthusiasm whatever.

HE CAME TO an abrupt halt and behind him I lifted my head. Before us, two thirds buried in the earth, was a concrete structure. Four steps led down to a steel door which was its entrance. Its roof was buried beneath thick grassy sod. At the rear a chimney thrust itself a foot above the earth.

I blinked at the sight with the rain splattering down in my face. Sackler plodded around to the rear and looked up at the chimney top. The aperture had been covered with tarpaulin, lashed tightly to the bricks, apparently to keep the rain out.

Sackler rejoined me and grunted. We stood for a moment in silence, then Sackler, whose ears were as keen as a scimitar, spun around swiftly on his heel and said: "What's that?"

I turned my head. I saw something black move behind

the thick bole of an elm tree. The pair of us moved quickly toward it. As we came up the wet and wispy figure of Westerly emerged from behind the tree trunk.

He was wearing a raincoat and a rubber hat. He smiled at us and bade us good morning.

Sackler studied him for a long silent moment before he spoke. Then he said, indicating the dugout: "What's that?"

"That? Oh, that's Memberson's air-raid shelter. Had it built some time ago. It contains every modern improvement. You ought to see it."

"I'd like to," said Sackler. "Is it open?"

Westerly shook his head. "Unfortunately not. Memberson carries the key with him."

Sackler gave out with his most suspicious grunt. "May I ask," he said heavily, "what you are doing out here in the rain?"

"I might ask the same of you," said Westerly, smiling. "However, I like rain. I'm interested in flora. I walk in the rain quite often."

"Most interesting," said Sackler. "Have you seen the sheriff?"

"He's out on the mountain again. He says he's going to get Richard if he stays out all night. Since Greaves was killed he says we're all in danger. He's going to take him dead or alive."

Sackler made no comment. He led the way back to the house.

This was Saturday and for almost twenty-four hours, Sackler did nothing but loll in a chair, smoke Memberson's cigars and brood. He made no effort to find Richard, no effort to persuade the sheriff to take the lad alive rather than dead which was what he was being paid for.

We ate with the others and it came home to me that Sackler's observation of the previous evening was perhaps more significant than I had thought.

Sammy, Westerly and Atherton *never were together!*

One of them was always missing. I puzzled over it for a long time, then arrived at the not unreasonable conclusion that perhaps there was valuable stuff in the workshop which they did not care to leave unguarded.

I mentioned this to Sackler who promptly informed me that I was a direct descendant of the Jukes family, an unmitigated fool and an idiot. After that I kept my mouth shut.

Early Sunday afternoon Henry Memberson arrived. He spoke privately to Atherton and Westerly for a short time then retired to a suite on the second floor, consisting of a sitting-room and bedroom. It was there, I understood, that he did most of his homework.

I WAITED IN the sitting-room while Sackler and Memberson closeted themselves in the inner chamber. I heard the steady drone of Sackler's voice but the door panels were too thick for successful eavesdropping.

About four o'clock Sackler emerged. He was wearing a grave frown.

"Joey," he said. "This is a filthier mess than I thought. In the meantime Memberson wants to rest for a while. He's not to be disturbed."

We went down to the living-room. There was no one there. We lounged about before an open fireplace for the better part of an hour. Then suddenly from outdoors we heard Atherton raise a mighty shout.

We raced to the terrace to see Atherton running like a madman away from the house toward the woods. There was something contagious about his straining pace. Sackler and I rushed out into the rain about a hundred yards behind him.

We came up to him, panting and leaning against a tree-trunk.

"I saw him," he gasped. "With my own eyes. He was running away from the house."

"You mean Richard Memberson?" asked Sackler, an odd glint in his eyes.

Atherton nodded. "God, I hope nothing happened." He paused and stared at Sackler in horror. "Memberson!" he ejaculated. "You don't think he's harmed his own father!"

The three of us spun around again and raced back to the house. Atherton, slightly in the lead, pulled up beneath the window of the sitting-room of Memberson's suite. He pointed a trembling finger downward.

"Look!" he gasped.

We looked to see a set of footprints similar to those we had seen when we had first entered the estate. The left print was bigger and more unwieldy than the right. They had obviously been made by a man with a club foot.

"He must've been in Memberson's suite," said Atherton hoarsely. "He must've dropped down from the window and run off. I saw him when he was halfway to the forest. You can tell by the prints."

I examined the prints more carefully. Two of them had been made while their owner faced the house, truly as if he had dropped from the window sill of the story above. Then the indentations turned and pointed off toward the mountain.

"For God's sake," cried Atherton. "We'd better see if Memberson's all right."

We all started for the doorway to the living-room.

"Wait," said Sackler. "Memberson's tired and upset. Told me positively he wasn't to be disturbed. I'll go alone. No use upsetting him further if no harm's been done."

Atherton and I remained in the living-room as Sackler raced up the stairs. We shifted uneasily in our seats for it was a long ten minutes before he returned.

"Everything's O.K.," he said. "Memberson saw and heard nothing. But he insists on rest. Says it's his only chance for any sleep. He must go back to Washington tomorrow. His doctor told him to get all the rest he can today. He positively refuses to be disturbed for anything."

Atherton looked at him oddly. He opened his mouth as if to speak, then closed it again. I observed that there was an angry glint in Sackler's eye and it seemed not unmixed with apprehension.

"As a matter of fact," he went on, "Memberson has asked me personally to see that no one bothers him. I'll remain upstairs in his sitting-room. I've got a lot of thinking to do anyway. Joey, you come up in a little while. I have an errand for you."

The errand, I discovered an hour later, was to mail a thick special delivery envelope to a New York address. It must have been important since Sackler actually had me call a taxi and advanced me the fare to take it in to the post office at Fredericksburg.

I returned in time for dinner which I ate in company with Westerly and Atherton. The ancient servant told me Sackler had ordered two trays sent upstairs, one for himself and one for Memberson.

Westerly and Atherton, I thought, regarded me with some suspicion. They were articulately resentful of the fact that

Memberson was spending his time exclusively with Sackler. It seemed they had important things to discuss with the industrialist.

I paid attention to my calories and ignored their complaints. As long as Sackler came through with my salary each week, I wasn't much interested in what he did about anything else.

4

Death Comes Silently

AT TEN O'CLOCK it was still raining. There was a dark, unfriendly and tense atmosphere in the house. Sackler was still upstairs with Memberson. I sat in the vast gloomy drawing-room with Atherton and Westerly. I hadn't seen Sammy since breakfast.

Sackler's observation that the three of them were never together recurred to me. It was a peculiarly consistent coincidence. I smoked a cigarette and mulled it over.

On the other side of the room Westerly and Atherton perched uneasily on their chairs. Constantly I intercepted their anxious interchanged glances. Once I thought I heard Atherton whisper hissingly to his partner.

At ten thirty Westerly stood up. There was annoyance, and I thought anxiety in his face.

"This is ridiculous," he said. "We have an important report to make to Memberson. I'm sure he is anxious to hear it. I'm beginning to believe Sackler is keeping him away from us against his will."

I shrugged. It looked odd to me, too. However, I was under Sackler's orders—orders he could always enforce by deducting part of my salary as punishment. For that reason alone I was on his side.

I heard his voice suddenly down the wide stairway. "Joey! Joey! Come up here, will you?"

With no reluctance whatever I got up and left the drawing-room. I climbed the stairs to find Sackler in the doorway
of Memberson's private suite. He stood aside as I entered and
closed the door behind me. I remarked the door which led to
the bedroom was shut and since Memberson was not in the
sitting-room it appeared that Sackler was even keeping him
away from me.

I looked at Sackler and noted that he, too, seemed worried.
"The boys downstairs are getting restive," I reported. "They're
beginning to think you're keeping Memberson to yourself for
private and reprehensible reasons. I'm beginning to think so
myself."

"You keep them out of here," said Sackler and I thought I
detected a note of panic in his voice. "That's your job in this
case, Joey, and I'll hold you responsible."

I stared at him. Sackler, when working on a case, was invariably cold as the Yukon River. He never became excited, never
lost his head. Now, however, he seemed definitely panicky. My
immediate thought was that somehow money was involved.
But after a moment I couldn't do anything with that theory.

"Now look," he said. "There's that library downstairs. It's got
a million books in it. Doubtless it has an encyclopedia. Look
up Morse Code. The encyclopedia will give the entire thing,
the whole alphabet reduced to dots and dashes. Tear that page
out and bring it up to me."

I blinked. "But you already know the Morse Code."

"Of course I do. What's that to do with it? Bring me that
page. Quickly."

I shrugged and went downstairs to the library. A few
moments later I returned. Sackler snatched the page from

my hand as if the whereabouts of Richard Memberson were printed upon it.

"Joey," he said, "have you a pocketknife?"

I produced one and handed it to him, staring at him in bewilderment all the time.

"All right," he said. "Now Mr. Memberson is in the bedroom there. The door is locked with a spring lock. Only I have the key. He must under no circumstances be disturbed by those guys downstairs. You stay on guard here. Don't let them see Memberson under any circumstances. I'll be back in less than half an hour."

He took a deep breath and strode from the room as if he were marching to the defense of the Caucasus. There was an expression of grim resolve on his face which I didn't understand. Any jobs which came up calling for those two qualities were invariably left to me. Sackler wanted no part of them.

I sat down in the big armchair by the window and racked my brains for the answer to Sackler's peculiar conduct. I thought of the crazed Richard Memberson out there in the rain on the mountain top while the police combed the woods for him.

I didn't like any of the things I thought of. First, it seemed too damned easy for Richard to enter the house any time he felt like it. He possessed an unnerving quality of appearing and disappearing like a wraith. And even if he left a most unwraith-like trail of footprints behind him, it certainly had made it no easier a task to catch up with him.

I took a cigarette from my pocket and stuck it in my mouth. I groped through my suit for a match and didn't find one. I stood up and looked about the room with similar unsuccess.

I was about to go downstairs to procure a light when I

recalled how serious Sackler had been about permitting no one to see Memberson. I decided I had better not desert my post. Besides, I was overcome with curiosity myself. Since his arrival, I hadn't seen Henry Memberson either. Perhaps if I did it would throw some light on Sackler's grim and mysterious manner.

I made up my mind to massacre a brace of birds with a single stone. I would tap on the door and get a match from Memberson himself.

I KNOCKED GENTLY on the panel. I received no reply. I knocked loudly. I said in a carrying voice: "Mr. Memberson, it's Joey Graham. Sackler's assistant."

The rest was silence. I thought that over for a moment, then tried the door. It was locked all right. I searched my pockets and was lucky enough to come up with a nail file and a safety pin. I am no naive infant in the matter of locked doors. I went to work on the spring lock with neatness and dispatch. I had it open in something under four minutes.

I pushed the door in, peeped around the jamb, and said respectfully: "Mr. Memberson."

There was no answer. I stepped across the threshold, closing the door behind me. I stood there for a long time staring at Henry Memberson. He lay quietly upon the bed. His eyes were closed and he did not speak to me.

"Good evening, Mr. Memberson," I said politely. "I have come to get a match."

I found one on the bureau and I lit my cigarette. I took a long, thoughtful inhalation. I scratched my head and pondered so hard that I left a neuralgic ache in my temples. Then I nodded my head slowly, tiptoed silently from the room, closing the door behind me. The spring lock clicked back into place and once again I was alone in Memberson's sitting-room.

A half hour later Rex Sackler returned. He looked like a torpedoed mariner. His felt hat which had survived a thousand storms over a period of many years had at long last given up the ghost. It was a blob of saturated fabric hanging in melancholy fashion over his right eye.

His suit was as wet as the Atlantic Ocean during a monsoon and his collar was as wilted as a ten week old daisy who has borne more than its share of trouble. His shoes left huge moist spots upon the carpet and his teeth chattered like a feverish machine gun.

"Are you hunting pneumonia?" I asked. "Have you an insurance policy which grants double indemnity for suicide? Is that possibly your motive?"

Had my grandmother heard what he called me she would have assaulted him forthwith with gamp and reticule.

"Don't bother about me," he snapped. "Go downstairs again. Call the local coppers. Tell them to be here at ten tomorrow morning without fail. Moreover, phone that lawyer of Memberson's—Heatherington. Tell him to be here at that time, too. It's vitally important. Although you may find our friends downstairs have summoned him already."

I regarded him thoughtfully. I knew what I had to do. I was considering the method.

"Very well," I said at last. "I will make those two calls for you. Then I'll put through a long distance call on my own account."

"Long distance?" he said sharply, suspiciously. "Who are you calling long distance?"

"The *News*," I said. "The New York *Daily News*."

"What for?"

"To make an honest penny."

"What the devil are you talking about?"

"They pay for news tips," I told him. "If you come across something you phone it in. They pay for it. See?"

His face became a shade paler than usual and I felt a contented warmth in my heart.

"The price depends on the news value of the tip," I went on. "Now take a traffic accident. I don't suppose they'd pay more than five bucks for a thing like that. But, for a big kidnapping, say, or a jewel robbery, why I suppose it might even run a few hundred slugs. They might even—"

"Shut up," said Sackler, venomous as the Japanese radio.

We looked at each other. My gaze as bland and ingenuous as I could make it; Sackler's was an odd mixture of insensate rage and righteous indignation.

"Joey," he said in the tone of the bishop who has intruded on the crap game in the choir loft, "Joey, you have been inside Memberson's bedroom."

"I was looking for a match," I said without expecting any credulity.

He drew a deep breath. He closed his eyes and registered a man enduring unbearable suffering. He requested, as if he were being led to the rack: "State your proposition."

"I am not hungry," I said. "I am a simple man who needs but little from life. All I ask is the same amount the *News* might pay, plus a couple of bucks extra because of our long-standing friendship."

All the musical geniuses of the eighteenth century could not have put together the heart-rending notes which composed Sackler's groan at that moment.

"How much in cash?"

I did some rapid mental arithmetic. "I think five hundred dollars will be ample."

Sackler clapped his hand to his forehead and water splashed from his hat. "Ample!" he repeated in agonized accents.

With his other hand he hammered his breast. Then his shrewd eyes narrowed and a gleam of hope came into them.

"You understand my motive, of course, Joey? You understand why…?"

"Too well," I said. "It has something to do with a gentleman whose offices are just off Wall Street, doesn't it?"

The hope in his eyes vanished like sugar. He spoke in a voice that was dead and without expectancy: "Three hundred, Joey?"

"I am steel," I said. "Five."

"You are a blackmailing thief," he shrieked. "Four."

"I am the British Isles," I said. "Five."

"You are a crook and a scoundrel. Four fifty."

"I am the Marines in the Pacific," I said. "Five."

"Five," said Sackler, in a tone of utter defeat. "Now get downstairs and make those phone calls. I have a couple to make from this phone myself. And keep those three mugs and their damned synthetic quinine out of here and also keep your mouth shut."

He unlocked the bedroom door with trembling fingers and I left him. I tripped lightly down the stairs humming a gay, off-key ditty and reflecting that virtue, perhaps, is not always its own reward.

IT WAS TEN minutes past ten on Monday morning. The rain had stopped and the sun beat weakly through the clouds. Outside the window a score of desperately optimistic birds sang as they went about the business of digging up worms for breakfast.

Upstairs in the Memberson mansion a door slammed. A moment later Sackler came into the vast living-room. He was haggard and pale of face. His eyes held a pair of ebony rings beneath them. Yet there was an air of great relief about him. He looked like a father to whom triplets have been safely delivered after a nip and tuck night. I knew why.

He was greeted by five pairs of hostile eyes as he entered. I had been holding down the fort for the past twenty minutes. It had seemed to me that Atherton and Westerly were worried about something, while Heatherington, who had arrived an hour earlier, made no bones about the fact that he strongly suspected that Sackler was up to no good.

He had already voiced this opinion vociferously to Sheriff Desmond and his deputy and those doughty minions of the law were inclined to agree.

The sheriff cleared his throat ominously as Sackler bowed and wished everyone a croaking good morning.

"Now looka here," he said. "I don't know what's on your mind but you're taking up precious time. We ought to be out on the mountain looking for that boy. He's liable to commit murder again if we don't get him."

"Oh, no, he's not," said Sackler, helping himself to Memberson's humidor.

There was a startled silence in the room. Heatherington looked quickly at the others, then said sternly to Sackler: "Where's Mr. Memberson? I demand to speak with him."

"You can speak to him," said Sackler, "but he isn't going to speak to you."

"Just what do you mean by that?" asked the sheriff.

I watched Sackler with interest. I was intensely interested in learning just how he was going to handle this and keep his own neck off the chopping block.

"He's dead," said Sackler. "Murdered."

The sheriff started and dashed for the stairway. He was followed by his deputy and, after a moment's pause, by everyone else.

When we were alone Sackler unleashed a sigh from the depths of his being and sat down in an armchair.

"Well," I said, "what tale are you going to tell? It isn't going to take the Mayo brothers to establish the time of death within four or five hours."

Sackler didn't answer. He went to the door of the dining-room and called sharply: "George!"

The ancient Negro servant entered the room. Sackler took him out of earshot and whispered to him at length. He took something from his pocket and pressed it into George's palm.

I casually picked up the morning paper which lay on a taboret and turned to the financial page. What I saw there caused me to lift my brows and shrug my shoulders. I looked up again to find Sackler glaring at me. His lips moved in anger. But before he could speak several footfalls clattered down the stairway and everybody poured back into the living-room.

The whole five of them stared accusingly at Sackler. Heatherington pushed forward into the room, pointed an accusing finger.

"You killed him!" he cried. "You killed him sometime yesterday. It's obvious enough. You refused to permit anyone to see him until you destroyed evidence of your crime. You are a murderer!"

"You," said Sackler wearily, "are an idiot."

The sheriff, with the deputy on his heels, pushed his way in to the center of the room.

"You just reported Memberson dead, didn't you?"

Sackler nodded.

"How long have you known he was dead?"

"About nineteen hours."

"Why wasn't it reported?"

Before Sackler could answer, Atherton did. "Obviously so he could destroy evidence. Obviously—"

Sackler grunted. "So you have your story set already?" he said as he stood up.

The sheriff and his deputy exchanged uncertain glances. Heatherington pushed forward again exuding that pomposity peculiar to attorneys.

"I demand that you arrest that man. Suspicion of murder. Perhaps he's even in league with Richard Memberson."

"The only confederates of Richard Memberson at this moment," said Sackler, "are worms and apparitions."

The sheriff blinked. "You mean he's dead?"

"As isolationism," said Sackler.

"How long have you known *that?*"

"For two days," said Sackler.

The sheriff put a horny hand on Sackler's shoulder. "I guess I'll have to take you in. There's something mighty funny going on here."

"Indeed there is," said Sackler. "As for instance the fact of the shoes of a man who drops from a second story window making no deeper impression on muddy soil than when he walks normally."

It seemed to me that Atherton flinched.

"Arrest him," shouted Heatherington again.

The sheriff shook his head. "Let's take it easy," he said slowly. "Maybe this fellow has something. Go ahead, Mr. Sackler, have you got something you want to tell us?"

SACKLER SAID: "I'LL thank you to see that no one leaves the room until I've finished. But I note that we're not all here. Sheriff, will you send your deputy to bring in Sammy Blake?"

"What's Sammy got to do with it?" asked Westerly. "It may take half an hour to find him on an estate this size."

"You will find him," said Sackler, "leaning up against the trunk of an elm tree some twenty yards northeast of that air-raid shelter out there. If you will, Sheriff."

The sheriff nodded to his deputy who left the room. Everyone, including myself was looking at Sackler. I was beginning to be interested. If, as Sackler had said, Richard Memberson was dead, who had killed Alice Memberson, Greaves and the old man?

I was still cudgelling my brains about that when the deputy returned with Sammy in tow.

"Where did you find him?" asked the sheriff.

The deputy stared at Sackler as if he were one of Satan's retinue. "Leaning against the trunk of the elm tree," he said.

He pushed Sammy into the room and took up a dramatic position by the door with his hand on the butt of his holstered gun.

"Well?" said the sheriff to Sackler.

Rex Sackler ran his thin fingers through his black hair. He took three paces forward which put him in the dead center of the room. He cleared his throat.

"Let us assume," he began, "that there is an unpleasant character, who for reasons which I will expound later, desires to put Alice and Henry Memberson out of the way. Let us assume further that it is known that Richard Memberson is a violent lunatic, is confined in an asylum. Wouldn't it be a good idea to arrange Richard's escape, keep him concealed until the killings had been done, then pin the entire rap upon him?"

"This," shouted Heatherington as if he were in a courtroom, "is sheer conjecture."

"I continue," said Sackler, ignoring him. "The plan is to kill Alice Memberson first, then produce witnesses who swear they saw a face at the window and Richard's behind disappearing into the woods. In addition to this they plant footprints neatly. Even using one shoe that would fit the club foot with which Richard was afflicted."

I blinked as a little light dawned. Apparently the sheriff had the same thought as myself.

"Is that what you referred to when you mentioned the footprints of a falling man only being as deep as his normal prints?" he asked.

"Precisely. When that last set of footprints was planted beneath Memberson's window, the planter forgot that the force of the fall would make the impressions deeper directly beneath the sill than they would be as they trailed off in the distance."

For the first time the sheriff looked at Sackler as if he believed him guiltless of Memberson's murder.

"Now," went on Sackler, "it is essential that Alice Memberson be killed first. She was the chief benefactor under her brother's will. If she is killed he will change the will. First Richard is aided to escape, then the plot to kill Alice begins to work."

"So," said the sheriff, "it works all right. But how?"

"You are wrong," said Sackler. "It didn't work at all."

There was a taut silence in the room. Sammy Blake stared at Sackler with bright beady eyes. I looked around and wondered if the guilty man was in this room. God knew, with the exception of the sheriff and his deputy everyone seemed panicky.

"You mean they didn't kill Alice?" asked the sheriff.

"They did not. They killed Richard instead."

Something clicked in my mind like a bolt.

"I've got it," I announced. "Richard's body was burned in the air-raid shelter. That was the smoke we saw as we came up here. I've got the whole thing now. I—"

"You've got a diseased brain cell," said Sackler. "A fact to which Greaves could ably testify if he were here."

"Listen," said Westerly and his voice sounded like water hissing under pressure, "how do you know Alice Memberson wasn't killed? Didn't three of us—three of us and Greaves see her body?"

"None of you saw her body," said Sackler. "A fact which was apparent to me when I found a bill from her storage company for a fur coat."

That bill was beginning to annoy me. "So what?" I asked. "What has that to do with it?"

"The coat was delivered two days before the alleged murder," said Sackler. "Yet it wasn't in Alice's room. It was not, I ascertained, on her person when she was supposed to have been dead. Thus it was possible she was wearing it."

"All right," said the sheriff. "Nevertheless four people, including Greaves, saw her body."

"No," said Sackler. "They saw the body of Richard Memberson clad in his aunt's clothes."

A taut silence settled over the room as if it were almost a material thing.

5

Killers All

"YOU CAN KEEP right on explaining," said the sheriff grimly. "You say the murderer aided Richard to escape to plant the killing of Alice upon him. Why wasn't that done?"

"Because," said Sackler, "Alice Memberson accidentally overheard the plotters discussing their scheme. She screamed and ran, with them after her. But she escaped. Now it became necessary to achieve the effect of her death without actually killing her. Richard was killed. Dressed in his aunt's clothes. Greaves was permitted only to glance at the masquerading corpse from the doorway. Naturally he believed it was Alice. While he phoned his employer with the news, the body of Richard was removed and buried."

"Buried?" snapped Heatherington. "Where?"

"I do not know. Sammy Blake will doubtless tell us later."

The sheriff blinked, incredulous. Sammy uttered a gasp which could be heard across the room. Heatherington, with cheeks red as bougainvillea, shouted: "This is insane. A ridiculous lie. There is no evidence. There are no witnesses."

"The hell there aren't," said Sackler. "There is no one leaning against that elm tree any more." He lifted his voice. "George!"

The Negro shuffled in slowly from the serving pantry. His eyes were wide with apprehension. Behind came an apparition—an apparition clad in a torn and filthy two thousand dollar mink coat, with a white smudged face and a pair of blazing eyes that glared like hating headlights around the room.

"My God," said Sammy Blake and wiped his forehead with the back of his hand.

Sheriff Desmond and his deputy stared as if they saw a ghost, which in a manner of speaking, they did.

"Miss Memberson!" gasped the sheriff. "My God, how—"

Alice Memberson moved into the center of the room. "I'll tell you how," she said and her voice was thick with savage hate. "Moreover, I'll tell you why and who."

Sackler gave me a sudden nod. It was our danger signal. The gesture told me that there might be trouble—physical trouble, at any moment. I put my hand in my pocket and my fingers rested on the cold butt of my automatic.

"Those killers," said Alice Memberson, "they planned to kill me and my brother, letting my poor crazed nephew take the blame. I understand the others are dead now. It was sheer luck they didn't get me."

The sheriff's gaze in turn fell upon Heatherington, Westerly, Atherton and Sammy. Then it returned to Alice Memberson.

"Go on," he said grimly.

"I overheard them. I went into the basement and heard them talking. They planned to kill me that very night. They had Richard hidden in the cellar somewhere. Then one of them came out of the work-shop and saw me. He knew I'd listened. He gave the alarm. I ran, terrified, to the air-raid shelter. I locked myself in."

The sheriff blinked. "You mean you've been there all that time?"

"All that time. I half-opened the door once and a bullet dug up the grass at my feet. So I went inside again. The place was stocked with food and water. I didn't dare come out."

"The first day she was there," said Sackler, "she burnt some of her clothes in the fireplace hoping the smoke from the chimney would be observed and bring help. That's what killed Greaves. They stuffed up the chimney after that."

ALICE MEMBERSON SHOOK her head and her eyes were wet. "Poor Greaves," she said. "I have wept since Mr. Sackler told me about that last night."

"Last night?" snapped Atherton. "Sackler spoke to you last night?"

Westerly cried out: "Sammy, you fool!"

"I swear," said Sammy Blake and his voice broke, "I swear that I—"

"Shut up," roared Heatherington.

"Wait a moment," said the sheriff.

"Why was Greaves killed?"

"They stood watches by that elm tree," explained Sackler, "ready to murder Alice Memberson when she appeared. Greaves went out to investigate the smoke. Miss Memberson spoke to him up the chimney until he was spotted by the guard who went for him. Greaves ran to the house for help, little knowing he would get none. At the same time my assistant and myself were coming up the driveway. A knife killed Greaves as he tried to escape via the front door. The others raced about planting their phoney footprints, and pretending they were pursuing Richard Memberson."

"But what of motive?" asked the sheriff. "I still don't understand it."

"Will it help you to," said Alice Memberson, "if I tell you that under the terms of my brother's will several million dollars were left to his son, Richard, with myself and Mr. Heatherington as administrators of the estate?"

For the first time the law contributed a thought.

"I get it," he said. "First it was necessary to convince Memberson his sister was dead, then he would change his will making Heatherington, here, sole administrator of a tremendous estate. Richard would be put away as criminally insane, Memberson would be killed, and a fortune is won."

"Right," said Sackler. "Miss Memberson made them change their plans slightly but they figured it would come out the same in the long run. They'd kill Miss Memberson sooner or later and neither she nor Richard would ever appear again. Naturally everyone would blame Richard, especially with those footprints sowed all around the joint."

The sheriff flushed. I guess he was thinking of all those prints he had tracked over the mountainside.

"Listen," said Heatherington suddenly. "You can use another witness. Suppose—"

"No," said Sackler sharply. "I'll take Sammy. I'll take an obvious triggerman like that for state's evidence, not you, Heatherington. What do you say Sammy? Will you burn or take life in exchange for information regarding the location of those shoes used to plant the footprints and the grave of Richard Memberson?"

Sammy was suddenly pale. His little eyes burned and his lips moved dryly. "I'll tell you," he said. "I'll talk."

I heard a staccato crackle behind me. I turned to see Heatherington on his knees and the deputy with a gun in his hand.

Heatherington had fallen half way to the terrace in a wild effort to escape. The law had been in there before me.

"All right," said Sackler. "Take all four of them, Sheriff. Obviously Heatherington introduced Atherton and Westerly to Memberson, arranged the experiments here in order to gain access for them to the house."

The deputy rounded up his prisoners. The sheriff looked sharply at Sackler.

"You know," he said, "I could hold you, too. Accessory after the fact of murder. Why did you withhold the information of Memberson's death?"

"That's an easy one," I told him. "Memberson paid his fee in stock. If news of the death leaked out before Sackler sold it, he'd stand to lose a fortune. Memberson *was* Memberson Enterprises. His death will drop the stock twenty points. Sackler couldn't afford to announce Memberson's death until his letter containing the stock had reached his broker this morning and been sold."

Sackler flushed scarlet. His eyes blazed. "That, Sheriff," he shouted, "is a damnable calumny. I sat with Memberson's body trying to convince the killer that he really wasn't dead. I was trying to encourage another attempt on Memberson's life so I could nab the killer in the act."

I clapped a hand to my head and said: "Heaven will punish you for that."

The sheriff smiled faintly. "I know your reputation, Mr. Sackler," he said quietly and turned his head away.

THE SHERIFF'S DEPUTY drove us back to Fredericksburg. Sackler who, after all, had sold out his stock for a total of three thousand dollars had almost forgiven me for cutting myself in for a trifle.

There was one thing that puzzled me and I gave it voice. "I understand," I said, "that you communicated with Alice Memberson in Morse, but I don't quite get it."

"Simple, Joey," Sackler said expansively. "I sneaked around the rear of the shelter where whoever was on guard couldn't see me. I cut the rope that held the tarpaulin to the chimney and dropped that page from the encyclopedia down it. Then I communicated by tapping. Alice had the answers on that sheet of paper and she could reply to me."

"Neat," I said. "But if you had most of the answers at that point why didn't we take the guard outside? Since you had taken the shelter key from Memberson we could have released his sister and she could have hanged them all. Why all the masterminding?"

"Joey," he said. "You're a bright lad. You know I never thought of that."

"You are a honey-tongued liar," I said bitterly. "You didn't do it that way because it would've speeded up the denouement. It would have exposed the fact that Memberson was dead before the stock exchange opened up this morning."

"Joey," he said chidingly, "you wrong me. I am no miser. I do not even grudge you the cash you blackmailed from me. Within reason there is nothing I would not do for you. Friendship can not be bought. I snap my fingers at money."

Like Hitler snapping his fingers at a Flying Fortress, I thought, but I kept my mouth shut until the sheriff had let us down at the railroad station.

Then as we approached the ticket office, Sackler's fist

hammered against his breast and he uttered the cry of a dying nightingale.

"Oh God," he cried. "And now it's too late. Why does everything happen to me?"

"Have you dropped a nickel?" I inquired solicitously.

"A nickel?" he cried. "I forgot to ask Memberson for the carfare I laid out coming down here. And we had no written agreement. I can't even sue the estate."

I threw my head back and rocked with laughter.

He said to the ticket agent savagely: "Coach, New York. One way and *one ticket*."

My laughter ceased suddenly. I wonder if it's true about the camel, the needle's eye and the rich man entering Heaven?

www.ingramcontent.com/pod-product-compliance
Lightning Source LLC
Chambersburg PA
CBHW031207020726
47499CB00002B/518